CHASING DREAMS ON SUNSHINE ISLAND

GEORGINA TROY

First published in Great Britain in 2023 by Boldwood Books Ltd.

Cover Design by Alexandra Allden

Cover Photography: Shutterstock

A CIP catalogue record for this book is available from the British Library.

Paperback ISBN 978-1-80426-068-5

Large Print ISBN 978-1-80426-067-8

Hardback ISBN 978-1-80426-069-2

Ebook ISBN 978-1-80426-065-4

Kindle ISBN 978-1-80426-066-1

Audio CD ISBN 978-1-80426-074-6

MP3 CD ISBN 978-1-80426-073-9

Digital audio download ISBN 978-1-80426-072-2

Boldwood Books Ltd
23 Bowerdean Street
London SW6 3TN
www.boldwoodbooks.com

For my cousin, Jane Le Lievre, for all the fun times we've shared over the years and for those yet to come.

1

Jax carried the two metal buckets filled with mussels along the beach, barely noticing the seawater sloshing against his legs, despite the icy wind sweeping inland from the sea, as it spilled over the rim. Beth would probably be wrapping some of the presents she had bought for her little boy, Billy's third Christmas. He smiled as he recalled Beth's pretty face looking up at him that first time he had held her in his arms and they had danced together at Vicki and Dan's wedding five months before.

Jax whistled for his little rescue dog, Seamus, to come to him. Billy loved Seamus and Jax pictured the excited child, who he had become fond of since he and Beth had begun seeing each other soon after the wedding. It was the first time Jax had been in a relationship with someone who had a child and he had to admit he rather enjoyed spending time with the two of them. Being an only child with only his cousin, Piper, close to him in age, spending time with Billy had been a new experience. Jax enjoyed teaching the schoolchildren who came to him in their groups to learn how to forage, but apart from that he'd never really spent much time with youngsters.

Beth was good fun and although he sensed that their relationship wasn't progressing as quickly as his relationships usually did, he supposed it was because she had to put her son's needs before either of theirs, and it gave him an insight into how it must feel to have a child. Jax loved that they had fun with Billy over meals and were then able to enjoy relaxed evenings together when the little boy was asleep in his room. What had surprised Jax most was how close he had become to Billy. He had never really seen himself as a father before now. Probably, he thought with a wry grin, that until recently he had barely thought of himself as much of a grown-up.

He was beginning to think that it might be time to find his own place and finally move out of his parents' home when his toe connected with a large pebble and pain shot up through his foot making him wince.

'Hell, that was sore,' he grumbled, aware that most people would think him mad for walking barefoot on the beach in December. Lowering both buckets onto the sand, he reached down and gave his toe a gentle rub. He frowned to see that the tip of his big toe had already begun darkening. He was going to have a nasty bruise in a couple of hours.

That'll teach him not to wear shoes. He groaned, his pain turning to amusement at the thought of his mother, Sheila's words when she saw what he had done to himself when he dropped off the mussels he had collected for her before taking the others to Helen's home and then on to Marjorie's.

'Hey, Seamus! Come on, boy,' he shouted, patting his knees and waiting for his damp dog to lope up to him. 'We'd better get you home and dry you off otherwise Mum is not going to be happy with me, especially when I go out and leave you behind with her and Dad.'

He had promised Beth he would take her some mussels too

when she had mentioned a few weeks before how much she would love to try his *moules marinière* at some point. Jax was hoping to encourage her to let Billy try his first *moules* that evening but he would have to wait and see whether Beth agreed with him. Although Jax's father had introduced him to seafood at a very young age, he was aware that not everyone was so willing to do the same with their own children.

He reached the top of the slipway and made his way to his mother's home, leaving his damp leather sandals on the front door mat on his way in.

Sheila was walking out of the kitchen with a mug of tea in her hand when she looked up and saw him. 'Look at the state of you two,' she said, shaking her head in amusement as he held the door open until Seamus had run inside. She looked at the dog and wrinkled her nose. 'Are you barefoot?' She shook her head, frowning. 'For pity's sake, Jax. And you've hurt yourself by the looks of things.'

'It was only a little bump,' he fibbed, trying to avoid a telling-off.

'I can see that it wasn't by the shade of purple on your toe.' She grimaced in Seamus's direction. 'And you can dry that little shadow of yours off before you do anything else. I don't want him jumping up on my furniture while his fur is all wet and sandy.'

'Will do.'

'Honestly, Jax, I thought that now you had a girlfriend you might at least attempt to look a little less dishevelled.'

'Mum, I've just walked off the beach on a rainy December evening. I'm not sure how else you expect me to look just now.'

'Wearing shoes might be a good start.'

And there it was, he thought, amused, his mum telling him off again.

'Anyway, Beth likes me just the way I am,' he said, not exactly sure what she actually saw in him.

'Yes, but I wonder how long that will last after the honey-moon period ends.'

He wasn't sure what his mother was going on about but didn't argue. Then he watched her raise one eyebrow in that way she had of asking and answering a question at the same time. 'No one wants a man who looks as messy as you do right now.'

'Thanks for the vote of confidence, Mum.' Did he really look that bad?

'I'm only being honest and if I can't be straight with my own son then there's something very wrong with this world.'

'Fine.' He sighed heavily, aware that agreeing with her was the quickest way to encourage his mum to stop having a go at him. 'I'll think about what you've said and tidy myself up a bit.'

'That's all I'm suggesting you do,' she said, taking a sip of her tea and giving him a satisfied smile.

He lowered one of the buckets onto the mat by the front door and carried the other through to the kitchen. 'I'll give these a quick wash, then leave them in salted water to allow them to purge themselves.'

'Perfect,' Sheila said, following him back to the kitchen and leaning against the wall, cupping her mug of tea in her hands as she watched him decant some of his catch.

'How do you think you'll cook them?' he asked, always intrigued to know what recipe people intended trying out.

'I'm not sure,' she answered thoughtfully. 'I might fry up a little of that chorizo I bought from the market in town last week, then add a dash of red wine, possibly a little passata. What do you think?'

'Sounds delicious.' It did. If Beth hadn't specifically asked him to make his *moules marinière* recipe, that he had already told her included a finely chopped garlic clove, some shallots, Jersey double cream, local butter and a splash of Jersey cider, he might have asked his mother for some of her chorizo. 'I'll give that a try next time.' He thought of the crusty cabbage loaf he'd bought for him and Beth to use to dip into the delicious creamy sauce once they'd eaten their mussels. He suspected Billy would enjoy eating the sauce-soaked bread best of all.

'There you go, Mum,' Jax said three-quarters of an hour later, washing and drying his hands before giving Sheila a peck on her forehead. 'I hope you and Dad enjoy those. I might see you later if you're not in bed by the time I come home from Beth's.'

'Thanks, love.' She reached up and patted his right cheek. 'You're having a shower before you go, I hope.'

What did his mother take him for? 'Of course I am. I'll be back for that after I've dropped off the rest of these with Helen and Margery.'

'Righty-ho.'

* * *

Showered and feeling much warmer now he was wearing dry clothes, Jax left his clean, dry dog snoring in front of the fireplace as his mother watched one of her property renovation programmes.

'Have a good evening, Mum,' he said, grabbing the keys to his jeep from the key hook picture hanging from the wall near the door. 'Thanks for looking after Seamus for me.'

'It's no effort to sit in front of the telly with the little chap,' she said. 'You go and have a fun time.'

He smiled as he drove his jeep up to Beth's holiday cottage.

She was always great company as well as being the most attractive woman he had ever seen.

He neared the small stone cottage that she was renting from one of the local farmers for the time being until she found somewhere more permanent for her and Billy to move into.

He parked the jeep, picking up the basket of his mother's that he had borrowed, checked the bottle of red wine he had brought with him, along with the crusty cabbage loaf and the large plastic container with the *moules*, hoping she was going to enjoy the meal he was about to make for her. He was looking forward to his evening with Beth. Jax made sure that the smaller containers with the rest of his ingredients hadn't become loose before running the short way from the car to the small porch. It wouldn't give the right impression for him to arrive at Beth's door wet and dishevelled, especially when he had assured his mother he was trying to make an effort to look his best for her.

He tapped lightly on the door, not wishing to ring the doorbell in case Billy had fallen asleep early. That was another thing he had learnt from spending time with the pair of them, that if the little boy fell asleep it was tantamount to being a traitor to wake him up before Beth was ready for Billy to wake up.

He saw her figure hurrying towards the door through the mottled glass and his heartbeat quickened to picture her smiling face. The door pulled back and there she was. His Beth.

'Hello,' he said, unable to help from grinning at her.

'Hello, you,' she replied, stepping forward and kissing him before taking his free hand and leading him into the hallway.

Apart from a three-year relationship with his first serious girlfriend, which began when he was seventeen, most of his relationships had been short-lived. Most women, he discovered, didn't like spending time walking on cold beaches only to return to their boyfriend's parents' home afterwards. He hadn't minded not being a part of a couple, mostly because he was a little nervous that a serious relationship might alter his day-to-day life and the amount of time he was free to wander about the island with Seamus.

'Are you hobbling?' Beth asked, peering down at his foot.

'Stubbed my toe earlier.'

She shook her head and grinned at him. 'Barefoot again, I presume.' She didn't wait for him to answer. 'As long as you're all right.'

'I'm fine, thanks.'

'Come this way,' she said before turning and leading the way through to her small kitchen.

Jax immediately began cleaning the *moules*. He liked cooking for Beth and Billy and tried to picture his own kitchen and how much he would enjoy preparing meals for them both if he did move into his own place. He definitely needed to think about this idea more seriously, he decided.

'I'll leave you to sort out all those tasty bits you've brought for our supper and go and check on Billy,' she said, cocking her head in the direction of the living room. 'He's asleep on the sofa.'

'Not in his bed?' Jax asked. It wasn't like Beth not to put the little boy to bed once he fell asleep.

She shook her head. 'No,' she whispered. 'He was desperate to stay awake to see you, so I let him snooze in the living room and promised to bring you through to see him when you arrived.'

The thought that the little boy wanted to see him so much touched Jax's heart. 'He's such a great kid.'

Beth's smile slipped and Jax instinctively knew she was thinking about her late husband, Will.

'I'm sorry,' he said, reaching out to rub her upper arm. 'I should think before speaking.'

She shook her head. 'Don't be silly. You were being nice and I appreciate it. It's strange though how thoughts of Will come into my head when I don't expect them to.'

'They're bound to,' Jax sympathised. 'Especially when you're talking about or thinking about Billy.'

She hugged herself and Jax wanted to take her in his arms and comfort her but sensed it wasn't the right thing to do at that moment.

'I can't help being upset to think how much Will has already missed.' Her voice tightened with emotion. 'And all the things he's not going to experience with Billy going forward.'

Jax hated to think of how deeply Beth must have suffered since Will's sudden death the year before.

'I still find it hard to believe that someone as fit as Will could suddenly die. He was always so careful about his health.' Her voice trailed off.

Jax recalled his mother telling him how Will was an experienced cyclist and had had a heart attack while out cycling one morning.

They stilled, hearing Billy's voice calling out to Jax.

'Jax? Is that you?' the sweet voice called. His slight lisp seemed more obvious now that he was tired.

Jax smiled automatically and went through to the living room. 'It is.'

'Have you come to see me?'

Jax saw Beth enter the room and stand at the other end of the sofa, a wide smile on her face. 'I told you he would, didn't I?'

'Yes.' He kicked the blanket from his legs, stood and then ran around the sofa and into Jax's open arms as Jax crouched to welcome him. 'Did you bring those things for me to eat?'

'The mussels? I did.'

'Can I help you cook them?'

Jax followed Billy's gaze towards Beth. 'Can he, Mummy?' Jax asked, feeling sure that Beth would agree.

She tapped her lower lip with one of her fingers and pretended to give their request some thought. 'Hmm, I'm not sure you'll know what to do, Billy.'

Jax stood as Billy's hand slipped into his and pulled a pleading expression in her direction. 'I'll make sure he keeps well away from anything hot or sharp and we promise to clear up any mess.' He looked down at Billy. 'Don't we?'

'We will, Mummy. Every bit.'

'Then I'll leave you both to make supper.' She winked at Jax when Billy hugged him.

Jax ruffled Billy's hair with his free hand. 'We should get you an apron to make sure your pyjamas don't get any food on them. Shall we get started?'

Billy soon became bored watching Jax clean the mussels and decided to join his mummy in the living room. Jax wasn't surprised, he would have found it boring when he was little too. He carried on alone and was soon happily serving two bowls of the delicious seafood meal to Beth and a small bowl of the creamy sauce for Billy with two of the perfectly cooked mussels in it in case he wanted to try them.

'You didn't last long, young man,' Jax teased, setting down Billy's and Beth's bowls in front of them at the round table in the living room.

'It was boring,' Billy said, looking up at him and grinning. 'But only a bit.'

Jax pushed a plate of the sliced crusty loaf in front of the little boy. 'Take one of these,' he said, setting his own bowl onto the table and sitting down. 'Tear it apart like this,' he demonstrated what he meant and waited while Billy copied. 'Then you dip it into the sauce.'

Billy did as he suggested and, frowning, popped a dripping piece of bread into his mouth, oblivious to the sauce running down his chin. His eyes lit up the instant the concoction hit his tongue. 'That's good.'

Delighted with the little boy's verdict, Jax smiled. 'Now it's Mummy's turn to tell us what she thinks.'

He watched Beth making an elaborate display of tasting a *moule* then tearing a piece of bread, dipping it a couple of times into the sauce and eating it. 'Mmm, deelicious.'

Billy clapped his hands. 'I helped make it, Mummy.'

'Er, you did?' Jax teased.

* * *

When Billy was settled in bed sleeping, having insisted that Jax tuck him in, he and Beth did the dishes.

As Jax dried the last of the cutlery, he felt Beth watching him. He looked up and went to smile at her but noticed she had a serious, thoughtful expression on her face. 'Is something the matter?' he asked, a sense of foreboding coursing through him.

She reached out and took the cutlery from him, hurriedly putting it away in the cutlery drawer without taking her usual care to place the right piece in the correct section. Pushing the drawer closed with her hip, Beth took a deep breath.

She's going to finish with me. Jax's heart raced and he focused on remaining calm and not revealing his slight panic. He waited for her to speak, wishing she would do so quickly and put him out of his misery.

'We've had a lovely evening tonight, Jax,' she said quietly. 'Thank you for always being so kind and including Billy. He's so fond of you and I'm grateful to you for all that you've done for us both since the summer. It's been good for him to have a caring male figure, especially since his dad isn't here any more.' She squeezed her eyes shut for a second.

He realised she was building up to a massive 'but'. He needed to say something and struggled for a moment to think what might help dissuade her. 'I'm grateful that the two of you welcomed me so openly into your little family.'

When her gaze dropped to the floor, Jax placed the tea towel he was holding onto the work surface and took Beth's hands in his.

'What is it?' She looked up at him, pain in her eyes but didn't reply. 'Beth, please speak to me. Whatever it is, I promise I'll understand.'

She slowly withdrew her hands from his and crossed her arms over her chest. 'I was trying to think of the best way to tell you.'

His panic increased. *Was she ill?* 'Tell me what, Beth?'

'I can't do this, Jax.'

He shook his head miserably. 'Do what?'

'This. Have a relationship. I'm just not ready. Not yet.'

So that's what was upsetting her. Aware that to try and persuade her otherwise would be selfish, Jax nodded. 'It's fine. I understand.'

Her eyes brightened. 'You do? Really?'

'Yes,' he said, wishing there was something he could do about her decision. 'You were, sorry, are, still very much in love with Will, aren't you?'

She nodded slowly. 'I am. I'm so sorry.'

'Don't be.'

'I never meant to hurt you, Jax, I hope you know that.'

'Of course I do.' He did, but understanding her reasons didn't help lessen the sting of what she was telling him.

'And I'm not sorry we've spent time together since Vicki's

wedding, but I think you're ready for something more out of this relationship and I've no idea when I'll be ready to take that next step.'

Jax thought back to how happy he had been with Beth and Billy, but realised that as much as he had enjoyed kissing her, he had never even tried to take their relationship further, probably because he had felt in his heart that she was still very much in love with her late husband.

'It's fine, Beth. I've never suffered a loss like you did losing Will, so I can only imagine how heartbreaking it is for you. You must do what's best for you and Billy.' Picturing the little boy and how much fun they had together, Jax decided that it was worth asking if they might still go on outings occasionally. 'I'll understand if you want a complete break,' he fibbed. 'But as well as being attracted to you, Beth, I also like you very much as a friend. And Billy is the greatest little boy. I don't want him to think I've forgotten him, just because we don't date any longer. If it's OK with you, maybe I could take him out to the beach occasionally with Seamus.' He saw her consider his request. 'With you, too, if you'd prefer. It's just a thought, I don't want you to feel pushed into doing anything you don't wish to do.'

She smiled. 'Thanks, Jax. I think we'd both like that very much.' Her smile slipped. 'I'm sorry for it ending this way.'

He took her in his arms and hugged her. 'Don't be,' Jax soothed. 'I'm a big boy and can take disappointment on the chin.' He held her silently for a moment as she slipped her arms around his back and rested her head on his chest. 'I've enjoyed getting to know you both.' He let his arms drop. 'I'd like to drop off a small Christmas present for Billy at some point, if that's all right with you?'

She smiled. 'That's very kind. He'd love that.'

'Great. I'd better be going.' He forced a smile.

Beth sighed. 'Thanks, Jax.'

'What for?' he asked.

'For understanding.' She reached up and rested her hand against his left cheek. 'And for being you.'

2

Jax walked deep in thought as he covered the short distance along the pier from his parked jeep to his parent's house. His phone buzzed. His immediate hope that Beth might have changed her mind vanished almost instantly. Beth wasn't the type of person who came to a decision lightly and he knew her well enough to know she would not have finished with him unless she was completely certain it was what she wanted to do.

Worried she might need him for something, he checked the message. It was from Piper. He smiled to himself, thinking how much better his cousin had become at using her mobile since starting to date Alex.

The text said:

Spreading the word about a Thank You Christmas Party up at the Cabbage Patch. Meg and Amy Ecobichon want to invite all the artisans as well as anyone who helped clean the second barn for Vicki and Dan's wedding to a party on Christmas Eve. Partners welcome. Should be great fun! Hopefully Beth can arrange a babysitter and come with you.

Jax stared at the screen for a moment before pressing the phone off and returning it into his back pocket. He was going to have to let his family know that he and Beth were no longer seeing one another. Feeling too miserable to want to return home, but aware that Seamus would need a bedtime walk, he went home and collected his dog.

'Let's go to the beach,' he said, the familiar words causing the little dog's tail to wag frantically.

They reached the slipway and began walking down onto the beath. The tide was a little way out and, relieved to have some time alone to think, Jax took off his boots. He was comforted by the familiar feeling of cold, wet sand under the soles of his feet.

Most people hated the darker winter nights but he didn't mind them too much. He enjoyed each season for different reasons and winter to him meant that the island was quieter and now that most of the hotels and guest houses had closed, life seemed calmer and slower, which suited his current mood perfectly. He followed Seamus along the beach, the lights from the houses on the pier reflected in the wet sand below. He loved moments like these when he and Seamus had the beach to themselves and everything in his world was peaceful. It helped soothe his bruised heart.

'Oi,' a voice he recognised bellowed.

'So much for having some alone time,' Jax moaned to Seamus. He heard footsteps running towards him and turned to see Piper, her puffy jacket zipped up as far as it would go and a woolly beanie pulled down over her ears.

'Wait for me.'

'What are you doing out here at this time?' he asked. 'I thought you might be cuddled up with Alex on a sofa watching television.'

'He's on the mainland at the moment visiting his parents.' She reached down to ruffle Seamus's scruffy head. 'He had to go back to make sure Fliss returned home like she was supposed to do.' Piper pulled a face. 'She wasn't ready to leave the island really but her parents insisted it was time she did. They told her that until she starts earning her own living and stops relying on them for everything she'll do as she's told and will stay there until after Christmas. Alex said she's furious with them and is in a massive strop. Poor Alex.'

At the mention of Alex's spoilt sister's name, Jax grimaced. 'You're not kidding. She's not the easiest person to deal with; I don't envy him that job.'

Piper nudged his side. 'You had a lucky escape there. I had no idea what you saw in her.'

Neither did Jax now. He thought of the beautiful but petulant girl and then Beth, so gentle and sweet; they were complete opposites. He wondered if maybe him believing he had liked Fliss might have been nothing more than being intrigued by her. Fliss had been unlike any other woman he had ever met, and now never wanted to meet.

He gave Piper's comment some thought and checking Seamus was still nearby, he pushed his cold hands into his jacket pocket. 'I suppose she was a bit of a whirlwind when she arrived on the island. And you must admit she is pretty, in a confident, worldly kind of way.'

'I suppose so.' Piper laughed. 'But when have you gone for someone like her? You know, the sort of high-maintenance woman you occasionally see around here? Never, that's when.'

'All right, clever clogs. Just because you're all loved up with Alex...' He noticed Seamus start to run after something and shouted out to him. 'Here, boy. Come on.' When Seamus took no notice, Jax groaned and began to run after him. 'Little bugger. Seamus! Here!'

He was used to his little dog charging off on occasion but could have done without it this late at night. 'Seamus!' What the hell was his dog doing? He was never this disobedient. Then Jax saw what looked like a heap of clothes. He squinted to try and see better in the darkness but couldn't make out what it might be. Seamus reached it and began nuzzling whatever it was, then lay down next to it.

'What on earth is Seamus doing?' Piper asked. 'Seamus, here, boy.'

Seamus continued to ignore them. 'Something's very wrong,' Jax said, breaking into a run. 'Even Seamus doesn't usually ignore me for this long.'

As he drew near he peered down at the heap of clothes and realised with horror that it was a person. They weren't very tall and if it wasn't for the style of the trousers and boots he might have mistaken them for an older child.

Jax crouched down next to the prone individual, worried about turning them onto their back in case they were injured. 'Good boy, Seamus,' he said quietly stroking the dog's head.

'Can you hear me?' he asked loudly. The person groaned. They were still alive. Relieved, Jack took off his coat just as Piper reached them. 'Call an ambulance,' he said without looking up.

She didn't argue and, seconds later, he heard her pressing the emergency number as he covered what he now realised was an elderly woman with his coat. 'Can you tell me your name?'

She mumbled something but he couldn't make out what. He heard a gasp next to him.

'Dilys? Is that you?' Piper immediately took off her own coat and covered the lady's legs with it.

Piper and Jax sat on the damp sand next to Dilys in an effort to keep her as warm as possible. Seamus hadn't moved at all and was tucked up against the woman's stomach. Jax relaxed slightly when the woman's hand moved to rest on Seamus's head.

'He's a good little dog,' the woman said, sounding a little stronger.

Aware he needed to keep her talking, Jax asked, 'Have you been here long? Do you know what happened?'

'I'm not sure.' She thought for a moment. 'I felt a bit dizzy and then woke up lying here. What time is it now?'

Piper checked her watch. 'It's a little after eight thirty.'

'Then I've been here for about ten minutes. It feels much longer though.'

Jax pushed away the thought of what might have happened to Dilys if he hadn't chosen to walk Seamus on the beach at that time. Or, he reminded himself, Seamus hadn't chosen to run off and inspect what Jax had presumed to be a pile of clothes.

'I'm rather cold,' Dilys said and Jax noticed she was shivering.

He began to rub her back very lightly, hoping to warm her as much as possible. 'Try not to worry. We'll have you warmed up in no time,' he reassured her.

'The ambulance should be here very soon,' Piper added gently, rubbing her hands along Dilys's legs.

Spotting blue flashing lights coming along the road and turning down to the pier, Jax watched the ambulance drive as far down the pier as they dared. Piper switched on the torch on her phone and waved it.

'Over here,' Jax called, grateful for the full moon lighting what would otherwise be a dark beach.

* * *

'Heavens,' Helen said when Jax escorted Piper home and explained what had happened. 'Poor Dilys. It sounds as if she had a lucky escape there.'

'She did.' Piper indicated the kettle. 'I'm a bit shaky myself, for some reason.'

'It'll be the shock, lovey,' Helen said, wrapping her arms around Piper in a hug. 'Want a cuppa, Jax? You're looking a little peaky yourself.'

He shook his head. 'No thanks, Aunty Helen. I'd better get this little guy home.' He pictured Dilys's pale face as they took her in the ambulance and shuddered. 'I wish she would have let one of us accompany her to the hospital.'

'So do I,' Piper agreed. 'But I promised to give her daughter a call once I get her number from Gran.'

'At least she'll have someone to look after her,' Jax said, relieved.

Helen shook her head and switched on the kettle. 'She doesn't. Dilys lives alone,' Helen said thoughtfully. 'Her daughter lives near Dinard. Has done since she married about ten years ago.'

'That's a shame.' Jax didn't like to think of the older lady returning home to an empty house. 'I suppose she's used to not relying on anyone else for anything. It sounds as if she had some sort of turn.'

'It does.' Piper took down two cups. 'Mum?' she asked, holding one up.

'Yes, please.' Helen crossed her arms. 'I'll give the hospital a call in the morning and see how she's getting on. Maybe I'll ask if she can come and stay here with us for a bit. I know she only lives in the village but she can't be alone if she's unwell and especially not at Christmas time.'

'That's a lovely idea, Mum. At least there'll always be one of us to look after her if she stays with us.'

'It is a good idea, Aunty Helen.' Jax gave his aunt a hug. 'Thank you. I'm so relieved Seamus found her. Dilys looked so helpless out there on the sand. She must have been freezing by the time we reached her.'

Helen unfolded her arms and rested each hand on his broad shoulders. 'Now you listen to me. I don't want you worrying about what might have happened,' she said. 'Seamus found her, you two helped her and she's now in safe hands. Hopefully she'll be fine with no harm done. All right?'

His aunt knew him too well. 'Yes.' He smiled.

3

'I bumped into Helen at the shop this morning,' his mother said, looking up from dusting her sideboard as Jax walked into the house the following day. 'She phoned the hospital and the nurse there reassured her that Dilys had had a comfortable night's sleep and they're pretty sure she'll be fine.'

'Are they discharging her then?'

Sheila shook her head. 'Not until they've carried out more tests and worked out what caused her to collapse. Soon though, I should imagine.'

'That's good,' he said, relieved. 'I hope she does agree to stay with Helen and Piper at The Blue Haven, then she'll only be a few doors down from us and I can pop in to see her if she needs me to collect anything from her home.'

'Before I forget, Piper asked that you call in to see her when you have a minute to spare, she has something to tell you.'

'Thanks, Mum.' He glanced up at the carriage clock on the mantelpiece and checked the time. 'I'll go and see her now.'

As he always did, Jax knocked a couple of times on the front door to Piper's house and, without waiting for an answer, walked straight in and through to the kitchen where he expected to find his aunt and Piper. They weren't there.

'We're through here,' Helen shouted. 'Dining room.'

Retracing his steps, he joined them. 'Good morning. I hear that Dilys is doing well.'

'She is,' Helen said. 'I also mentioned to the nurse that I'm happy for Dilys to come and stay with us until she's well enough to return home.'

'I hope she takes you up on that offer,' Jax looked at Piper and waited while she finished her mouthful of breakfast. 'Mum said you wanted me for something. Did you manage to get hold of Dilys's daughter?'

'No. Apparently she and her husband have taken a short holiday somewhere in the Canary Islands. Their neighbour told me they should be back in a few days, so I'll call again then.'

'Right. If that's it, then I'd better get going.' Jax went to leave the room.

'Wait,' Piper said. 'That wasn't why I asked you to pop round.'

'Something wrong?'

'It was regarding the party that I texted you about.'

'Yes.' Jax pictured the two octogenarian sisters who owned and lived in the large farmhouse, which had two barns at the back, the largest of which was called The Cabbage Patch and which was where Piper and other artisans had stalls and sold their wares. It was usually a hive of activity, although not somewhere he had visited often. 'That's nice of them,' he said, unsure what she was expecting from him.

'It is.' Piper pulled a face. 'So? Will you be coming?'

He wasn't sure what this had to do with him. He worked for himself and helped Dan with boat trips from Gorey taking groups of islanders and holidaymakers from Jersey to Carteret on the French coast during the summer, or to Les Ecrehous, a small group of islands. He had nothing to do with the sisters or their farmstead. 'I'm not sure why I'd be invited. I only helped clean the barn for the wedding.'

Piper groaned. 'I know, but I was asked to send you that text about the party because they are including you in their invitation. You and anyone else who helped make the smaller barn look so lovely. Since Matteo's photographer took those photos of the wedding reception and medieval hall at the castle as a thank you to Casey and Tara for helping him out with his music video, the sisters have been inundated with requests for events to be held at the barn. It's another income stream for them and they're enormously grateful to everyone who helped make it happen.'

'I did very little though,' he said, still unsure why he should be included.

Piper buttered her last piece of toast before looking up at him again. 'If you were anyone else I'd assume you've just woken up and that's why you're being so dense this morning but I know you'll have already been up for hours.'

Jax had always been an early riser but after the upset of Beth ending their fledgling relationship and then the shock of finding Dilys, his mind had raced so much that he had barely slept more than an hour and that had been in fits and starts.

He realised his cousin was saying his name. 'Jax, are you listening to anything I'm saying?'

Seeing the concern on his cousin's face he pulled out a chair and sat down at the table.

'I can see you two have something to talk about,' Helen said, excusing herself and standing. 'Can I fetch you some toast and tea, Jax? An egg or two maybe?'

'No thanks, Aunty Helen, I'm fine.'

Helen frowned and he knew it was because he hardly ever refused a cooked breakfast from his aunt. She shrugged and left them to it though. Piper lowered her knife next to her uneaten piece of buttered toast, sat back in her chair and stared at him with an intensity he knew meant he was going nowhere until he had told her what was on his mind.

'Speak to me,' Piper said. 'This isn't just about Dilys, is it?'

His cousin knew him far too well to be fobbed off with any old excuse, unfortunately. Jax shook his head and sighed. He may as well tell her now. Piper was like a terrier when she suspected he was keeping a secret from her and was bound to hound him until he admitted what was wrong with him.

'Beth finished with me last night.'

Piper didn't speak for a few seconds. He could see by the stunned expression on her face that she hadn't seen that coming.

'Jax, I'm so sorry. Did she say why?'

'She still loves Will,' he said. 'I can't say I'm surprised.' He rubbed his face. 'I was more surprised that she agreed to go out with me when I asked her after Dan and Vicki's wedding, to be honest.'

'Are you very upset?'

He went to answer that he was, then stopped. *Was he? Really?* 'I did like her,' he said, trying to find the right words to explain his feelings. 'And I am sorry that she didn't want to continue seeing me but I think it's probably more that I enjoyed spending time with her and little Billy.' He waited for Piper to react.

Her expression softened.

'What?'

'Well, it's just that I've never thought of you as being the type to want a family. It seems that I was wrong.'

He supposed she had a point. 'Up until now I'd never thought of myself that way either,' he admitted.

'Do you think Beth will let you still spend some time with Billy? I'm sure she would if you asked her.'

'I did and she said it was fine. We've agreed that I'll take them both out walking sometimes.' He thought of the sweet little boy he had unexpectedly grown fond of over the past few months.

'I'm glad,' Piper said. 'It would be unfair to Billy for you to simply disappear out of his life, especially as that's essentially what happened when his daddy died.'

Jax sighed. 'Poor little boy.'

'I know, it's horrible to think of him having to go through something so cruel when he's only, what? Three?'

'Yes.' Jax could feel his spirits dipping. Mooning over Beth and what had happened wasn't going to help him get over the end of their relationship. 'Anyway,' he said, determined to snap out of his miserable mood. 'Tell me more about this party. When did you say it was going to be held?'

'Christmas Eve, or maybe the night before that, I'm not quite sure.'

'But that's only a few days away. Can they get everything ready by then?'

Piper shrugged. 'I don't think there's too much to do. The artisans have all agreed to stay late and help dust the barn, wash floors and all that to make it look nice and we've each offered to make some food and bring drink to the party, so they won't have to do too much.'

'So a relaxed party then, rather than anything too formal,' he said, feeling much more positive about attending.

'It won't be anything fussy, I know that much. They just want everyone to get together and have a bit of fun.' She frowned. 'I think now is the perfect time for you to go to a party and take your mind off what's happened between you and Beth, don't you?'

He wasn't sure. 'Maybe,' he said doubtfully. Then, seeing his cousin's determined stare, he knew he may as well give in, it wasn't as if he had anything else to do. 'Fine. If I must, but I won't drink though. I'll drive you and I up there. Will your gran be coming?'

'I imagine so.'

'Then tell her I'll take her there and home again.'

Piper beamed at him. 'Yes. I'll tell them that you'll be there then?'

'Go on, why not,' he said, aware that spending time with Piper and others that he knew from The Cabbage Patch might be fun. 'Just let me know if I can help in any way and what you'd like me to bring on the night.' It would have been nice to be able to attend with Beth but he presumed she wouldn't have been able to go anyway unless her mother or sister were available to babysit and Vicki would more than likely be going to the party with Dan.

'Phoebe's going,' Piper said unexpectedly.

Jax wasn't sure why Piper was telling him. 'Does that mean Fliss will be there too?' Had he misheard his cousin when she had told him that Fliss was having to stay in Poole for Christmas?

Piper shook her head and rolled her eyes heavenward. Jax was confused. 'Nope. I told you she's back in Poole. Remember?'

'Sorry. My mind is all over the place this morning. But I am glad that Fliss won't be there.' He'd had enough of Fliss and her exhausting ways back in the summer and was relieved to know he wouldn't be confronted by her and her silly games during the party. He realised Piper was still speaking.

'...Phoebe helped out when we prepared the reception so I invited her yesterday afternoon.' She narrowed her eyes. 'That's not a problem for you, is it?'

'No. Why would it be?'

'I wasn't sure how it was between you after Fliss was such a pain to you in the summer,' Piper said. 'I mean Phoebe seems nice enough but she is Fliss's best friend so they can't be too different, can they?'

'How should I know?' He pictured the pretty girl who had been in their group most of the time Alex's spoilt sister, Fliss, had been there. 'Phoebe seems much nicer than Fliss, but she's...' He struggled to work out what it was about the beautiful girl with the sleek, dark hair that he had a problem with.

'A bit too glossy for you?' Piper teased, her eyes twinkling with amusement.

Jax knew his cousin was having a dig at his clothes, unshaven face and untidy, sun-bleached hair. 'There's nothing wrong with how I dress.'

'Really? Are you sure about that?' She laughed. 'How many other people do you see going out in late December wearing shorts and a T-shirt?'

'Er, I'm wearing a jacket now it's cold, and boots.'

'That's not much of a concession to the cold,' Piper laughed. 'You should be wearing jeans and a pullover in this weather, maybe a hat too.'

'Now I know you're joking.' He had thought about wearing jeans but decided that foraging on a wet beach would only mean they would get wet anyway and what use would they be then at trying to warm his legs. None, that's what.

'Am I though?' She raised an eyebrow.

4

CHRISTMAS EVE

Jax took Dilys's hand and slipped it around his forearm to assist her into Helen's guest house from the front seat of his jeep.

'You're such a kind boy,' Dilys said as she and Jax walked slowly down the hallway behind Helen towards the dining room. Helen had asked Piper to prepare a bowl of soup and some bread for Dilys before she was settled up in the bedroom they had made ready for her stay.

'It's my pleasure,' Jax said honestly. 'You must be pleased to be out of hospital now.'

'I am, and just in time for Christmas.' She spotted Piper carrying a tray towards her. 'Ahh, Piper dear, that looks delicious.'

'Sit here, Dilys,' Piper said, putting the tray onto the nearby table and pulling back a chair for Dilys to take a seat. 'If you don't like ham and pea soup I'll happily make you something different.'

'Not at all. This looks and smells delicious.'

'Do you want me to take Dilys's bags upstairs, Aunty Helen?' Jax asked, feeling happier than he had in days now that Dilys was well and looking so delighted to be at The Blue Haven.

'No thanks, lovey, I can do that. You get on now.'

'Shall I come to yours later?' Piper asked, looking expectantly at him.

'Sure. I'm dropping off a present for Billy first but I'll come back and fetch you straight afterwards.'

Piper frowned. 'Look, why don't I make my own way there. I don't want you to be worried about time if you and Beth have things to say to each other.'

'No, it's fine.' As far as he was concerned, Beth had made up her mind and he was simply going to have to navigate his emotions in his own way.

She looked concerned, which didn't surprise him. Piper always looked out for him when things were difficult. 'Are you sure though? We mostly need a lift back home after the party.'

'It's no problem at all. I'm happy to take you there as well as bringing you home.'

Jax said goodbye to the three women and walked the short distance along the pier to his parents' home. He decided that he was looking forward to Christmas Day and spending time with them, Piper, and his aunt. It was a tradition he always looked forward to and this year Dilys being included could only add to the festive celebrations. As usual, he and his parents would walk to The Blue Haven guest house at around noon, when his mother would help his aunt with final preparations for a mid-afternoon meal. He thought of Dilys and how happy she had seemed to be spending Christmas with both families. Yes, he mused, Christmas was going to be fun.

He pushed his hands deep into his shorts pockets to protect them against the cold. Stopping at the harbour wall, Jax breathed in deeply. He suspected they were about to be hit by a storm. He noticed the blue-grey altostratus clouds making their way from the French coast. Not a storm, snow. And soon by the looks of things, he decided.

He didn't have long to walk Seamus if he was going to get to Beth's before Billy's bedtime. He found Seamus lying in front of the fire in the living room and reached down to stroke his head.

'Come along, little guy.' Seamus looked up at him but didn't move. Jax knew his dog loved his walks but wasn't a fan of very cold weather. 'You'll enjoy it when you get going,' he laughed, amused by Seamus's laziness. 'Do you want to go for a walk?'

At the words 'Do you want', Seamus's ears twitched and a second later he was standing and wagging his tail.

'Is that you, Jax?' his mother called from the direction of the kitchen.

'Yes, Mum. Just going to the beach quickly with Seamus.' He went to find her and saw she was making her famous pork stuffing for the turkey the following day. 'Do you need me to fetch anything for you?'

She shook her head. 'No, I have everything I need. Your dad is out buying a few last-minute bits for me now. You just go out and enjoy yourself.'

'I think we're going to have some snow,' Jax said.

'It's a good thing then that we only live a few doors down from Helen's guest house then, isn't it?' She grinned.

'It is.'

He patted his right thigh and Seamus immediately raced to the front door where he raised a front paw and dabbed it against the door, impatient for Jax to open it and let him out. They strolled along the pier, the drop in temperature taking Jax a little by surprise. The snow clouds had already covered the entire sky and by the time they reached the top of the slipway he felt the first snowflake land on his forehead. He had been right. He hoped that the snow would hold off until everyone was back home after the party had ended. They occasionally had snow on the island and sometimes even had it bad enough to be snowed in, especially in the outer parishes where the land was more exposed to the elements. It wasn't often though that the snow settled and if they were lucky, this would be one of those times.

He whistled for Seamus to slow down and not race off too far ahead of him; it was getting dark and Jax was still a little shaken by finding Dilys lying on the sand a couple of days before.

Maybe a smattering of snow over the landscape might be perfect to give the island a Christmas card-like appearance before the festivities began in earnest the following morning.

He spotted a piece of yellow sea glass and picked it up to give to Piper later to add to her collection. Brushing the damp sand off the cold, opaque glass, he sighed. He wasn't looking forward to seeing Beth again. He stared out at the rolling waves not far from where he stood and wished he could muster up the festive mood he usually had at this point. Even the sight of Seamus playing with a discarded tennis ball that he had come across didn't raise his spirits as much as it usually would.

He wasn't sure what was getting him down so much. He had liked Beth very much but he hadn't been in love with her. It dawned on him that he was sad for her and for Billy. They should be preparing to spend Christmas with Will.

'Poor things,' he sighed, dropping the sea glass into his pocket. He realised the temperature had dipped even more and, holding his hand out, watched as snowflakes dropped in quick succession onto his palm. Time to head back inside.

'Come on, Seamus,' he called. When the little dog ignored him, Jax bellowed. 'Do you want supper?'

At the question, Seamus's sandy ears pricked up and he turned to stare at Jax, an expectant look in his eyes. Still he didn't move though.

'You can bring your ball. Come on.'

Happy to have Jax's approval, Seamus bounded over to him

across the sand, ball in mouth, his fox-like tail wagging back and forth.

As much as Jax would like to have made Beth happy, and Billy, he wasn't her answer, he knew that now and was grateful to Beth for being honest with him about her feelings before he had begun to fall in love with her and get too used to being around Billy.

He trudged to the slipway, wishing he hadn't agreed to go to the Ecobichon sisters' party. It wasn't as if he really knew them or had done much for them. Jax glanced at the Christmas tree lights glowing from the guest house. It was too late to change his mind now, especially as he had offered to give Piper and Margery a lift. He smiled to himself. His cousin would never let him stay at home when there was a party being held. Maybe it wouldn't be so bad seeing Beth and Billy after all, he mused, passing Piper's home and arriving at his own front door.

He opened it and let Seamus inside, still thinking about what lay ahead that evening.

'For pity's sake, Jax,' his mother yelled. 'You've given that dog of yours another ruddy ball. Now we're going to have bits of rubber and felt stuff all over the damn floors.'

'Sorry, Mum.'

'What's the matter with your mother?' his father asked, his voice barely above a whisper as he followed Jax inside the house.

'Sorry, Dad,' Jax said, surprised to see him there. 'I didn't realise you were following us.' Jax took the two bags of shopping from his father. 'Seamus found an old tennis ball on the beach and Mum's not very happy about it.'

'Not another ball,' his father grumbled. 'That dog has an extra sense for sniffing out those things, then when he's finished with them discards them in all sorts of annoying places. I nearly broke my neck the other week tripping over one in the bathroom when I got up before daylight.'

'Sorry, Dad.'

'Is that your father back already?'

'It is,' Jax replied. 'I'll take these through to the kitchen for you, if you like.'

'That'll be grand. I'll go and change. There's some good stuff on the telly tonight.'

Jax left his father and made his way down the hallway to the kitchen. The thought of going out tonight was becoming more appealing by the minute.

5

It was 6.30 p.m. when Jax drove to Beth's house, glad to have a jeep now that the weather had turned. The party was due to start at seven but there was already a couple of inches of snow and everything around him was now white. If the snow didn't let up they were going to risk finding some of the roads impassable by Christmas morning.

He parked and carried the gift Beth had approved for Billy's Christmas to her front door. He was relieved that he had thought to check with her that the present was suitable, not wishing to overstep any boundaries. He knocked on the door and after hearing Billy's excited voice saw the door open and Beth and Billy's faces smiling up at him.

'Come in, quickly,' Beth said, stepping back and taking Billy with her. 'It looks freezing out there.'

'It is a bit chilly,' he said, aware it was an understatement but knowing Beth wouldn't expect him to be bothered by the wintry weather.

'Is that present for me?' Billy asked, his smile wide.

'It is,' Jax said. 'But you need to wait until at least tomorrow morning to open it. He handed the box into the little boy's outstretched hands. 'Be careful with it, won't you?'

Billy nodded enthusiastically. 'What is it?'

Jax's heart swelled to see Billy being so excited. He wished he could spend Christmas Day with him and see his face as he opened the present.

Beth laughed. 'You'll have to wait and see,' she said, ruffling his hair. 'Take it through to the living room and put it under the tree with the other presents.'

They watched the little boy run off to do as his mum had instructed and once he had gone, Beth turned to Jax. 'How are you?'

He cleared his throat, not wishing to betray his emotions. 'Fine, thanks. You?'

'All right.' She stared at him for a moment. 'Thank you for bringing a present for Billy,' she said, glancing at the living room door. 'He will love his dinosaurs.'

'I've read a few of his books to him and his favourite seemed to be the one about dinosaurs, so I thought he'd like them.'

'I know he's missed seeing you the past few days but I wasn't sure how else to handle things between us. I thought I was ready for a relationship—'

Jax shook his head. 'It's fine. I said I understood why we had ended and I do.' Feeling the need to reassure her, he added. 'Maybe I could take you and Billy out somewhere sometime next week, or the week after? Would that be all right?'

'He'd love that.' She smiled. 'And so would I.'

'Great. We'll arrange when suits you best after Christmas is over with.' Jax heard Billy's footsteps and fixed a smile on his face. 'Looking forward to tomorrow?'

Billy nodded. 'It's Christmas tomorrow,' he said palms up. 'Father Christmas is coming down our chimley.'

'It's chimney, Billy,' Beth corrected lovingly. 'And yes, he's on his way now.'

'Look at our tree,' Billy said, taking Jax's hand without waiting for him to reply.

He let the little boy lead him into the living room where a four foot tree stood in one corner, coloured lights and baubles arranged in a haphazard fashion around it. Jax noticed that most of the baubles hung low within Billy's reach.

'I helped Mummy make it nice.'

'You did a brilliant job,' Jax said. 'And are those all your presents?'

'That one is for Mummy.' Billy pointed to a neatly wrapped box in the middle of the selection. 'Nana helped me buy it and wrapped it for me. I wrote the note.'

Jax saw a mismatched label tied to the ribbon around the present. 'Did you do your best writing?'

Billy nodded proudly.

'Well done.' He looked towards the window and seeing that it was still snowing decided he should not spend any longer chatting. 'I suppose I'd better get a move on.'

'Happy Christmas, Jax,' Billy said, running to the tree and bringing back a present and handing it to Jax. 'For you.'

Jax's voice caught in his throat and, unable to speak, he crouched down and hugged Billy. 'Thank you,' he said.

He stood and Beth put her arms around him. 'Happy Christmas, Jax. Are you off to the Ecobichon party tonight?'

'I am.' He wished he hadn't accepted the invitation now. Having seen Beth and Billy all he really felt like doing was going home and spending time watching something senseless on television.

'Have a fun time. Vicki, and Dan will be there, too.'

He forced a smile. 'I will. If you need anything, please call me or send me a message. It's getting a little treacherous out there and I have the right vehicle for it.'

'I doubt I'll need anything but thanks for the offer anyway.' She led the way to the front door and opened it. 'See you soon, Jax.'

He smiled, gave Billy a quick wave and left feeling more miserable than he had before.

The wind had picked up quite a bit in the short time he had been at Beth's and Jax knew it didn't bode well, not when the snow was falling heavily like it was now. Not wishing to dwell on his low mood, he concentrated on driving carefully back to the pier to collect Piper and her gran. The snow wasn't too much of an issue yet.

Jax rushed into his home and collected the two bottles of red wine and boxes of truffles his mother had bought for the sisters and placed them in a bag, then went to Margery's cottage to collect her. It was a little icy and he didn't intend letting her slip and injure herself.

'I'm not sure about going out tonight,' Margery said, shaking her head as he held the jeep door with one hand and proffered his other for her to help her up into the vehicle. 'I'd rather be stuck at home if the weather gets too bad. I don't want to spend Christmas in someone else's house.'

'I don't blame you,' Jax said, wishing he could do the same.

'Come on, Gran,' Piper said, walking up to them from the guest house. 'It's almost Christmas and we're bound to have fun when we get there.'

'Are we though?' Jax asked, unsure whether his cousin was right.

'I'm with Jax on this one,' Margery grumbled, giving a dramatic shiver.

'Neither of you are backing out now,' Piper said, smiling.

'We're going to the party, we'll have fun and then Jax will bring us both home. I promise you'll be glad you made the effort once you get there.'

'You'd better be right.' Margery settled herself onto the passenger seat.

Piper stepped up and sat next to her and Jax left her to help Margery to fasten her seat belt.

'Ready?' he asked when he was seated. He drove to the main road and up Gorey Hill. The drive there took slightly longer than usual with the snow on the roads and other drivers taking more care but eventually Jax steered off the main road towards the farm. As he drove up the bumpy driveway, he glanced at the farmhouse, thinking how lucky the two sisters were to have lived their entire lives in such a beautiful, although run-down, place. He reached the designated parking area at the back of the largest barn where the artisans sold their work and parked.

Getting out of his jeep, Jax grabbed the bag of items from his mother for the sisters, who she knew loved chocolates. He then helped Margery and Piper down from the vehicle before he and Piper linked arms with Margery on either side and accompanied her to the entrance of the smaller barn.

'Doesn't that look Christmassy?' Margery said, stopping and gazing up at the holly, ivy and ribboned garland, which was almost completely covered in snow already.

Jax wondered if maybe it would be a good idea to suggest they took it inside to hang up in the barn. At least that way everyone could enjoy the benefit of it.

The sound of laughter and music filtered out of the barn increasing massively when he pulled open the door and stepped inside. Maybe coming here had been a good idea after all.

6

PHOEBE

It was a little strange being at the party and not really knowing anyone, Phoebe thought, taking yet another sip of her drink. She was only half listening to the woman she had just met who was explaining to Phoebe and two others how she sourced costume jewellery for her stall. Maybe she should have thought this through before accepting Piper's invitation to come along, Phoebe mused. It was a surprise to have been asked in the first place and not having anything else to do this Christmas Eve, she thought it might be a good way to spend what would otherwise be an evening alone at home.

Amused at her attempt to lie to herself, Phoebe shook her head. She wasn't here for that reason at all, she was here on the off-chance that Jax might be here too. Her stomach flipped over at the thought of the tall, handsome man she had developed a massive crush on over the summer. He was a nice chap too. Far too good for her friend, Fliss, who seemed to see men as prey to play mind games with and somehow enjoyed their torment when she hurt them.

Phoebe suspected it might be Fliss's weird way of wanting

them to prove how much they liked her. She had been the same when they were at boarding school, always vying for people's attention. Phoebe had been so grateful when Fliss, the outgoing, popular girl, had taken her, the shy new student, into her inner circle that she had chosen to overlook Fliss's less appealing qualities. Phoebe knew that although she was slightly more self-assured now, she still battled with the feeling that she had little to offer others, unlike Fliss. Since the summer Phoebe had begun to notice more and more just how badly Fliss behaved, especially towards kind people like Jax. Not cool, Phoebe thought. Not cool at all.

She thought back to how difficult it had been watching Jax fall under Fliss's spell, albeit for a short time, and knowing her friend wasn't nearly as interested in him as she was pretending to be on the odd occasion she did pay him attention. Phoebe had been attracted to him the instant she saw him at St Catherine's Bay the day he and Dan had taken a party of them to the Ecrehous by boat. It had been Jax's birthday too, she recalled, wondering if she would have the courage to send him a birthday card the following summer when that date came around again. Would that be an odd thing to do though? Probably, she decided.

A rush of cold air entered the room as the barn door opened. Instinctively, Phoebe looked over towards the entrance to see who had arrived. She saw Piper and the lady she seemed to recall was her grandmother walk in and then her heart seemed to still for a few seconds as the tall, still relatively suntanned, man of her dreams walked in after them. 'Jax is here,' she whispered, almost not daring to believe he was actually standing there as he seemed to search faces in the crowd.

Then he looked straight at her. For a moment neither moved, transfixed. Phoebe wished she could force herself to smile, or wave, or do something, but her brain seemed unable to come up with anything at all.

'Jax!' Dan's voice rang out and Jax looked away. 'You look like you could do with a drink,' Phoebe heard him say as she struggled to regain her composure.

She turned back, trying to appear as if she was listening to the woman who was still chattering about her stall, but couldn't help overhear what Dan and Jax were saying.

'Thanks, but I'm sticking to soft drinks tonight,' Jax said. 'I'll need to drive home once the party's over and with the weather as it is out there, I'll probably be needed to do a few trips and drop people home.'

'Fair enough. I'm not drinking much because we have the family around tomorrow for the usual traditional lunch. Beth's coming with Billy,' Dan said, his voice dropping. Phoebe heard the pointed way he spoke but wasn't sure why he had changed his tone. 'I had expected you to pitch up at some point but Vicki said you weren't joining us.'

Phoebe could hear the confusion in Dan's voice and sensed something was wrong.

'We're, um, not seeing one another any more,' Jax said, clearly sad by the change in his circumstances.

Phoebe's mood dipped. She hadn't realised Jax had been seeing Beth. Was that the same woman he had been dancing with at Vicki's wedding reception? she wondered.

Phoebe had to force herself not to turn and look over her left shoulder at Jax. This was none of her business and it wasn't as if she really knew him to be able to offer any words of comfort to him, much as she might like the chance to do so.

'I'm sorry, mate, I hadn't realised it was all over,' Dan sympathised. 'Are you all right?'

'Sure. I'm fine,' Jax replied. 'I suppose, if I'm honest, it was more of a friendship between us than anything else.'

Was it? Phoebe wondered hopefully.

'There's more people here than I expected,' she heard Jax say. 'Ah, there's the Ecobichon sisters, I've got a couple of bits I need to give to them. I'll catch up with you in a bit, Dan.'

'No worries. Chat soon.'

'Don't you agree?' Phoebe realised the woman was asking her a question and knew she had to admit not having heard it. 'I'm sorry,' Phoebe said. 'I spotted a friend arriving and missed what you said.'

The woman didn't look pleased and Phoebe thought that now might be the perfect time to excuse herself from their conversation.

'What a thoughtful boy you are,' Meg was saying to Jax as she took one of the bottles of wine he was holding and placed it behind her on the table.

'These are for you, too,' he said.

Phoebe saw the lady's face light up and how happy Jax seemed to have pleased her.

'Truffles are my favourite,' she was saying. 'And these are particularly delicious. I'll not be sharing these with anyone.'

'Neither will I,' Amy, the other sister, said taking hers and holding onto them. 'Very kind of you to bring us something, young Jax.'

'I thought it was the very least I could do when you'd invited me to your party.' He looked about, and Phoebe, not wanting to be caught watching him, took a sip of her drink. 'The barn looks very festive and you've had a big turnout too.'

'We have,' Meg said. 'I just hope there's enough food and drink to go round.'

'These bottles will help,' her sister said, nudging her and almost causing her to drop her box of truffles. The sisters glared at each other and Phoebe could see Jax looking as if he needed to be rescued.

Without giving herself the chance to back out, she stepped forward. 'You made it then?'

He looked to his side to see who had spoken and smiled when he saw her. 'Hello there.' Jax turned, cocking his head to one side. 'Shall we go this way?'

Trying not to grin, Phoebe nodded. 'Yes, let's do that.'

They made their way past other guests to a space in one of the corners. 'That's better.' Jax smiled.

'It is.'

'Thanks for rescuing me. I have a feeling it was in the nick of time.'

'I wasn't sure if I should come over but thought I'd take a chance.'

'I'm grateful.' He looked over her shoulder. 'I'm not sure if the sisters are about to fall out.'

'Hopefully they'll forget their differences and start enjoying the party again.' Phoebe looked up at him and saw that, like her, he was a little lost for words. She needed to think of something to say. 'I hadn't expected to see you here?'

He looked relieved to hear her question. 'I wasn't sure about coming but if anything will get me in the Christmas spirit I think this might be it.'

Was he referring to seeing her? She hoped so, but doubted it very much. 'Something wrong?'

'Not really,' he said. 'I just can't seem to get into the right frame of mind. I'm sure I will do soon though.'

Unable to hide her amusement, Phoebe narrowed her eyes. 'You'd better get a move on, it's New Year soon.'

Jax laughed. 'Sorry. You're right, I'm being a misery. Can I fetch you a drink?'

She held up her glass. 'Tonic water and a slice of lemon. I didn't want to drink tonight, not with the weather being as it is. I've borrowed my dad's Range Rover and would hate to damage it getting home.'

'Wise move. I'm only on soft drinks too for the same reason. Although my old jeep isn't remotely as pristine as your dad's car probably is it's great for driving on rough roads.' He pointed to her drink. 'I'll go and get us a refill.'

She waited for him to go and fetch them some drinks, watching the cheerful faces of the other guests as they laughed and chatted with each other. Then Phoebe noticed some excitement seemed to be growing near the door.

'What's going on over there?' Jax asked, appearing at her side and handing her a drink.

'I've no idea.'

He was tall enough to peer over most people's heads and she waited for him to try and get a good look.

'What is it, can you see?' Phoebe asked, intrigued.

'It looks like Matteo and Casey have just arrived.'

'Really?'

'I didn't realise he was back here for Christmas.'

Phoebe wasn't surprised. From what she had seen at the wedding reception that summer, Matteo and Casey seemed very much in love, or at least in the first flushes of a big romance. It was like something out of a movie, she mused, wishing she could have something similar. She looked up at Jax, who was still focused on the new arrivals and thought what a perfect leading man he would be for any romcom. She sighed.

'Something the matter?' he asked, looking concerned.

Mortified that he had heard her, Phoebe had to remind

herself that Jax only heard her sighing and wouldn't have had any clue about why.

'I was just thinking how perfectly suited they seem,' she said, pleased she'd diverted any attention from herself.

He looked over at them once again. 'I suppose they are. They certainly seem happy enough. I'm pleased. Casey is a great girl and Matteo seems like a decent bloke.'

Casey waved over to Jax and gave Phoebe a cheerful nod.

She did look incredibly happy, Phoebe thought. She felt her mood lifting. She loved seeing people happy and this was turning out to be the perfect antidote to her earlier mood when she discovered that her parents had decided to stay on in the Caribbean for Christmas, believing Fliss to be staying with her. Although, why they hadn't thought Fliss might be with her own family, Phoebe couldn't imagine.

'I wonder if he's going to sing?' Phoebe asked, determined not to give her parents another thought.

Jax laughed. 'Knowing the locals as I do, I doubt he'll have much choice.'

'Good.'

The barn door opened again and someone walked in. The woman, Vivienne, who had been speaking to Phoebe earlier shrieked.

'What's wrong with her do you think?' Phoebe asked, hoping Jax might know the woman better than she did and have an inkling as to what was going on.

Jax threw his head back and laughed. 'I think she's just seen Ernie. I don't know his last name but I think he works on one of the farms nearby. He must have walked here because he's covered in snow.'

'But why would that bother her?'

'Because he looks like something resembling the Abominable

Snowman right now,' Jax laughed.

Phoebe struggled to think of what to say next. Why did she get so tongue-tied when she was around Jax? She knew why. It was because she liked him so much. Maybe she shouldn't have spent so much time with outgoing people like Fliss. It was always easier being around someone like her who pushed themselves and their opinions forward, it meant people didn't realise how little Phoebe had to offer.

'You all right?' Jax gave her a quizzical look.

Phoebe forced a smile. 'Of course. Just thinking, that's all.'

'About anything in particular?'

How could she tell him? 'I was, er, thinking how everyone seems to know each other.'

'I suppose we've all lived here most of our lives, so it's not surprising.' He studied her face for a moment. 'How long have you lived on the island?'

Phoebe sensed he was wondering why she didn't seem to have any friends. 'My parents moved here when I was ten but I was at boarding school and tended to stay with friends during the holidays.'

He seemed surprised. 'You didn't want to come home to the island?'

'I was here some of the time but always with friends from boarding school.' She shrugged. 'I didn't really get to know any of the local kids growing up.'

'That's a shame.'

He was right. It had been short-sighted of her not to make an effort before now to get to know people here. 'I can see that now.'

Jax waved his arm in an arc, taking in the group of people near the door. 'You're bound to get to know a few of them this evening.'

She hoped so. Things could be much worse, Phoebe decided,

amused, as she leant to Jax's side and peered through the crowd, spotting the grumpy-looking man shaking snow off his cloth cap and glaring at Vivienne. She might be about to spend Christmas Day alone, but for tonight she was in great company and spending time with Jax was enough to keep her going through the following few lonely days.

7

JAX

Casey, Matteo, Tara and a tall, gangly-looking chap Jax vaguely recognised from The Cabbage Patch made their way over to join him and Phoebe. He had been enjoying chatting to her but, aware they had very little in common, was unsure what to speak about next, so welcomed his friends joining them.

Tara introduced the tall man as Perry and Jax discovered that he was a sculptor from Cornwall who had been living on the island for a couple of years and made pottery. And, by the look of adoration on Tara's face as she gazed up at him, Jax suspected that this man was probably the one he had heard Casey mention Tara having a massive crush on. I wonder if he realises? Jax pondered, suspecting that Perry was oblivious to her barely concealed attraction to him. Poor Tara.

'Jax, how are you doing?' Matteo asked, patting Jax on the back. 'Hello, Phoebe, nice to see you again.'

'Thank you,' Phoebe said. 'It's good to be here with everyone.'

'I hope you're all impressed that Jax is wearing jeans rather than shorts?' Piper teased, coming up to join them. 'He has even worn a jacket, though I suppose it is Christmas, so dressing up once a year isn't too unexpected.' She grinned at Jax and he pulled a face at her. 'You know I'm only teasing, don't you?'

'I do.'

'Good to see you, Matteo,' he said, noticing how tired the usually relaxed looking man seemed. He was holding Casey's hand in his and was smiling but Jax couldn't miss the strain. He imagined all those concerts and travelling to different places day after day for the past few months had exhausted Matteo. 'How's the tour going?'

'Very well, thanks.'

'Did you know Matteo was coming to the island?' Phoebe asked Casey.

'I did,' she said, smiling up at the man she had fallen in love with that summer. 'I'm travelling back with him to London for a couple of weeks on the twenty-seventh.'

'Sounds exciting.'

'I'll be glad of a break,' Matteo said, raising Casey's hand and kissing the back of it as he looked lovingly into her eyes. 'It's been very successful but it gets a bit tiring being away from the woman you love and moving from one hotel to another most days.'

'I can imagine,' Jax said, having no clue at all how that must feel. His idea of being busy was out earlier than usual in the mornings with a group of schoolkids or lively corporate groups. The thought of spending months in hotels didn't appeal to him for one minute.

He watched as the Ecobichon sisters walked over to Matteo and quietly spoke to him. They seemed to be enjoying whatever it was they were discussing and after a brief hesitation, Matteo smiled at them and nodded.

'Right,' Matteo said, clapping his hands together as the sisters stepped back and waited. 'I've been asked to sing a couple of songs to get this party underway. However, I'll need a few backing singers. Eight should do.' He laughed as hands were raised and excited voices called out for him to choose them. He pointed to two men and two women, then to Casey, Tara, Piper and Phoebe. 'Come along, I don't want any excuses. Let's have some fun.'

Phoebe looked up at Jax doubtfully, making Jax laugh. 'Go on,' he said, trying to encourage her. 'You'll enjoy it.'

'But I'm a dreadful singer.'

'Who's going to hear you when you're one of eight?' He shook his head and pointed towards where Matteo was waving for his designated singers to join him. 'Go on.'

He watched Matteo singing, surprised to find that he quite liked the song. The best part was, Jax thought, when the backing singers tried to harmonise, laughing with each other as each one made a mistake, or was overcome with embarrassment.

Matteo was right, Jax decided, clapping along with the rest of the guests as the first song ended, this really was fun.

* * *

The next couple of hours passed by in a happy, noisy blur. Most of the food had been eaten and Matteo had been persuaded to sing two of his latest songs, delighting everyone at the party. Jax realised he was having a fun time with everyone.

'Ask Phoebe to dance,' Piper whispered to him as Tara and Perry chatted to Phoebe while others enjoyed the music at one end of the room.

'Why?'

'Because I'm sure she'd like to dance with you.'

He narrowed his eyes. 'You know I don't like dancing.'

He saw his cousin place her hands on her hips and give him one of her 'don't-bother-arguing-with-me' stares. Jax groaned. 'Fine then, I will.'

He waited for a break in Phoebe and Tara's conversation. 'Would you like to dance, Phoebe?'

She looked surprised for some reason, maybe because he didn't seem like the type to dance, whatever that was, Jax wondered. Or maybe she'd seen him dancing with Beth at the wedding reception and was trying to think of a way to let him down gently.

'I'd like that,' she said, surprising him.

He led her to the makeshift dance floor and reached it just as the music slowed. He stared at her awkwardly for a moment and then held out his arms inviting her to step into them. 'May as well, I suppose.'

Phoebe shrugged. 'Why not.'

She didn't seem to mind too much, and as he put one arm behind her back and took her left hand in the other one, it occurred to him that he was actually rather enjoying himself. 'I am apologising straight away in case I step on your toes,' he said. 'I'm not the most delicate of people.'

'I can see that.' She grinned. 'But you're doing just fine.'

He was relieved to hear it. He took her in his arms, ignoring the surprised look on Piper's face to see him dancing. Jax looked down and saw Phoebe staring up at him. She smiled shyly and Jax went to return her smile when pain shot through the toes on his right foot.

'Ouch.' He dropped his arms from her and wriggled his toes.

'Oh, sorry. That was terribly clumsy of me.' She looked down at his feet.

Seeing Phoebe's discomfort, Jax shook his head wanting to reassure her despite the terrible ache he now felt in his already bruised toe. 'I don't think anything's broken.'

'Are you sure?' She looked up into his eyes. 'You're teasing me, aren't you?'

'I am.' He saw her relax slightly. 'Now, if you promise not to stamp on my other foot we can carry on dancing.'

Phoebe laughed. 'I'll do my best.'

'It's been fun getting to know you a bit better tonight,' he admitted, slipping his arms around her again.

'Thank you. Apart from damaging your foot I've enjoyed myself too.'

He was about to ask her if she might consider meeting him for a coffee sometime after the Christmas festivities were over when a hand landed heavily on his right shoulder.

He looked to his side to see Tara looking concerned. 'What's the matter?'

'Have you got your jeep here?'

He nodded. 'Of course.'

She gave Phoebe an apologetic smile. 'I'm sorry to interrupt your evening but we need someone to drop a couple of people off at their homes before it gets too late.'

'Right.' Did she need to ask him? Surely other guests had their cars, Jax thought. 'Do you really need me though?'

Tara nodded. 'While we've all been in here having fun we've had a dumping of snow. It's really deep out there now and people are worried about driving in it. Would you mind very much dropping them off? They don't live too far away, only in St Mary.'

How could he say no? The country roads were narrower than the town ones and St Mary was one of the country parishes, so he understood people's reluctance to drive in these conditions, especially if they had little experience of doing so.

'I don't mind at all. Do they want to leave right away?' he asked, hoping she'd say no and realising that he didn't really want to stop dancing with Phoebe just yet.

'Yes, please.'

'I'm sorry to run off like this,' he said to Phoebe, surprised to note a hint of disappointment in her expression. It threw him slightly. 'Hopefully I shouldn't be too long and then maybe we can have another dance when I get back.'

'I'd like that.'

He left her and followed Tara to the door where two men and one woman were waiting and looking, he noticed, rather anxious.

'Jax is going to give you a lift home,' Tara explained. 'You can collect your cars tomorrow or the next day if you prefer.'

'That's very kind of you,' the woman said, clasping her handbag so tightly to her chest Jax knew he had to put her at her ease.

'Please don't worry about it. I should have you home in no time.' He pulled his keys from his jeans pocket and held them up. 'Give me a minute to bring the car to the door and then come out.'

He left the barn, the strong, freezing wind slapping him in the face with more vigour than he had expected. It really was rough outside.

He buttoned up his jacket against the cold and lowered his head as he walked quickly to his vehicle. 'Damn,' he shouted, seeing that not one but two cars had blocked his jeep against the wall. He brushed snow off the back of both cars to make sure he knew the right colours and makes to tell the owners, then cleared the number plates and ran back into the barn.

'Ready?' Tara asked.

'Not quite, I've been blocked in.' He walked over to where one of the guests was acting as a DJ and indicated for her to turn down the music. Clapping his hands to get everyone's attention, Jax waited for them to quieten down.

'I need to drop people at their homes but two cars – a red Mazda and a black Golf – have blocked my car in. Could the owners please come with me to move them?'

He was beginning to think no one was listening to him when there were raised voices and a man walked over to him. 'Mine is the Golf, I'll move it right now.'

'Do you know who owns the Mazda?'

'I think he left in a taxi about an hour and a half ago,' the man said, frowning. 'We can't seem to locate his keys so he can't have left them with anyone here and must have taken them with him.'

'Great,' Jax moaned, his voice heavy with sarcasm. 'How am I supposed to give people a lift if I can't move my car?'

'Sorry, mate. No idea. I'll move mine out of the way in case the other driver does return, but I doubt that's going to happen now.'

'I agree. Sorry to snap,' Jax said, realising he might have been a bit rude. 'And thanks for moving your car.'

'No problem.'

Jax went to tell his passengers what was happening when Phoebe caught up with him. 'I can drive them home if you like?'

'It's treacherous out there.'

'Are you saying you don't think I'm capable of driving in snow?'

Horrified that he might have insulted her, Jax shook his head. 'No, of course I wasn't. But you said you had your dad's car and I'd hate for you to slide into a wall or something.'

She smiled and Jax realised she had been teasing him. 'You have two choices from what I can gather,' Phoebe said. 'A, the guests stay here and wait for the other driver to return, or B, I drive them home. You can come with me if that would help reassure you?' Her eyes glinted mischievously. 'Then you can be certain I'm driving carefully enough.'

'Very funny. Fine, then you drive. I will come with you, but only if you really don't mind?'

'I don't.'

Wanting to give more of a reason for offering to accompany

her, Jax added, 'Who knows what you might find out there. Last time we had snow like this there were cars left in the lanes. They were hidden by the snow drifting from the high hedges on either side and impossible to see. I'd hate for you to drive into one and get stuck.'

'Fine, that's decided then.' She undid her small bag that he hadn't noticed hanging from her shoulder and took out a set of car keys.

'I'm sure the passengers will much prefer sitting in your father's luxurious car than my old banger anyway.'

'How do you know it's a new Range Rover?' She grinned over her shoulder at him before walking towards the door.

'I, er... Isn't it?'

'It is.' They reached the three guests who seemed surprised to see her. 'I'll be taking you all home now,' Phoebe explained. 'Shall we go?'

It hadn't occurred to Jax until they were all outside that her car could have also been blocked in but when they reached it he was relieved to see that it was fine. He helped the three passengers into the back and took note of the two home addresses, which were thankfully almost next door to each other, and got into the passenger side.

'This is very comfortable,' one of the ladies said. 'And very kind of you to take us.'

'It is,' another agreed. 'Thank you.'

'It's no problem at all,' Phoebe said when everyone had clicked their seat belts into place. She turned on the car's ignition and then the heater and lights. 'Right, shall we get going?'

She seemed much more confident now they were outside and on a mission of sorts.

'What a smart car,' the gentleman said from the back seat. 'And so warm.'

Not like my jeep would have been, Jax pondered. Maybe it wasn't a bad thing that Phoebe had ended up driving. He relaxed slightly but didn't take his gaze from the roads ahead. They seemed passable, but only just and he suspected that as the snow was continuing to fall heavily there would soon be little chance of driving anywhere far from the barn. They would need to return as soon as they had dropped the three guests off in case any other people required a lift. Aware that he was thinking of offering someone else's vehicle and time, he waited until the passengers had been dropped safely home and shared his thoughts with Phoebe.

'I don't mind a bit,' she said.

'But you'll want to be getting home too. I know this is an excellent vehicle but who knows how bad this will get.' He looked at the night sky, which was mostly white, snow swirling all around them. 'The wind has picked up even more now. It's pretty stormy out there.'

'It's fine, really. I'm happy to help in any way I can.'

'Won't your family be worried if you're out late on a night like this?'

'No,' she laughed. 'They won't mind one bit.'

'Well, if you're sure.'

She reached out and rested her hand on his. 'I am. Stop worrying and let me concentrate on what I'm doing.'

They eventually pulled into the driveway and drove past the farmhouse to the smaller barn. 'I'll leave the car here so I can get away more easily if anyone else needs taking home.'

She turned off the ignition and then the lights. As she went to open the car door, Jax spoke. 'Phoebe?'

'Yes?'

'I thought it might be nice if we were to meet up for a coffee in a week or so, when all this Christmas lark is over.'

'You'll have to choose where we go' she said in that understated way he was beginning to expect from her. 'I've not been out much for coffee recently on the island, so wouldn't know the best places to visit.'

He liked that she was opening up a bit more with him. He thought of Beth and how comfortable she had made him feel from their first moment together. But Phoebe wasn't Beth and his relationship with Beth had been a romantic one. 'That's no problem. I'll happily introduce you to my favourite places.'

She seemed to hesitate then turned to face him, her left arm on the back of her car seat. 'I was wondering something.'

'Go on,' he said, seeing she wasn't completely sure about asking whatever it was that was bothering her.

'Oh, I don't know.'

'Phoebe,' he soothed. 'Tell me.'

'Well, all right then. You never noticed me before. Was that because you liked Fliss so much, or...'

'Or, what?'

'I'm just not your type.' She sighed, her cheeks reddening. 'There, I've said it.'

He had to think about his answer before speaking. 'I had noticed you,' he admitted, recalling how he hadn't had much choice when she had flung her arms around his neck and kissed him briefly on his lips on his birthday when a group of them had gone to Les Ecrehous. 'But I...' He laughed. 'I'm going to sound ridiculous.'

'Tell me.' She glanced out of the window, then back at him... 'I presumed I'd put you off me when I launched myself at you on your birthday,' she said, as if she had been reading his thoughts.

She had taken him aback when she had kissed him out of the blue, he realised. 'Fine. I actually noticed you that first day when we were going out on the RIB.'

'So why did you spend time with Fliss?'

Jax felt embarrassed to answer truthfully but knew he must even if she didn't understand what he meant. 'I know you're the quieter one of the two of you and I suppose I wasn't sure if you were messing about when you kissed me. Fliss was a bit over the top but seemed easier to read.'

She stared at him thoughtfully. 'You thought I was phony?'

'No. It was more that both of you were different to the other women I know and I wasn't sure how to take either of you.'

'But you felt more comfortable with Fliss?'

Was this a trick question? He had no idea. He hurriedly tried to find the right way to explain himself. 'No. I mean.' He sighed. 'I've no idea what I mean.' Then he had a thought. 'For example, if I was a car, I'd be like my jeep, rusty in places, a bit dishevelled despite doing my best to appear as I should for tonight's party, but you can see exactly what kind of life I have. Fliss is like a bright red Mercedes. You can't miss her and you know people are impressed by her. Whereas you look...'

She laughed, clearly amused. 'Go on.'

Embarrassed, he struggled to find the appropriate words. 'Like your father's Range Rover.'

'What? Big and hefty?'

He knew she was teasing him this time. 'No, sleek, shiny and perfect but somehow understated.'

Damn, he hadn't meant to say perfect. That was too much. Jax cringed.

'It's OK,' Phoebe laughed, her voice quieter. 'I think I understand what you're trying to tell me, and as much as it shows to me how little you know the real me, I can't expect you to think otherwise.'

'I'm not entirely sure what you've just said, but as long as I haven't offended you that's fine.'

'You haven't.' She tilted her head to one side. 'I suppose we should go inside and see if anyone else needs us to take them home.'

He liked that idea and was enjoying the evening far more than he had expected.

They entered the barn and both shook off the snow from their clothes. Jax brushed snowflakes from his unruly hair, moving out of the way when a couple exited the barn hand in hand, discussing their walk to their nearby home. Another group followed immediately after.

'We'll have you back to your babysitter in no time,' a woman said, holding up a pair of keys. 'Our four-by-four can get through most weathers.'

Jax was glad that some of the partygoers were making their way home. 'Good idea, it's getting really bad out there now.'

'That's what we thought,' the woman said, shivering as she stepped outside.

He waited as Phoebe explained to Piper that the roads were getting to the point that they would be impassable for any car that wasn't a four-by-four. As he watched her speaking, her hands animated and facial expressions adding to her description of their drive, he tried to picture her as Fliss's friend. They always seemed so close, yet despite his original assumptions about her, he was now seeing that Phoebe seemed quite unlike Fliss after all. It was a relief.

8

Jax was grateful to Phoebe for her offer to take others home. He looked around for Margery. He had promised to get her back home and knew that he wouldn't have much time left to do it before the roads became impassable. Spotting her, he walked over to where she was laughing with a large group of friends.

'Sorry to interrupt,' he said, touching her arm lightly. 'But I think I should be getting you home now.'

'What?' Margery looked at him as if she had no idea what he was talking about.

'You wanted to be home early to spend time with Dilys,' he reminded her in case she might have forgotten.

Margery narrowed her eyes. 'I haven't lost my memory,' she snapped and Jax realised he had spoken out of turn. 'I'm not ready to leave just yet though.' She indicated her friends, most of whom smiled up at him. 'We're making arrangements for our New Year's Day swim.'

'But it's getting really bad out there,' he said, doubting she understood how deep the snow now was. 'If we leave it much longer I think we might all end up having to stay here for the night.'

Margery burst out laughing, and after a couple of her friends seeming momentarily concerned, they began teasing him. 'You youngsters love a bit of drama,' Margery teased. 'I'll be ready in, say, fifteen minutes?'

'I don't think we have that long though,' Jax argued.

Margery turned to face him, her back towards her friends. She lowered her voice. 'Dear boy, I know you mean well, but you're becoming a little tiresome. I promise I won't be much longer. Now,' she said, waving him away. 'Why not go and find Piper while I finish off my conversation.'

Aware that he had little choice, Jax walked away to look for his cousin.

'Jax,' Phoebe said, hurrying over to him. 'Do you have time to come with me to drop off another couple?' When he looked doubtfully at her, she added, 'Their farm is nearby and they have two dogs and a cat they need to get back to. They walked here and wanted to try walking home again, but I've persuaded them that it will be far safer if I drive them home, and quicker.'

Aware that others might be worried about getting home to their children or pets, Jax hurried over to the DJ. After apologising for interrupting her, he took the woman's microphone and called for everyone's attention. 'Excuse me, but if any of you need to urgently get home to your families or pets, please raise your hands.'

One woman put a hand in the air. 'I do,' she said, a stricken look on her face. 'Those people who just left didn't have space for me in their car.'

'Don't worry, we'll think of something. Do you live far from here?' Phoebe asked, reaching Jax. 'Because I don't know if we can make it to the south of the island, or very far west.'

'You could phone a neighbour maybe?' Jax suggested.

'No, I'm just a couple of minutes that way.' She indicated north, which was where they were headed with the other couple.

'Come along with us now then,' Phoebe said.

Jax looked back to where Margery was still holding court. 'Go on then, I still have a little time.'

'Thank you,' Phoebe sighed. 'I feel better with you accompanying me.'

* * *

As Phoebe parked the car on their return to the barn, Jax turned to her. 'That was more difficult than I had imagined.'

'Same here.' She turned off the ignition. 'I'm not sure I'm happy to drive all the way to Gorey,' she said, looking guilty. 'Of course I'll try if you think we can make it there.'

Concerned, he shook his head. 'I can't ask you to do that. You'd still need to get back to your house and I worry about you driving in these conditions by yourself.'

'I admit I'm a bit concerned too. Although I do have a mobile if I get stuck,' she said, but he could see she was trying to sound more confident than she felt by the worried look on her face. 'We don't have much longer until we really are going to be stuck here.'

'I agree. We need to tell everyone and I need to speak to Piper and Margery. Maybe the person parked behind my car has moved it,' he added, aware that was more wishful thinking on his part rather than a likely occurrence.

As they hurried back to the barn, Jax noticed its wooden walls were now completely white and the pathway where he and Phoebe had walked out to the car barely twenty minutes before was almost invisible. What was he going to say to Margery?

'You were longer than you were supposed to be,' Piper's

grandmother grumbled when Jax explained how treacherous the lanes from the farm now were.

'You weren't ready to leave when Jax asked you,' Piper reminded her gran. 'You told me that yourself.'

'I said fifteen minutes,' Margery argued. She tapped her watch. 'It's been over twenty since then.'

Jax had known Margery his entire life and loved her but was also aware that when she was in one of her difficult moods there was little reasoning with her. 'I'm not asking Phoebe to drive again unless it's to try and get herself home.'

'Then how are you going to take me home?' Margery asked, tapping her right foot impatiently.

Jax shrugged. 'I'll have to ask some of the guests to help me try and move the Mazda out of the way so I can take you in my jeep.'

'How?' Piper asked.

'There are enough of us left here to lift one end and pull it back,' he replied, realising that even if it was possible that to try in slippery conditions was irresponsible. He shook his head. 'No, we can't do that, it's too dangerous and we don't want anyone getting hurt, especially when it will be difficult for emergency services to reach us quickly.'

'Well then, what do you suggest we do, stay the night here?' Margery asked, raising an eyebrow.

'Would that be so bad?' Jax asked, regretting doing so the second the words left his mouth and he saw Margery's eyes widen in horror.

'Don't be ridiculous, of course it would.' She glared at him. 'I was being sarcastic. What if the weather's worse tomorrow? It's Christmas Day for pity's sake. I have to be back at the pier to help Helen look after Dilys and cook tomorrow's lunch. I can't have her without me or Piper at Christmas time.'

Jax heard the panic in Margery's voice and supposed that she, Helen and Piper had always been a small unit, depending on each other. 'I'll do my best to think of something,' he said, hoping to reassure her.

'Thank you.'

'Gran, why don't you come over here and sit down while we leave Jax to think,' Piper said, giving Jax an apologetic grimace as she led her grandmother away.

They couldn't have walked a metre when all the lights went out and the music stopped. Several people shrieked in fright and those guests who were still there began wondering loudly what might have happened.

'A bloody power cut, that's all we need now,' Ernie bellowed. 'Everyone stay where you are while we try to find some torches.'

Jax doubted that there would be any lying around the barn. He pulled his mobile from his jeans pocket, located the torch and turned it on, just as several of the other guests did the same thing.

'This better come on before tomorrow,' a woman grumbled somewhere to Jax's left. 'Otherwise we won't be able to cook Christmas lunch.'

'When I was a kid in the war my mother cooked ours in a straw box.'

Jax hadn't heard of a straw box before and wondered what that entailed.

'Don't be silly,' the woman snapped. 'You have to part cook it first before putting it in the box for it to keep cooking. Don't you know that?'

'Maybe I'm not as old as you.'

'I think we should stop worrying about Christmas lunch right now. Nobody panic,' he heard a male guest say. 'Try to familiarise yourself with the room and find somewhere to sit so you don't trip over anyone else.'

Jax heard mumbles of chatter fill the large space as he had an idea. Seeing Piper in his torchlight, Jax went over to join her. 'I'm going to go and find the sisters and ask them if they have any torches, lanterns, and candles so that we can bring some light into this place.'

'Good plan,' Piper said.

'Did you mention candles?' he heard Tara ask.

'Yes, would you mind if we used some of yours for this evening. I'll settle up with you after Christmas.'

'There's no need to do that, Jax,' Tara said, raising a hand to shield her eyes from his torch light.

'Oh, sorry.' Jax lowered his phone.

'I'll find Casey and we can go and fetch some of our larger candles for you.'

'That's brilliant. Thank you.' Jax heard singing in one of the corners. Turning to check that Phoebe was still nearby he took her hand briefly. 'You OK?'

'Fine thanks. I'm rather enjoying myself.'

'I would be too if I wasn't so worried about people getting home somehow.'

'I've looked out of the window,' Piper said. 'There aren't any lights on in the main house either and I couldn't see any from the couple of houses across the field, so it must be an area power cut.'

'Probably an island-wide one,' someone else moaned unhelpfully. 'I wonder if they turned the power off from France again like they did on Liberation Day that year.'

'That wasn't done on purpose,' a woman argued.

'That only happened because the energy company in France was doing planned maintenance,' a woman insisted. 'It should have been fine but the secondary cable tripped.'

'Maybe that's what's happened now?' another suggested.

'Either way,' Perry the sculptor said. 'We need to figure out what to do next. I've just looked outside and seen how bad the snowstorm is and doubt any of us will be going anywhere in the next few hours, at the very least.'

'Well, I'm enjoying myself,' an elderly voice said, immediately followed by another agreeing with him. 'All I've got to look forward to tomorrow is a meal-for-one in my microwave. This is much more fun.'

Jax relaxed slightly knowing that most people seemed to be fine about the lack of lighting.

'We can't stay out here,' someone argued, lowering his mood. 'There's no heat and this place will soon cool right down. If only there was a fireplace, we could light a fire.'

'I need to get home,' Margery said, the panic in her voice clear. 'I can't stay here all night.'

'Don't worry, Gran,' Jax heard Piper attempting to soothe her gran.

Someone clapped their hands and Jax turned his torch in the direction of the sound and saw it was Meg, one of the sisters. 'Amy and I have been talking and we'd like to invite you all into our home for the night.'

'Or as long as necessary,' Amy added.

'Yes. We have fireplaces there and if people can carry chairs, food, drink and the table across the yard then I'm sure we can all help to set ourselves up nicely in our two main living areas. There should be enough room to comfortably fit everyone.'

Relieved that someone had come up with a plan, Jax thanked them. The torches on people's phones would soon drain their batteries, so it made sense to move into the house where at least they could light fires to give them light and heat.

'Those of you who can do, help others across to the house,' Jax said, giving pointed looks to those he needed to stay behind. 'Then the rest of us who don't need help can carry everything necessary back to the house. I'm sure we'll be organised in no time.'

'Great idea,' Piper said, giving him a wink. 'Come along, Gran, let's get you to the farmhouse and we can work out what to do from there.'

Jax heard Margery grumbling but not what she was saying. He shone his torch to light the way to the door and noticed one of the female guests then shine hers across the yard.

Spotting Phoebe in the dim light, he walked over to her. 'How are you doing?'

'Fine, thanks,' she said. 'In fact I'm finding it a little exciting, aren't you?'

He thought about her question. 'I would be if I didn't feel so guilty about Margery being stuck here.'

'Yes, she is rather upset but I can't see how that's your fault.' She rested a hand on his forearm. 'Maybe she'll calm down when she's inside the house and she feels more secure.'

'Maybe,' Jax said, doubting it very much but hoping she was right.

When most of the guests had made their way gingerly across the yard, Jax, Piper, Phoebe, Tara and about ten others gathered what they could and made several trips to the farmhouse. Each time Jax stepped outside with an armful of bottles, chairs, cutlery, or food, the icy wind took his breath away. It really was a nasty, wintery night. Not at all the Christmas Eve he had imagined.

It was a bigger struggle taking the heavy oak dining table from the barn back to the house. A couple of them slipped, almost causing Jax to drop his end of the table, but with a little patience they managed to get the antique piece of furniture into the house, down the wide hallway and into the dining room.

The sisters were already instructing two guests to light fires in the large fireplaces, one in the living room and the other in the dining room. He noticed that there were double doors joining the two rooms, which had been folded back making one large entertainment room.

'This is brilliant,' he said, causing the sister nearest to him to smile.

'I'm glad you think so.'

'We should be comfortable enough in here,' Jax said, joining Phoebe.

'I agree. Although...' she lowered her voice and leant closer to him, 'I have heard a couple of them moaning that they could do with a cup of tea or hot cocoa.'

He guessed that Margery was one of them. 'Not much we can do about that right now though.'

'Maybe the power cut won't last too long.'

He crossed his fingers on both hands and held them up. 'Please let that be the case.'

Phoebe giggled.

He lowered his hands and stared at her, marvelling at how unfazed she had been by all that had happened that evening.

'What?' she asked.

'I was just thinking how good you've been about all this,' he admitted. 'Doesn't it worry you that you probably won't be able to get home to your parents before morning, if then?'

'Sorry, but can I interrupt,' Perry said, holding up a string bag with some supplies in it.

'Of course.' Jax nodded.

'There's a neighbouring farmer here. He's come on his tractor to check on the sisters. He asked me to give these bits to them. Do you know where they are?'

Jax scanned the room and spotted them in the living room over by an overstuffed sofa. 'They're over there,' he pointed.

Perry left to speak to them and it dawned on Jax that maybe

the farmer might be the answer to at least one of his problems. 'I won't be a minute,' he said to Phoebe.

'Where are you going?'

'Follow me and you'll find out.' As he rushed through the house to the back door, he hoped that the farmer hadn't come on an older tractor without a cabin. If he had then he wasn't going to be able to help Jax out.

The man was standing inside the back door, so Jax went up to him. 'Do you mind if I have a look at your tractor?'

The farmer shrugged. 'Do what you like, son.'

Jax opened the door willing to find what he hoped to see. 'Yes!' He felt as if all his Christmas presents had come at once. He went back inside.

'You're looking pleased with yourself,' the farmer said.

'What it is?' Phoebe asked frowning.

'I think I've found Margery's transport home.'

9

'What?' Piper said her eyes widening in shock when Jax explained his idea. 'Gran can't get up there?' She pointed to the cabin high off the ground.

'If I can,' the older farmer said. 'Then this young lady will be fine.'

Margery gave a satisfied nod. 'There, you see, Piper? Not everyone thinks that I'm past it yet, my girl.'

'But, Gran, are you sure you don't mind?'

'I think your gran is perfectly happy about it,' Jax said, seeing the excited grin on Margery's face. 'At least this way she'll be able to spend the night in her own cottage and check up on Dilys. She can also let my mum and yours know that we'll be stuck here for the night.' He checked that Margery didn't mind being his messenger. 'Is that all right, Margery?'

'Of course it is. Now, Piper, fetch my bag, will you?' Margery said. 'It's in the dining room on the sideboard at the far end.'

As soon as Piper had left to do as she had been asked, Margery shook the farmer's hand. 'This is kind of you, I'm very grateful. I'm longing for a cup of tea.'

'Not at all, ma love. I'll have you home in a jiffy.' He cocked his head in the direction Piper had gone. 'I can come back for her afterwards if you like.'

'You'd better ask her about that,' Margery said. 'Anyway, what brought you here in the first place?'

'When the lights went my wife suggested I bring bread, milk and some cheese, and come to check on the Ecobichon sisters. She was worried they might be concerned about the power cut, but we should have known better. They're tough, those two. Lived through the Occupation as young girls, they did. From good farming stock, like me.' He tapped his chest proudly. 'People like us don't let little mishaps like this get us down.'

'No, we don't,' Margery said, although Jax knew perfectly well she hadn't come to the island until the seventies. He caught Phoebe trying not to smile out of the side of his eye. 'Well, we're very grateful to you, Mr... er?'

'Just call me Len. I live on the farm down to the left at the end of the lane. Ah, here's your handbag now. Best be getting you up in that cabin then, Margery.'

'Don't you worry, Jax can help me.' She waved for Jax to assist her to the other side of the enormous vehicle. Then Jax opened the door of the cab, and after a little heaving, managed to get her up into the glass box and settled onto the smaller seat next to the driver's larger one.

'All good?' Jax asked, having stepped up into the cabin with her. Margery nodded and he could see by the glint in her eyes that she was enjoying every unexpected moment. 'Let me do that for you,' he said, taking the seat belt, pulling it around her and clicking it firmly into place. 'There you go,' he said. 'I'll ring ahead and let Helen know you're on your way, then I'll call Dad and ask him to meet you from the tractor.'

'Thanks, lovey,' she said, resting a hand on his left cheek. 'And

I'm sorry if I was a bit snappy earlier. I just got a bit of a fright, that's all.'

'It's fine. Forget all about it.' Jax jumped down.

'I could come back and clear the driveway tonight,' Len said, standing near him. 'But I don't think it's worth it, not when the roads are impassable to cars. 'I'll come back in the morning and see what I can do then though.'

'Great, thank you. I'll let Meg and Amy know.'

Len took Margery's bag from Piper and passed it up to her. 'Will you want me to come back and fetch you, young lady?' he asked. 'I don't mind doing it, so don't worry on my account.'

Jax could see Piper wasn't sure whether to ask him to do so, or not. 'I suppose I should go home if I can get there,' she said. 'Yes, please if you really wouldn't mind.'

'No problem. I'll be back for you in no time.'

Piper went back to stand next to Jax. He moved over, placing an arm around her and Phoebe and pulling them closer to him so that they could huddle out of the wind in the doorway. They watched Len climb up into the cab and set off.

'Look.' Piper laughed. 'Gran's having a fun time up there.'

She was, Jax thought, seeing Margery waving merrily at them.

'Thank heavens he came to check on the sisters,' Phoebe said as they turned and went back inside the house.

'You're not kidding,' Piper agreed. 'Jax would never have heard the end of it if she hadn't been able to get home to her own bed tonight.'

'I thought she wanted to go home to check on Dilys.' Jax frowned.

'She will do that,' Piper said knowingly. 'But Gran loves her routine, so would have missed not having her last cuppa, and she loves sleeping in her own bed.'

'If this power cut is island-wide then she won't be enjoying that cuppa, but at least she'll be in her own home, so that's something,' Jax said, thinking of the floor in the farmhouse where he would most likely be sleeping tonight.

'I wonder how long Len will be coming back for me?' Piper asked, covering her mouth as she began to yawn.

'No idea,' Jax said, wishing he was going home too. 'I'd better phone your mum and my dad before I forget. I don't need Margery getting to the pier and not have them waiting to help her to her cottage.'

After making his calls he went back to the two adjoining reception rooms to let the sisters know what Len had said about coming back to clear the drive in the morning.

'That's good of him,' Meg said. 'Typical Len to be so thoughtful, although I know his wife will have been the one to suggest it.'

'She will,' Amy agreed.

'Is there anything you need me to do?' Jax asked. 'If we're all stopping here for the night then we should probably organise ourselves and figure out where people should sleep.'

The sisters swapped glances that seemed to pass a message from one to the other because they then nodded.

'We were talking about this when you were outside with Len,' Amy said. 'We're not set up for guests but we do have four guest rooms that can be made up for people who would rather sleep on a bed. I'm afraid the younger ones will need to make do with the floors. And those of the guests who would rather not be in a freezing cold room might choose to sleep on the sofa or on a chair down here, where at least it's a little warmer.'

'Sounds good to me,' Jax agreed, having a quick look at the sofa and realising that even though it was fairly large it would still be too short for him to lie on comfortably. 'Do you want to tell them, or shall I?'

'You have a louder voice than us, so you can,' Meg said.

Jax clapped his hands and called for everyone's attention, then shared the sisters' suggestions about sleeping arrangements. 'Anyone who needs help making up rooms just let me know.'

'Or me,' Phoebe added. 'I'm happy to help anyone.'

'There's an airing cupboard full of sheets, pillows and blankets over there,' Meg said pointing to a door at the top of the stairs. 'Take whatever you need to make yourselves comfortable downstairs. You should find a few torches in there too.'

Jax opened the door, amazed at the array of bedlinen and towels stacked neatly on shelves reaching high up towards the ceiling on either side of a room slightly bigger than his bedroom at home. 'I think we'll have more than enough to keep us warm with this lot,' he said gratefully. 'I'll start to take what I think we need downstairs to the others.'

* * *

Half an hour later, the extra rooms were made up and Jax and several of the others set fires in the small bedroom fireplaces to warm the rooms and help give a little light. The eldest couple took one bedroom and two sisters shared another, with other older guests taking the remaining rooms. He had also found several torches and, leaving one in each room upstairs, brought the spare two downstairs for the rest of the guests to use together with a mixed load of bedding.

Jax handed the bedding to Phoebe when she appeared outside the room. 'Wow, we got stuck in the right place,' she said. 'I'll send some of the others up to help you.'

Jax carried on downstairs, pointing the way up to the airing cupboard to Perry, Tara, Casey and Matteo as he passed them on the staircase.

He found Phoebe standing in the doorway between the two

rooms. 'I'm not sure where to set up,' she said looking from one side and then the other.

'Ah, good point. I think we need to make more floor space for those who'll be sleeping down here. I'm sure the sisters won't mind us moving furniture as long as we're careful and put it all back in the morning.'

Tara and Casey brought in a couple of large lanterns they used for displaying their candles on their stall and set one down in the kitchen for when people went to find something to drink and another in the hallway leading to the bathroom. There were two smaller candleholders in the bathroom, too.

With everyone helping, they soon had the sofa, chairs and any tables pushed back against walls leaving the floorspace in front of both fires free for bedding. The firelight gave the room a cosy glow and for the first time Jax found he was beginning to feel a little festive.

'I'm going to sleep under the dining room table,' he whispered to Phoebe. 'It's out of the way and hopefully no one will trip over my gangly legs if they're tucked away.'

Phoebe laughed. 'I've seen your legs, remember? There's nothing wrong with them, although I have to admit they are rather long.' She giggled, clearly amused at her teasing.

He liked this side of her. She was fun and much more relaxed now that they had spent a few hours together. Her amusement vanished and Jax wondered what could be wrong.

'Is everything OK?'

She nodded. 'I was wondering something, but it's a little embarrassing.'

'Go on, I'm intrigued.'

He saw her hesitate, then shrug. 'Would you mind very much if I slept under the table next to you? Would that seem odd?'

He decided it wouldn't. 'No, I don't think so. We're in a room full of people and you have to sleep somewhere, don't you? Anyway, these are unusual circumstances.'

'It's just that I don't really know anyone apart from you.' She frowned thoughtfully. 'I vaguely know Casey and Tara, but don't want to impose on them.'

Jax followed Phoebe's gaze to where Tara and Casey were sitting cross-legged on the floor on top of their makeshift beds playing backgammon with Perry and Matteo. He smiled, wanting to put her at her ease. 'It's fine, really. I do understand.'

'Thank you, that's kind.'

'I wouldn't say that too soon,' he said, trying to look serious.

Phoebe frowned. 'What do you mean?'

'You don't know if I snore yet.'

Her expression softened. 'Do you?'

'I don't know.'

'Well, if you do, I'll cover your face with a pillow.'

Jax laughed. 'Great. The first time we sleep together and you want to suffocate me.'

'The first time?'

He realised what he had said and grimaced. 'I meant...' What did he mean? he wondered.

Phoebe pushed him in the shoulder. 'I think maybe we should change the subject.'

Relieved not to have made an even bigger fool of himself, Jax nodded. 'I agree.'

Now that everyone at the house was settled he couldn't help thinking about Beth and Billy. Were they all right? Their cottage was away from any neighbours and, although he knew she had planned to spend Christmas Day with her parents, Vicki and Dan, Jax wondered if Beth had made it there. He checked the time. It was just before 9 p.m. so she would still be awake. He found her number in his contacts and decided to give her a quick call. Nothing.

'Damn.'

'What's the matter?' Phoebe asked.

'I've just tried to call Beth,' he said, now anxious to speak to her and reassure himself she and Billy were fine. He noticed Phoebe's expression alter slightly but didn't know why and thought he should explain. 'I think the phone lines must be down now. I was hoping to check up on them.'

Phoebe stared at him for a moment. 'If you want, we could try and get to them. Are they far from here?'

'Not very,' he said, liking the idea. 'About five minutes usually.'

'Would you like us to try?' Phoebe asked.

Jax stared at the sweet girl in front of him. 'I hate bothering you with this,' he admitted, aware that he had little choice if he was to reassure himself. 'We're finally settled down in here and I'm suggesting we go back outside into the storm.' He groaned in frustration. 'If only my jeep wasn't blocked in, then I wouldn't have to ask you to take me.'

Phoebe smiled. 'It's fine. I really don't mind.' She narrowed her eyes. 'Would it be awkward, me coming along?'

'No.' *Why would it be?* 'It's not as if there's anything between you and me, is there?'

'No,' she said a little shortly, taking him by surprise.

'And Beth and I aren't a couple any longer. I'm only checking up on her as a friend.'

'Are you really though?'

Jax hadn't expected Phoebe's question and by the look of surprise on her face she hadn't expected to say it. *Was he lying to himself about his feelings towards Beth? No.* 'Yes, I really am.'

'You had to think about it first before being able to answer,' she said quietly, as if not really wanting to voice her thoughts.

He couldn't understand why she was questioning him. What difference did it make to Phoebe anyway? He felt her hand on his forearm.

'Ignore me,' she said. 'I'm tired. If you want to check up on them, then I think we should go now. This snow isn't going to go anywhere overnight and if it's still snowing out there then it'll only get worse.'

'I agree. We'd better get our coats back on then.'

10

PHOEBE

They hadn't driven far down the lane before Phoebe wished she hadn't been so quick to offer to take Jax. *What had she been thinking to come out on these roads again?* Then she thought of the young widow and little boy and felt guilty for moaning, if only to herself.

'I do appreciate you doing this for me,' Jax said. 'When this is over we'll have to go out for a drink, or something to eat. My treat as a thank you.'

Phoebe's mood soared just before the tyres hit some black ice and skidded sideways. She only just managed to right the vehicle before it connected with the granite wall on the side of the road. She needed to concentrate. 'Good thing I was only going slowly then,' she said almost to herself.

'Sorry, I shouldn't be interrupting your concentration,' Jax said, focusing on looking ahead of them.

'It's not your fault,' she said hurriedly, not ready to finish their conversation until they had arranged something concrete. Who knew when he would ever invite her out on a date again? When he didn't say anything, Phoebe decided it was up to her to get their conversation back on track. 'So when were you thinking of taking me out for that thank you meal?'

She saw his head turn her way and smiled inwardly. 'Er, we can go out whenever you like.'

'Not much happens between Christmas and New Year, does it?'

'I suppose not. Where would you like us to go?'

If she left it up to Jax, Phoebe had a feeling they might end up foraging for their meal and enduring a damp picnic on a beach somewhere. That might be an exciting thought for summer, she decided, but no so much in the depth of winter. 'I don't mind,' she said honestly. 'Wherever you choose to take me.' She took her eyes off the road when they reached the end of the lane. 'As long as it's warm,' she added, smiling at him.

Jax's expression softened and his mouth drew back into a smile. The effect lit up his entire face and Phoebe felt her stomach flip over wishing he might lean forward and kiss her. Instead, his attention was diverted and he pointed to the left. 'Beth's place is down that way.'

Beth. 'Right,' Phoebe said grumpily.

The depth of the snow made their journey a slow one and Phoebe had to concentrate on keeping to the middle of the road where the snow was shallowest, only moving to the left if she saw another vehicle coming in the opposite direction. Thankfully that only happened twice.

'Most people clearly have the sense to stay at home tonight,' she said.

'Maybe we should have followed their example,' Jax said. 'It's worse out here than I had expected.'

'Good thing I borrowed my dad's car then.'

'It is.' Jax pointed to a cottage up a short driveway. 'There it is.'

'I'm happy to stay here and wait if you'd rather I do that,' she offered, hoping he would insist she accompany him. She had only seen Beth once and was interested to see the woman who had recently dumped someone as gorgeous as Jax.

Jax looked horrified. 'You can't stay out here, it's freezing.'

'I can keep the engine running and the heater on.'

'I wouldn't be comfortable leaving you out here.' He frowned. 'Unless you'd rather not come in?'

'No, I'm happy to come with you.' Before he had a chance to change his mind, she turned off the engine and stepped out of the car.

'Here,' Jax said, holding out his hand. 'Take my arm and we'll work our way through this snow together.'

She did as he asked, not needing him to ask twice. Phoebe slipped her arm through his, enjoying the warmth of his side against hers. He held her close as they walked up to the front door.

He knocked on the door, which was opened almost immediately by a beautiful woman Phoebe recognised as Beth. She seemed relieved to see Jax, but as her eyes moved from his face she seemed taken aback to notice that he and Phoebe were arm in arm.

Jax let go of Phoebe. 'I hope we're not disturbing you. We only wanted to check that you and Billy were all right with the power cut.'

Beth smiled, first at Jax and then at Phoebe. Then she stepped back and waved them in. 'You'd better come in, it's freezing out there.'

Jax waited for Phoebe to enter the hallway before following and closing the front door quietly behind them. 'I hope we haven't woken Billy,' he asked quietly as Phoebe looked around her, trying not to seem as if she was being nosy. It was such a pretty home, which was evident despite the lights not working.

'I love your lanterns,' she said, wanting to be friendly to this woman whose home she had pitched up at.

'You should see them when they're lit up. They do look rather lovely, don't they?' Beth said smiling. 'Although the ones in the kitchen have skulls on them because they were left over from Halloween.'

Phoebe laughed. 'Very resourceful.'

'Well, no point in wasting them, is there?'

Phoebe decided she liked this friendly woman. She seemed welcoming and rather gentle. She realised Jax wasn't speaking. Presuming he felt awkward turning up uninvited at the home of the woman who had recently dumped him, Phoebe thought she should say something. She could see the reflection of flames on the wall. 'You have a fire going?'

'Yes,' Beth said. 'I was grateful to have a working fireplace when we moved in and now this has happened I've decided I'm not going to move into another place unless it also has one.' She waved her arm in the direction of the living room. 'Would you like to come in for a bit? I would offer you a drink but unfortunately it will have to be a cold one and I only have tap water or mango juice.'

Phoebe shook her head not wishing to use anything that Beth might need for her little boy. 'I'm fine, thanks.' She looked from Beth to Jax, both fair and tall, and couldn't help thinking how perfect they had looked dancing together in the summer at Vicki's wedding. Her heart lurched. She was so different to Beth, dark-haired, and despite being taller than most of her friends, was shorter and clearly very different to the women Jax was attracted to. The thought saddened her.

'Me too,' Jax said. 'I can see you're warm enough here and you seem fine, so we'll leave you in peace. Would you like me to check up on you both tomorrow?'

Beth smiled and shook her head. 'No, we'll be OK. My dad will no doubt find a way of getting to us, so we should be fine.' She glanced in the direction of the door. 'Billy is going to be beside himself with excitement when he wakes up to all this snow.'

Jax smiled. 'He will. Well, Happy Christmas, Beth. Take care now and please tell Billy to throw a few snowballs just for me.'

She laughed. It was a soft, warm laugh Phoebe noticed. 'I will do.' Her eyes met Phoebe's. 'Thank you for coming to check on us tonight, Phoebe. I appreciate it. Happy Christmas both of you.'

'Happy Christmas, Beth,' Phoebe said.

As she and Jax trudged slowly back to the car, Phoebe couldn't help wondering if Beth hadn't still been grieving for her late husband she and Jax might have made a lovely couple. They certainly looked beautiful together. *What the hell was she thinking?* She was torturing herself unnecessarily. She decided to push all thoughts of Beth and Jax together aside and try to be in the moment and enjoy every second she had with him while she could. Who knew what might happen after Christmas and New Year and when the snow melted and everyone went back to their usual lives.

Once they were strapped back into their seats, Phoebe turned to Jax. 'She's lovely.'

'She is,' he agreed quietly, giving her a strange look.

'What?'

'I was just thinking how different you are.'

Phoebe turned on the ignition. 'I was thinking the same thing earlier.' Why did he have to say that? She turned the car with a little difficulty and began driving back towards the farm. Her earlier happy mood had dissipated and now all she wanted to do was drop Jax off at the Ecobichons' house and slowly make her way home. So what if her parents were away over Christmas?

Right now all she wanted to do was go to her bed and wallow in her misery. It didn't matter how much she liked Jax, he clearly didn't see her romantically, otherwise he would have let her know by now, surely?

The snow was still falling but didn't seem to be quite as heavy as earlier. Good, thought Phoebe. She liked the countryside all white and looking as if it had been painted especially for a Christmas card, but snowdrifts were no fun, not when you wanted to get somewhere.

Phoebe slowed the car and parked at a bus stop but kept the engine running. Jax turned his upper body to face her. 'Are you wanting to go somewhere else?'

'I'm going home, Jax,' she said, aware that her tone was short.

'What? You can't!'

She tilted her head to one side and frowned at him, annoyed that he should presume to tell her she couldn't do something. 'Er, I can do whatever I like.'

He looked stunned by her reaction and she was instantly embarrassed for her outburst. 'I'm not telling you that you can't, Phoebe. It's more that I'm suggesting you probably shouldn't.' He stared at her intently for a moment and Phoebe wished he wouldn't. 'Have I said something to upset you? Because if I did it wasn't intentional.'

She sighed, irritated with herself and her own sensitivity. 'No,' Phoebe lied. 'I just want to sleep in my own bed, that's all.'

He turned to face the front of the car again. 'Then I'm coming with you.'

'What?' She might fancy him, but she had no intention of accepting Jax telling her he was coming back with her to her bed. 'You'll do no such thing.'

He seemed confused and didn't speak for a few seconds. Then

his eyes widened and his mouth dropped open. 'No! I didn't mean it that way.' He grimaced.

Phoebe wondered if he needed to look quite so horrified by the prospect and gritted her teeth to try and hide her hurt.

'Hell, no. All I meant was that I'd come home with you to make sure you got back safely. I'd sleep on the sofa, or something.' He rubbed his face. 'I'd never presume anything like that.'

Mortified to have misunderstood him, Phoebe cringed. 'I'm sorry. I'm being ridiculous. It's not your fault.'

'Something is wrong though. Will you tell me what it is?'

Should she? She wasn't sure she wanted to let him know. What if he felt sorry for her, she would hate that almost as much as him being appalled at the thought of going to bed with her. Almost.

She took a deep breath and shrugged. 'I suppose I may as well be honest.' She saw him waiting patiently for her to continue. 'It's just that my parents told me yesterday that they're not coming home for Christmas as we had planned.'

He seemed confused. 'Not... they're away then?'

'The Caribbean. St Kitts to be precise.'

'Wow, nice.' Then he frowned. 'Not for you though. Did they know you would be alone for Christmas?'

She shook her head. 'I think they presumed I'd spend it with Fliss.' She liked to think that was the case anyway. 'And they did offer to fly me to spend the holidays with them.'

'And you didn't want to go? Even when Fliss had to return to Poole?'

She shook her head. 'I didn't fancy travelling all that way only to return a week later.'

He stared at her thoughtfully. 'I've never been to the Caribbean but I've always imagined it to be beautiful. All those golden sandy beaches, turquoise oceans and green hillsides. And I thought the vibe was very chilled. What's not to love?'

He appeared genuinely confused that she had chosen to remain on the island. 'You'd rather go away from here for Christmas then?'

'What, me? Hell, no. I love it here. I can't imagine anywhere else I'd rather be.'

Double standards? 'So why should I choose differently then?' She waited for him to consider his reply, interested to hear what he thought.

Jax shook his head. 'No, it's just that I had thought you'd choose spending time with your parents over being alone, that's all. Don't you get along well with them then?' He winced. 'Don't answer that. It was wrong of me to ask such a personal question. I don't mean to pry.'

Phoebe thought about her relationship with her parents. She loved them both, very much, but she suspected Jax's relationship with his mum and dad was a closer one than hers with her parents. She didn't want him to think she didn't love them, but decided she wanted to explain a little bit about their relationship.

'Mum and Dad are great people,' she said, 'but whereas a lot of parents base their lives around their home, mine have been very focused on their careers.' She realised that hadn't come out as she meant it to. 'I don't mean in the nine-to-five way that most parents work, but it's like they've both been competing with each other in their professions.'

'What do they do, if you don't mind me asking?'

'Dad designs luxury yachts and Mum has her own collection of jewellery. They're both extremely driven and rarely take time away from their phones.' She pictured them both how they probably were right at that moment. 'Even though they're staying in a luxurious house borrowed from one of their friends, I'm fairly certain they'll both be working in some capacity.'

'Do you have siblings?'

Phoebe shook her head. She had prayed for a younger brother or sister for years growing up, but had long given up on that ever happening now.

'Don't you ever get lonely?'

Was he starting to feel sorry for her? She hoped not. 'I don't, but neither, I thought, did you.'

'I don't, but I live a few doors down from Piper and we've been brought up seeing each other most days, like siblings.'

'Of course.' Determined to put him right, she smiled. 'I might be an only child but I've always had friends coming to stay, or been to stay with them, so I've never minded too much.' She shrugged. 'Anyway, this is how my life's always been, so it's not as if I really know anything different.'

'But you'll be alone in that big house over Christmas?'

Phoebe shrugged. 'It's not so bad. Anyway, I'm used to the house, it's where I've always lived.'

'I suppose not.' She saw his handsome face light up in a smile. 'I'd like you to spend Christmas with us, with me.'

'With you?' What did he mean?

'Well, not me so much as with my family.'

'Really? Your family wouldn't mind me imposing on them with no notice?'

She watched his expression change as he seemed to think over what he had just said. Clearly he hadn't thought that far.

'Piper's mum has a guest house a couple of doors down from our house,' Jax explained. 'I'm sure she'd be happy to put you up. Helen is great at making guests in her home feel very welcome. I would offer for you to stay with me...' He shook his head, realising what he'd said. 'I mean, with my family, but our place is tiny.'

'That sounds nice,' she said quietly. 'But I'm not sure. I don't like the thought of imposing myself on your aunt.'

'Not at all.' He thought for a moment. 'Why don't I ask her? I won't let Helen know that I've already made the suggestion to you. That way you'll know she hadn't felt pressured to agree to you staying at the guest house.'

Liking the thought of spending time with the close family, Phoebe nodded. 'I'd like that.'

'Good, that's settled then.'

'I suppose we'd better get back there now.'

She looked at Jax's handsome face and, recalling how she had thrown herself at him on the Ecrehous during his birthday trip in the summer and kissed him, she reminded herself that he wasn't actually interested in her. Would it be so bad simply having him as a friend?

Jax frowned. 'Is something wrong?'

'Yes, why?' she asked, embarrassed that he had noticed.

'You've got a bit pink in the face. You're not coming down with something, are you?'

Phoebe saw the panic in his face and after a moment's struggle to decide whether to pretend she was fine, she decided to confess to what had caused her embarrassment. 'I'm fine. I just remembered flinging myself at you on your birthday and kissing you.'

Jax frowned thoughtfully. Surely he remembered her making such a berk of herself? His eyebrows rose and he grinned at her. 'Ah, that. Yes, you took me by surprise when you did that.'

'I did?'

'Yes!'

'I'm sorry. It was out of order.'

'It was a little awkward, that's all.'

She wasn't sure what he meant. 'What, my kiss?'

Jax laughed. 'No, my reaction.'

'I promise I won't do it again.'

He grinned at her and she presumed he was relieved. The thought stung a little, but she had no intention of making a fool of herself again as she had when she had been going round with Fliss. Even her father had remarked, after seeing the two of them together by their swimming pool that summer, how silly she was when she was with Fliss. The realisation had mortified her.

'Shall we?'

'Sorry?' *What had he just said?*

'I said I thought we should probably get moving again.'

He was right. Phoebe pulled back onto the road. 'I wonder how the others are getting on at the farmhouse?'

'They should be fine as long as this power cut doesn't last too long.'

11

JAX

Jax watched Phoebe as she drove. She seemed deep in thought but was probably concentrating on driving in the difficult conditions. He had forgotten about Phoebe kissing him on his birthday. She had seemed so different then, but it had only been a few months before. Maybe Fliss was a bad influence on her, he decided. She had certainly appeared to like being the one to get the attention, unlike Phoebe, who came across as the gentler character out of the two women. Phoebe was very different now, or seemed to be. All he had witnessed of Phoebe recently had been her hard work helping others and being incredibly kind.

Had she had a bit of a crush on him in the summer? He thought back to her kiss when they had been on the Ecrehous and realised he should have probably considered why she might have done it. Her kiss hadn't been a shy peck on the cheek. She had surprised him by flinging her arms around him and plonking a great big smacker on his lips. Jax recalled how embarrassed she had seemed as soon as she had done it and all he had wanted to do then was cover his surprise at the unexpected kiss.

Hearing her promise that it would never happen again, Jax

supposed Phoebe had expected him to be relieved, or certainly pleased with her assurances. Instead, he found that he was saddened by them.

Her eyes moved to him briefly before returning to the road. 'Why are you staring at me?'

Damn! 'I was er...' Jax tried to think of a reasonable excuse. 'I was thinking how kind of you it is to come out again in this dreadful weather so I could check up on Beth.'

'It's nothing,' Phoebe said. 'Don't worry about it. I was happy to take you there.'

Relieved that she had bought his excuse, Jax relaxed again. 'I hope Billy's Christmas isn't ruined,' he said thinking of the little boy waking the following morning to no electricity.

'Why? As long as Santa has visited him and the snow is still covering his garden, which...' she laughed, 'I'm sure it will be, I should imagine he'll think it's the very best of Christmases.'

'But if the rest of their family can't reach them and there's no electricity Beth won't be able to cook their Christmas lunch.'

Phoebe tilted her head to one side. 'And you think a three-year-old is going to be bothered by that?' She slowed the car even further as they reached the farm. 'Do you recall any of your Christmas lunches from when you were small, or do you mostly remember the gifts you received and the excitement of the day.'

Phoebe had a point. 'True. I have no idea what we ate, or anything apart from my presents,' Jax said.

'Well then. He's safe with his mum and their home is cosy with that lovely fire and their pretty decorations. I think Billy will have a wonderful day regardless of whether the lights work or not.'

'Thanks, Phoebe,' he said, feeling reassured.

'Here we are.' She parked the car. 'At least the snow seems to be lighter now. Let's hope it stops altogether overnight.'

'I agree.'

Once inside the living rooms they were greeted by the other guests, most of whom seemed a little tipsy but comfortable enough in the conjoined rooms.

'How was it out there?' Ernie asked. 'Treacherous, I imagine?'

'It was rather,' Phoebe said. 'I'm glad to be back here.' She covered her mouth with her hand as she yawned.

Jax supposed she must be tired after all that had happened and having to concentrate for so long. He looked around the room but couldn't see Piper anywhere. 'Did the farmer come back then?'

'Yes, he picked up Piper and also a lady who lived on the way,' Perry said. 'Shouldn't have done, of course, but it was probably safer not to make the trip twice and both needed to get to the same place.'

Jax was relieved his cousin had managed to get home. Helen and Margery would have been worried about her. He supposed Piper would also let his mum know that he was staying the night with the others at the farmhouse and relaxed.

'Maybe we should find ourselves something to eat and drink,' he suggested, handing her a couple of blankets and a pillow from the ones they'd found in the well-stocked airing cupboard.

Phoebe took them and unfolded one of the blankets. 'Why don't we pull some chairs together and hang the blanket over them.'

Enjoying her light-hearted banter, Jack grinned. 'We could if the chairs weren't already being sat upon.' He tried to think of an alternative. 'Maybe there's a corner we could find to set up our own place to sleep?'

Phoebe laughed and hit him lightly with the pillow. 'We sound like a couple of children playing forts.'

Jax laughed. 'I suppose we do.' He smiled at her. 'I hope you're enjoying yourself, even if only a little bit.'

She nodded. 'I am. This certainly beats sitting at home alone.'

He remembered what she had told him about her parents not returning from the Caribbean. 'I wish you had told me sooner about that.'

'Why?' She shrugged. 'It's not as if we're able to make any arrangements with your family either way under the circumstances. It's not as if the phones are even working right now.'

'I suppose you're right.' He led the way to what remained of the food and handed Phoebe a plate. 'I'm not sure there's much choice here but I hope you can find something you like.' He picked up a cheese and tomato sandwich and waved it in the air. 'It doesn't look all that tasty any more,' he joked as it flopped from side to side. 'The bread is a little dry at the edges but it's probably better than nothing at all. Depends on how hungry you are, I suppose.'

She giggled. 'I'm hungry and will probably eat anything right now.'

'Me too.'

They took their plates with a few sandwiches and sausage rolls and, after pouring themselves a glass of wine each, went and sat at the large dining room table.

'At least it's warm in here,' Jax said, aware that he was stating the obvious but feeling strangely awkward with Phoebe for some reason. What was wrong with him? They had spent hours together and he had been fine with her then. He watched her take a bite of her sandwich and eat it. 'How is it?' he asked, wanting to get back to some form of conversation with her.

She shrugged. 'Not too bad.' She smiled at him and Jax felt like he had been hit by a thunderbolt. Why was he being this way? This wasn't like him at all. He'd been attracted to all the women he had dated, but apart from his childhood sweetheart, Sophie, he hadn't fallen in love with any of them. Even Beth, who he had liked very much, hadn't upset him too much when she had ended their budding relationship. Even so, it still felt odd thinking about pursuing a relationship with Phoebe so soon after his and Beth's split.

Phoebe was so different to him in every way. Their lives were at opposite ends of the social scale on the island. Now he thought about it, everything about Phoebe seemed well polished, shiny and immaculate; the opposite to him in every way. Determined to hide his surprise at his unexpected feelings towards her, Jax, seeing he had one sandwich left, pushed his plate closer to Phoebe.

'Here, have the last one.'

She looked at the sandwich and then up at him suspiciously. 'Why? What's wrong with it?'

Hurt that she could imagine him giving her anything that was unsavoury he pulled back the plate. 'You said you were hungry and I was trying to be a gentleman.'

Mistaking his hurt for teasing, Phoebe took hold of the side of the plate and pulled it closer to her again and picked up the sandwich with her other hand. 'Then I'll happily accept it.'

Jax was relieved she had mistaken his actions and smiled. He really needed to get a grip of himself. This wasn't like him at all and he wasn't enjoying feeling so vulnerable. 'Good.'

She rubbed his upper arm with her right hand. 'I'm glad I'm here with you,' she said quietly. 'I've enjoyed getting to know you a little better.'

'I'm pleased,' he said, wondering if maybe he should ask her out on a date sometime rather than just the friendly lunch or coffee he had already asked her out for. She had said she fancied him in the summer and now that he had realised his own feelings mirrored hers, there was no reason why not. 'Phoebe,' he said at exactly the same time she said his name.

They laughed.

'Sorry,' Phoebe said. 'You go first.'

Wanting to but not wishing to be rude, he shook his head. 'No, you say what you were going to.'

'All right, then,' she said, taking a deep breath. 'I wanted to say that as well as enjoying spending time with you, I'm over my crush on you now.'

'What?' Jax felt like he'd received a slap to his face.

'Yes, and I don't want you to feel awkward around me and worry that I might take it upon myself to fling myself at you again.' She took a sip of her wine and placed the glass back onto the table thoughtfully. 'I want us to be friends and it would only be weird for you to have to worry each time you spoke to me that I might take your meaning the wrong way.'

Crushed at his lousy timing, Jax nodded his agreement. 'That's fine then.' To cover his disappointment he drank some of his wine and forced a smile onto his face. 'I suppose we should think about getting some sleep. Who knows what the morning will bring?'

'Not Santa, I'm imagining.' Phoebe grinned.

They finished their drinks and left their glasses and plates neatly on the table before making up two beds underneath it. After settling down on the blankets and pillows, Jax closed his eyes. 'Goodnight, Phoebe. I hope you get some sleep.'

'You too,' she said. 'This might not be the most comfortable bed I've slept on but it does feel rather cosy under here.'

She turned her back to him and Jax rested his head on his left arm, his back close to the wall. He could smell her perfume and, as he stared at the back of her dark hair, he doubted that he would end up getting much sleep at all. Eventually he heard her breathing change and sensed she was asleep.

He wished he had managed to get to know her a little better in the summer instead of being taken in by Fliss and her antics. He might have woken up to her very quickly but that had soured his image of her and her friend, presuming them to be similar in the way they treated people. He sensed that his assumptions might have messed up his chances of anything serious with Phoebe and that she could possibly have made him very happy. He hoped not, but after what Phoebe had said earlier it seemed very much as if that was the case.

12

PHOEBE

For a moment Phoebe couldn't work out where she was. Her body ached and it dawned on her that there was a heavy weight across her upper body. She opened her eyes, and seeing a tanned arm, bit her lower lip to stop from exclaiming. Jax. He had his arm around her and she liked it. She closed her eyes, relishing the feeling of being in his arms. She felt the heat of his body behind her and his warm breath on the back of her neck. The sensation made her shiver happily.

Hold on a minute? she thought, waking a little more. Why was he pressed up against her? They had been lying close to each other when she fell asleep but they hadn't been touching.

Jax had been lying between her and the wall, she remembered. She tried her best to peer over her shoulder and saw that he was pressed up against it. As she came round a little more she realised she must have shuffled back against him. *Bugger*. The poor man had had very little option but to *be* lying up against her like he was.

Mortified, Phoebe wanted to move away but the moment she moved he seemed to wake up a bit. She didn't want him to get the wrong idea and think that she had done this on purpose, especially not since she had made such a big deal about not fancying him any more. Which was a bare-faced lie. How could she have been so stupid?

What was Jax going to think of her when he woke? Hadn't it been bad enough for her to throw herself at him in the summer? Now she had pressed the length of her body up against him so much that the poor man was trapped between her and a wall.

Phoebe gritted her teeth together, urging her brain to think of something before Jax woke up. She couldn't move to look at her watch but it still seemed dark and was either very late or very early. At least everyone else seemed to be asleep, she thought. The only sound in the room was a ticking carriage clock and snoring, oh, and someone whispering somewhere on the other side of the dining room. So she wasn't the only one awake then. Phoebe closed her eyes, grateful that Jax was still fast asleep and that they were slightly hidden from most of the other occupants of the rooms. She needed time to think.

Phoebe edged away from him again, but Jax stirred and mumbled something under his breath. Not wanting to disturb him, Phoebe carefully moved his arm to lie over the blanket, then moved back so that she wasn't right next to him. Relieved to have saved herself any embarrassment, Phoebe yawned and closed her eyes, giving into her need for sleep.

13

JAX

Jax vaguely heard the sound of a clock somewhere and the smell of jasmine. He opened his eyes, only just managing to hold himself back from groaning. The jasmine must have been Phoebe's shampoo. It dawned on him that his right arm was lying over Phoebe's upper arm and over her body. Oh hell. He was lying against her.

Trying not to panic, he hurriedly tried to think.

'It's all right,' Phoebe whispered. 'It was me, not you.' She moved forward and Jax raised his arm so that she could turn and face him. Phoebe didn't sound shocked or angry, he thought, relieved.

'I'm so sorry,' he said, keeping his voice low so that no one else could hear what he was saying. He wanted to apologise. 'I've no...'

She rested her head on her arm, facing him. 'It's fine,' she whispered. 'You have nothing to apologise for.'

'I don't?' he asked, only barely daring to hope it was the case.

'Look where you are.' She indicated over his shoulder and it was then that he realised he might have been lying against her but his back was pressed up against the cold wall. Relief flooded through him.

'It's me who should apologise,' she said. 'I must have moved back against you in the night giving you nowhere else to move to.'

'That's a relief.'

She grimaced. 'It is?'

Was there hope in her eyes? He realised that she must have been as shocked to wake up and realise what she had done just as he had been. Wanting to reassure her, he nodded. 'Yes, for a moment there I thought I had disgraced myself.'

Her smile vanished. 'You think that's what I've done?'

Horrified that Phoebe had taken his comment the wrong way, Jax shook his head. 'No, of course not.'

'But you just said.'

'I know what I said, but I was referring to me, not you.'

'I don't see how that makes things different,' she said, raising her voice and causing others nearby to stir in their sleep.

'Shh.' Jax closed his eyes, not wishing to annoy her. 'Please, it's far too early to have a sensible argument.'

'Is that what we're doing?' she whispered through gritted teeth.

Hearing the annoyance in her voice, he wished he hadn't said anything. 'I hope not.'

They stared at one another for a moment then Phoebe looked away and he realised she was embarrassed, just as he had been. 'Phoebe, I only meant that...' What had he meant and how to put it into words? 'Shall we agree that you were the one to move back against me.' He smiled at her. 'Which, I might add, is fine. And that I was the one to put my arm around you.'

She studied his face for a moment and then sighed. 'Fine. It's just one of those things, I suppose.'

He had a thought. 'Yes, and at least we were under the dining table so it's doubtful anyone would have seen us lying there like that.'

All amusement left her face and without knowing how, he saw that he had upset her. 'What did I say?'

'Nothing.' She moved backwards. 'I need to find the bathroom.'

He watched her go, trying to work out how he had managed to get on the wrong side of her, again. Piper could be tricky to work out sometimes but she was never this confusing for him. Then again, he knew her very well whereas he barely knew Phoebe. And, he thought, wanting to put the morning's experience behind him, maybe it was a good idea that they kept things that way, for both their sakes.

He needed to take his mind off Phoebe and focus on the day ahead. It was Christmas Day after all and he needed to find a way to get back to the pier and his family once he had helped the others to get home. He was also determined to help tidy up the house and not leave until he had satisfied himself that the Ecobichon sisters were fine.

Jax slid out from under the table. He folded his and Phoebe's bedding into a neat pile. Others began stirring and getting up. He wondered about the situation outside and walked over to the window and pulled back one of the curtains.

'Hey, close that, will you?' a man bellowed.

'Sorry,' Jax said, lowering the curtain so that he could peek out of a small gap. The snow was still very thick but no longer falling. He tried to gauge how long it might take him to walk home. A couple of hours maybe, looking at the depth of the snow. It would be worth it though, to be with his family and know that he had a comfortable bed to sleep in that night.

He turned to pick up the bundle of bedding and thought of Phoebe. They might have had cross words but he couldn't leave her here, especially as she didn't really know anyone. He had already invited her to spend Christmas with them and if she wasn't happy to do that he would have to help her get home somehow if she wasn't able to drive the Range Rover back to her house and then find his own way back to the pier.

He wondered where Phoebe had got to and hoped that she was all right. Deciding to make the most of his time until she returned from the bathroom, he began collecting plates and piling them up while a couple of people he recognised from The Cabbage Patch started collecting glasses, tins and bottles.

Jax was at the kitchen sink washing plates in cold, soapy water when Phoebe walked in. The electricity was still off and he knew his mother would be fretting about the meat in their freezer defrosting.

'There you are,' she said as if he had been trying to avoid her. 'Let me fetch a tea towel and dry those.'

She seemed to have calmed down, he was happy to note. 'I didn't want the sisters to come down to a mess,' Jax explained. 'Did you see how things were doing in the living rooms?'

'Yes. Everyone is up now and moving furniture back to the right places. Someone else is wiping down surfaces and hopefully everything should look spick and span when the sisters come downstairs.'

'That's great.' He sensed her watching him and wondered if she was trying to make up her mind whether or not to say something else to him. Jax rinsed a plate and went to put it in the draining rack when Phoebe's hand reached out to pick it up and the back of their hands touched. He pulled his back to give her space to take the plate. He was being ridiculous. He turned to her. 'Listen, Phoebe, this is ridiculous.'

'I know,' she sighed. 'I think we both had a bit of a shock when we woke up in that position and both felt...'

When she didn't continue, he said, 'Embarrassed?'

'Yes, that. Which is silly. We had such a lovely time together last night and I would hate for us to fall out, or find things strained between us for no reason whatsoever.'

Relieved, Jax nodded. 'I agree. Let's start our morning again.'

'Yes, let's do that.'

'Merry Christmas, Phoebe.'

She smiled. 'Merry Christmas, Jax.'

Jax still had no idea what he had said to upset her before she raced out of the room to go to the bathroom but decided that now wasn't the time to ask. He was just grateful that they seemed to be on a friendly footing once again.

'I've had a look outside,' he said, picking up the next dirty plate and washing it. 'And I think we should be able to get home today.'

'That's good.'

She didn't sound as happy as he had expected. 'You're welcome to come to my place, like I mentioned last night. I'm pretty sure my Aunty Helen will put you up in one of the rooms in her guest house and my mum will be very happy to include you in our family lunch.'

When Phoebe didn't reply he turned his head to look at her. 'I mean it, Phoebe, I'd love for you to spend Christmas with my family.'

'Really? You're not just saying this because you feel sorry for me?'

That was exactly why he was inviting her, he realised. It would be much easier for him to see her safely to her home and not have to worry about saying anything else that might upset her, or embarrassing himself by having a couple of drinks and admitting he had feelings for her. 'Of course not,' he fibbed, aware that to admit his concern would risk annoying her again.

'My extended family is a bit noisy and probably not quite what you're used to, but they're good people and will make you feel very welcome.'

She bit her lower lip and he sensed she was trying not to smile. 'What?' he asked.

'My parents might have smart clothes and cars but they're probably not that different to yours,' she hesitated. 'Although yours probably wouldn't change their mind at the last minute and spend Christmas on the other side of the world to you.'

They wouldn't, he thought but refrained from agreeing with her. 'They did invite you to join them though, didn't they?'

She sighed. 'They did, aware that I would probably arrive halfway through Christmas Day with the little amount of notice they gave me.'

Jax hated to think that Phoebe had been shoddily treated by her parents, especially when she didn't have her best friend on the island to keep her company.

'Don't look at me that way.' She took the clean plate from his hand and began drying it.

'What way?'

'Like you feel sorry for me. I'm fine, although maybe a bit annoyed with them, but I certainly don't need anyone's pity. I told you that.'

'You did. Anyway I wasn't thinking that.'

She narrowed her eyes. 'You were thinking something, I can tell by the look on your face.'

'If you must know I was thinking what a shame it was that Fliss was made to go home. I'm sure you would have had much more fun spending time with her at your home than you're probably going to in my parents' tiny cottage on the pier.'

'If you must know I was glad Fliss was sent home.'

Shocked by her admission, Jax stopped washing up and stared at her. 'Seriously? Why?'

'Because I think we've begun to outgrow each other,' she said quietly as if she was confessing something she felt uncomfortable revealing.

'Why?' They had seemed so close over the summer. It was why he had presumed Phoebe was probably attempting to make a bit of a fool of him when she kissed him, he thought, recalling his reaction to the incident fully. Teasing him, or hoping to get a reaction out of him, or maybe to make Fliss jealous.

'Because the things that amuse her don't amuse me.' She finished drying the plate and placed it on the pile next to the draining board. 'We've been friends for years, though didn't see very much of each other until she came to stay with me at the beginning of the summer season.'

'But I thought you were close.'

'We are. Were. Well, we had fun together at school, but I don't know if Fliss has changed since then, or if I simply didn't know her as well as I imagined I did.' She thought for a moment before looking up into his eyes.

'Go on,' he encouraged, wanting to hear her thoughts before she changed her mind.

'It's just that she seemed so unfeeling, unkind really, the way she was with you, and then when she stirred up trouble upsetting Dan before his and Vicki's wedding and nearly causing the whole thing to be cancelled, I have to admit that I was horrified that everyone might assume we were similar in that way. You know, being nasty and completely lacking in empathy for others' feelings.'

Jax was stunned to hear her being so open about her true feelings towards her friend. He went to speak but heard footsteps and then Tara's voice.

'Can I do anything to help?' she asked cheerfully. 'Perry's outside speaking to the farmer with a couple of the others. They're helping him clear the driveway for the sisters.'

Not wanting to leave Phoebe without finishing their conversation but aware that he should offer to go and help the others outside, he turned to her. 'You can finish this washing up with Phoebe if you like,' he said. 'I'd better go and see what I can do to help them.'

'Sure.'

He moved away to give Tara space and turned to Phoebe. Her shoulders were set and he didn't want her to think she had opened up to him and that he was disinterested in what she had said. 'I'll come back as soon as we're finished and then we can see about getting back to Gorey,' he said. He lowered his voice, 'We can chat more then.'

Phoebe shook her head. 'It's fine, I think there's nothing more to say really. You go and help and Tara and I will finish sorting out the kitchen. I'll see you in a bit.'

Aware that there was nothing left to say, Jax walked out of the room.

'What was that all about?' he heard Tara ask.

'Nothing important,' Phoebe replied.

Jax knew he had probably done it again but resigned himself to speaking to her and clearing up any misunderstanding later on. It was a relief to know that Phoebe had been as shocked as him about Fliss and her unacceptable behaviour to others. He had been wrong about Fliss, but thankfully for only a short period of time. At least now though he knew that Phoebe wasn't like her at all and that made him happy.

He found his jacket and put it on, then went outside to find the others.

14

Two hours later, Jax's car still blocked in at the farm, Phoebe drove them both to the pier. Jax led Phoebe to his parents' cottage. 'Don't look so worried,' he said, wanting to reassure her.

'But they're not expecting me.'

'It's fine. They'll be happy to see you.'

'They will? Are you sure?'

Grateful to have arrived at his front door so that he didn't have to listen to Phoebe's concerns for another moment, Jax opened it and waited for Phoebe to step inside. 'This way,' he said as the familiar scent of his mother's baking filled his nose.

'Whatever's baking smells delicious,' Phoebe said, taking a deep breath, then giving a shriek as Seamus raced past her to get to Jax.

'Hello, little guy,' Jax said, lifting him up and kissing the top of his tatty head. 'Hey, stop wriggling.' He lowered his overexcited dog back onto the floor.

'That's some welcome,' Phoebe laughed, bending to pat Seamus who sniffed at her trousers for a few seconds, then wagged his tail.

'He's trying to work out where we've been,' Jax explained. Then, recalling that Phoebe had mentioned his mother's baking, added. 'My mother loves to bake when she's not working at her salon. She loves hairdressing but I think it's baking that relaxes her the most.'

'Lucky you.' She turned to him. 'Do you think she'll let us try whatever it is?' she whispered.

'If we're very lucky.' He led her into the small living room off the hallway. It took him a moment to notice that the coloured lights on his mother's Christmas tree were sparkling brightly. 'The electricity is back on,' he announced cheerfully.

'I had assumed as much,' Phoebe teased.

'You did?'

Why was she looking at him like that? he wondered.

Phoebe stared at him for a moment. 'The smell of baking? It tipped me off. Unless you have an Aga or Rayburn, or some other stove.'

'No, just a regular oven.' He clearly wasn't thinking too well today and hoped that he might have a chance to catch up on his sleep a bit later. 'At least Christmas lunch can go ahead as planned.'

'I'm so pleased.' Phoebe beamed at him.

'You're not the only one. What a relief.' It would mean that his mother was happier than he had expected.

'I imagine there'll be more cooking going on than usual,' Jax said, thinking of all those freezers and the food in them that no one would want spoilt. 'Come this way.' He led her down the corridor towards the kitchen at the back of the house. 'Mum? Where are you?'

'This way, Jax. You've arrived just in time to help peel potatoes for me. I...' She stopped speaking when Phoebe entered the room behind Jax. 'Hello? Who do we have here?' she asked, glancing quickly at Jax then back at Phoebe. 'Ooh, I know,' she said. 'You're Alex's sister's friend...' She raised a finger to stop either one of them answering. 'Phillipa? No, Phoebe. That's it. I always remember a face,' Sheila said. 'It's from spending years running my hairdressing salon. Customers feel slighted when you don't recall who they are.' She winked at Phoebe. 'And some of them even expect you to remember exactly what they were talking about the last time they came to you, too.'

'They do?'

'Yup.' Sheila narrowed her eyes. 'I saw you at Vicki and Dan's wedding reception, didn't I?'

'That's right,' Phoebe said.

'Phoebe also helped set up the barn beforehand.'

'That was kind of you. I'm Sheila, Jax's mum.'

'Hi, Sheila,' Phoebe replied, smiling. 'Jax hoped you wouldn't mind me joining you but I have to admit that I'm a little embarrassed to gate-crash your festivities.'

Sheila batted her hand in the air. 'Well, don't be, Phoebe. You're more than welcome to join us.' She carried on mixing the stuffing in a large glass bowl. 'So, were you stuck up at The Cabbage Patch like Jax then?'

'I was.'

Jax spotted two racks on the worktop. One with cooling bread rolls and the other, by the smell of it, his mother's famous winter buns with a hint of cinnamon. 'Can we try one of these?'

Sheila glanced at the cooling buns. 'You can each take one of those but not the bread rolls, they're going with us to Helen's guest house for our meal.'

'Go on then,' he said to Phoebe. 'Quickly, before she changes her mind.'

Phoebe clearly didn't need telling twice. Jax watched her take a bun, tear a bit off the side and pop it into her mouth, closing her eyes in delight as she ate it. He loved his food and enjoyed seeing that Phoebe seemed to do so as well.

'Mmm, these are heavenly.'

His mum raised her eyebrows. 'They should be, I've been making the things for decades.'

Jax kissed his mum on her cheek. 'Thanks, Mum.'

Sheila kept mixing the stuffing. 'So, tell me more.'

'Phoebe kindly drove me to check up on Beth and Billy last night before the snow got too bad,' Jax said, wanting his mother to know how caring she was. 'They're fine, by the way.'

'Good, I'm glad. That little boy must be loving all this snow.' Sheila looked over her shoulder at them. 'I could do without it though. Not that we get it too badly here, of course, but I presume it was the bad weather that messed up the power across the island last night.'

'Yes, more than likely,' Jax agreed.

'Is there anything I can do to help?' Phoebe asked, finishing off the last mouthful of her bun.

'I'm sure there is,' Jax's mum said. 'In fact since that lousy power cut I'm having to cook far more than I had expected today. How are you with a potato peeler?'

'Not brilliant, but if you don't mind untidy potatoes I'll give them my best shot.'

Jax watched his mother's interaction with Phoebe, fascinated with their easy banter. It was as if they had known each other for years rather than minutes. Why couldn't he feel that relaxed with Phoebe? Then again, he reminded himself, his mother ran her own hairdressing salon along the pier so she was used to making people feel welcome and relaxed. He was too, but unlike his mother he had to make very little small talk with his clients, spending most of his time with them teaching them about what and where to forage for food.

'If Phoebe's doing the peeling, what would you like me to do, Mum?'

'I was wondering when you were going to offer to help,' his mother teased, winking in Phoebe's direction. 'He's a good boy really.'

Jax groaned. He braced himself for his mother embarrassing him. Not that she meant to, he knew she was only trying to make his friend welcome. But he hadn't missed the interested glint in her eyes when she saw Phoebe enter the kitchen.

Phoebe looked over her shoulder at him and smiled. 'He's been helping everyone up at The Cabbage Patch and insisted I join you here today. I really am grateful to be included.'

Sheila inclined her head in Jax's direction. 'Any friend of my son's is welcome here.' She moved her elbow sideways to indicate the cutlery drawer. 'Don't just stand there, Jax, grab a potato peeler and start helping Phoebe by working through that lot in the bag over there.'

Jax saw the large paper sack in the corner. 'Flippin heck, Mum! How many people are you catering for?'

'You don't need to do all of them. Just about twenty-five or thirty. We'll cut the bigger ones in half.' She seemed to realise that she hadn't answered his question. 'I'm doing the potatoes and the stuffing and some of the veg. Helen is seeing to the turkey and other bits at the guest house. Margery will be doing a few things too. Then we'll take what we've cooked down to them and all eat there.' She smiled at Phoebe. 'They have more room than us, which is why we always go to the guest house for family get-togethers like Christmas.'

'Very organised,' Jax said, grinning at Phoebe who seemed a little stunned. 'But I wouldn't expect anything less.'

'Good. Now, take a couple of saucepans, add cold water and take them and the potatoes through to the dining room and get started. Better take a couple of old newspapers for the scraps too.'

Once they were settled in the dining room, Jax looked across the table where they were working. 'I'm sorry you've been roped into doing this,' he said. 'We don't usually expect our guests to help prepare their food.'

Phoebe smiled and after finishing peeling the potato she was working on dropped it into the saucepan of cold water and looked at him. 'I'm enjoying myself.'

'Really?' he asked, doubtful that anyone wouldn't mind spending Christmas morning preparing vegetables.

'Yes.' She selected another potato from the sack and shrugged. 'In fact I've loved yesterday and today.'

Jax frowned. Could she really have done?

'Don't look so doubtful,' she laughed, flicking cold water at him.

'Oi,' Jax flicked her back. 'I'm sure you would usually be opening beautiful presents in a perfectly decorated room somewhere.'

'That's true.' She focused on what she was doing and didn't return his gaze.

'Then, why would you find this fun?'

Phoebe stopped what she was doing and looked up at him. 'Because this is fun.'

Jas wasn't sure about that. 'I wouldn't call it fun exactly.'

'Then that's where we differ.' She thought for a moment. 'Maybe it's because what we're doing is different for me.'

Her cheeks reddened slightly and Jax wondered what she was about to say.

'Maybe it's spending time with you, Jax.'

He was taken aback, unsure if she was intimating that she actually did still have feelings for him. 'I'm not sure I understand.'

'I don't mean this to sound odd, but you're very different to any of the men I've spent time with before.'

He pictured the clean-cut, smart-suited men his father spent his working days with and presumed she meant people like that. Jax rubbed the side of his chin with the back of his hand and felt the stubble rough against his skin. 'I can imagine.'

Phoebe should her head. 'Don't get me wrong, most of them were perfectly lovely.'

'But I'm different.'

She grinned at him, her eyes twinkling in amusement. 'In a good way.'

He tried to picture her father. 'I suppose your dad is always well dressed.'

She narrowed her eyes thoughtfully. 'Dad is smart even when he thinks he's dressed casually,' she said as if it was something she didn't like about him. 'I think it's how he feels he's expected to dress.'

'Sorry, I'm not sure I understand what you mean.'

Phoebe popped the peeled potato she had just finished into the pot and rested her hands on the table. 'Dad is a self-made man. He made his money from designing luxury yachts. He seems very self-confident but tends to worry about how people perceive us and likes Mum and me to have the best of everything.'

'Good for him for doing so well though,' Jax said. He thought of his father working hard in finance and trying to persuade Jax's mum to move from the pier to a bigger house for the past ten years. Jax was relieved she had always refused to leave. He couldn't imagine living anywhere else. 'Is he retired now then?'

'He retired when he was thirty-nine and spends most of his time either playing golf, or travelling with Mum, or investing in new businesses. I think he'll always be a bit of a wheeler-dealer.

He loves the excitement of it all, but he's enjoying spending time relaxing more now he's getting a little older.'

Jax didn't like to ask Phoebe's father's age. He wondered what her father would think of him, if the situation had been different and he and Phoebe were seeing each other.

'What are you thinking?' Phoebe asked. 'I can tell it's something about Dad.'

'How?'

She shrugged. 'A lucky guess. Go on then, tell me.'

Jax wasn't sure he wanted to. He finished peeling the potato in his hand and decided there was no harm in it. They had spoken honestly to each other the previous evening, after all. Well, Phoebe had been honest as far as he could tell, he might have resisted being completely straight with her.

'Go on, ask me.'

'I was trying to picture your dad and wondered how he would react if you took me home.'

Phoebe threw her head back and laughed until tears ran down her cheeks.

Jax glared at her, taken aback by her unexpected reaction. 'I hadn't imagined he would like the idea,' Jax said when she eventually gathered herself and wiped her eyes. 'But I didn't think it was that funny.'

She seemed to notice that he was upset by her laughter. 'Oh, Jax, I didn't mean to offend you,' she said, reaching out to rest her hand on his. 'I'm sorry.' She grimaced. 'There's nothing at all wrong with you. It's just that the first thing Dad always notices about people, especially other men, is what they're wearing and by which designer. He probably wouldn't know what to make of your foraging clothes.'

'I see.' Was that supposed to make him feel better? Jax didn't want Phoebe to see how deeply her amusement had cut him. He picked up another potato and began peeling it in silence. He could feel her watching him and wanted to say something amusing to change the subject away from him but his mind was blank. At least they had agreed that there was nothing between them, he reasoned. The last thing he needed was to get close to a woman who found his appearance amusing.

'How are you...' Sheila stopped at the doorway. Jax looked up to see her scowling. 'What's the matter with you two? I know this is a boring job but I presumed you'd keep each other entertained while you did it.'

Jax didn't like to think his mother felt responsible for their silence. 'We're fine, Mum,' he tried to assure her. 'Aren't we, Phoebe?'

'What? Oh yes. Fine.'

'You could have fooled me. Did no one tell you both it's Christmas Day?' she joked, pulling two red cone-shaped Father Christmas hats from behind her back and putting one on Jax's head, pulling the thin elastic down under his chin to keep it from falling off and then doing the same to Phoebe.

'Mum, no!' Jax felt foolish enough already after what Phoebe had told him without wanting to wear a stupid hat that made him look even more ridiculous. 'Phoebe doesn't want to wear a silly hat.'

'Rubbish,' Phoebe argued, surprising him. 'I think it's fun.'

Sheila stood behind Phoebe and rested her hands on the girl's shoulders. 'There, you see? It's only you who hasn't got into the spirit of things,' his mum said, winking at him.

Unsure what she meant by that wink, Jax sighed heavily. 'I suppose I have no choice but to try and join in then, do I?'

'You don't,' Sheila said. 'Stop being a grump. It's not like you at all.' She moved to stand at the side of the table. 'Lack of sleep,' she explained to Phoebe as if Jax wasn't in the room. 'That'll be what's ruined his mood. I'll make you both something to drink and maybe bring you some breakfast?'

'A tea would be lovely for me,' Phoebe said looking, Jax thought, rather relieved that his mother had lightened the atmosphere in the room. 'But nothing to eat, thanks. The bun was delicious and filled me up comfortably.'

'I'll just have a coffee thanks, Mum.' He shot a grateful smile in his mother's direction, pleased to see her looking happier as she left the room. 'Sorry about that,' he said when he and Phoebe were alone again once more.

'Your mum's fun and I think she's right, we do need to get into the Christmas spirit.'

'Not that,' he said, realising she had misunderstood him. 'I meant me being quiet before she came in.'

'I upset you,' Phoebe said. 'I didn't mean to. Sorry. We seem to keep on doing that to each other, don't we?'

'We do, though I'm not sure why,' he said, still unsure why she found his clothes quite so amusing but deciding to let it go. The last thing he wanted was to ruin her or anyone else's day.

The front door closed and he heard his father's familiar footsteps coming along the hallway. He passed the dining room and, seconds later, stepped back and peered in at them. 'Hello there,' he said smiling, looking first at Phoebe and then at Jax. 'And who do we have here then?' Before Jax had a chance to introduce Phoebe his father added, 'I'm Duncan, by the way. Jax's dad. I notice my wife has already put you to work.'

Phoebe laughed. 'I'm Phoebe,' she said. 'Jax's friend, and I've been invited to join you today, so I'm more than happy to help prepare the meal.'

'That's just as well by the looks of things.' He walked over and patted Jax on his head. 'Morning, son. Good to see you made it home. Your mother was worried that you'd miss out on your lunch today. Refused to believe me when I assured her you'd find a way to be here even if you had to trudge the entire way through all that snow.'

'I wouldn't miss it for anything, Dad,' Jax said, relieved he had been able to get home and be with his parents.

15

PHOEBE

Phoebe could have kicked herself for her lack of self-control. What had she been thinking, laughing hysterically like that when Jax had asked about how her father would react to seeing them together. She wished Jax hadn't assumed her amusement was caused by his appearance rather than her being tickled by her father's patronising beliefs about people's clothes and how important they were to show you 'were somebody'. It was the only thing she didn't like about her father but after all this time there was little chance of him ever changing his ways.

Jax had been so sweet inviting her to spend Christmas with his family and although they were so different to her own parents, their friendly, relaxed way with each other made her yearn for the same relationship with her mother and father.

Phoebe recalled the delicious smell of baking that had greeted her and Jax on their arrival. How she would have loved to have a mother who enjoyed baking, or cooking of any type. She pictured Jax arriving home from school on a cold winter's evening and being handed a warm bun fresh out of the oven and a glass of milk. She smiled to herself. For all she knew Jax didn't like milk, but the image was so perfect, almost like a drawing in one of her childhood children's books that she had loved to read about wholesome, large families with lots of laughter, chatter and cosy evenings in front of a roaring fire.

Phoebe thought of Jax's dad and how close to his wife and son he seemed. So relaxed and chilled. She bet they didn't try to compete with each other over how well read they were, their taste in fashion and who they had lunched with. Her parents knew how to have fun and enjoyed socialising, but she rarely saw them as relaxed as Jax's parents had been, even to her, if ever.

'I think we must have done enough now,' Jax said, interrupting her thoughts. 'I'll carry these through to the kitchen to Mum and then maybe you'd like to freshen up?'

'Thank you,' she said. 'I'd like that very much.'

She picked up her filled pan and followed Jax through to the kitchen with it.

'You two are stars,' Sheila said. 'Your drinks are there, I was about to bring them in to you.'

'Thanks, Mum,' Jax said. 'I was wondering about asking Helen if Phoebe might be able to stay the night in one of the guest house rooms.'

Sheila looked over her shoulder at Phoebe. 'Of course, I hadn't thought that you might not be able to get home. Have you phoned your parents and let them know yet?'

'Er, no.'

'The phones are working again?' Jax asked.

'Everything seems to be. It's just the roads that are impassable in some places out of town, or so your dad tells me. That's where he's been. Went out in his pal's jeep to have a recce.' She turned to Phoebe. 'Jax will take you to the guest house to speak to Helen. I'm sure she won't mind putting you up. She's already got Dilys staying anyway.'

'If you think she won't mind,' Phoebe asked, feeling anxious to be invading everyone's privacy at such a special time of year.

'She can only say no.' Sheila shrugged. 'Which I doubt she will. Why not go there as soon as you've had your drinks, then you'll know what's going on.'

Phoebe liked that idea.

* * *

'Of course I don't mind,' Helen said a few minutes later. 'You're more than welcome to stay with us.'

Jax explained about her parents being away.

'Then you must stay for a couple of days, if you'd like to, that is. The more the merrier, don't you think, Piper?'

'What was that?'

Phoebe saw Piper enter the kitchen where she and Jax had been speaking to Helen. 'Oh, hi, you two.'

'Your mum has kindly invited me to stay for a couple of days,' Phoebe explained, wanting to see Piper's reaction so that she knew for certain she didn't mind.

'That's great news,' Piper exclaimed. 'It'll be fun having you here.' Piper stared at her for a moment and Phoebe wondered what she was thinking. 'Aren't those the clothes you were wearing last night?'

'They are. I haven't been able to get home yet.'

'Then you can come with me. I'll find something for you to wear. I think we're about the same size and then I'll show you where the bathroom is so you can freshen up. You'll find a new toothbrush in the cupboard under the sink. We always have one in case a guest has forgotten theirs.'

'That's so kind of you, thanks.'

'This way.'

Phoebe followed Piper upstairs. 'This is such a pretty guest house,' she said as if she had never been in one before. 'You must love living here.'

'I do. I love life on the pier with all its chatter and the sound of the waves and the boats.'

'Have you always lived here then?'

'Yes, apart from when I was at university and as much as I enjoyed uni life, I missed being here every day.'

'I'm not surprised,' Phoebe said certain she would miss this too if it had been her home. It felt like there was an invisible comforting duvet around her somehow. As if nothing bad could breach the walls of the guest house and although she had always lived in much bigger and grander houses, for some reason she felt as if she had come home. It was the strangest but most wonderful feeling and she wished it could last forever.

16

JAX

'Come along then you,' Piper said, leading Jax through to the reception room and closing the door quietly behind them. 'What's the story between you and Phoebe?'

'What are you on about?' He doubted his bluff would work with Piper but thought it worth a try.

'Don't give me that. You know what I mean.' She folded her arms across her chest and stood with her back to the door so he couldn't leave. 'You seemed very comfortable with each other last night. Do you like her? Is that what's happening here?'

He shook his head. 'No.'

'Hmm, I'm not sure I believe you.'

'It's true,' he fibbed, not daring to catch his cousin's eye in case she saw he was trying to fob her off. 'Her family is away and I didn't like to think of her being at home by herself over the Christmas holidays.'

'Alone? In that enormous house?'

'Exactly! I thought she could do with some company.'

'I agree. I'm glad you brought Phoebe down to the pier.' She smiled at him. 'I imagine your mum was intrigued to meet her?'

Jax nodded. 'She tried to hide her delight when she saw Phoebe but I didn't miss the way her eyes lit up when we walked into the kitchen.'

Having grown up only a few doors away from each other they were both aware how each other's mother reacted to certain things and Jax finding someone he loved enough to settle down with was something his mother had been looking forward to for several years.

'Did Aunty Sheila sit Phoebe down and start asking her questions?'

'Mum was too busy for that, thankfully. She was nice to her, of course, and immediately invited Phoebe to join us for lunch, then gave us a mountain of potatoes to peel.'

Piper giggled. 'I love that. I hope Phoebe realises that being given a job to do means she's already been welcomed to your household.'

'Don't you think you're getting a little ahead of yourself?' he asked, unnerved.

Piper gave him a playful punch to his left shoulder. 'Don't look so terrified. Wimp. Anyway, I think it's funny and typical Aunt Sheila. I imagine Phoebe didn't mind at all either.'

Confused, Jax asked, 'What do you mean? Being thought of as one of the family?'

'No, silly. Being asked to help out. Despite being Fliss's friend, she seems quite different and actually rather nice.'

'She is,' Jax said, calming slightly, then realising he had replied more quickly and enthusiastically than he had intended.

'Ahh, so there is something going on between you then.' Piper pointed a finger at his chest looking very satisfied with herself. 'I knew it, you like her.'

'You know nothing of the sort.'

'Piper! Jax! Where are you?' Helen yelled.

'We'd better open the door before Phoebe comes back downstairs and thinks we're talking about her,' he said, taking hold of the doorknob and turning it. He pulled the door back just as his aunt went to open it.

'We were,' Piper whispered.

'What are you two conspiring in here?' Helen asked suspiciously as she entered the room.

'We're not doing anything of the sort,' Piper said, keeping her voice low and pressing a finger up against her lips. 'I was only asking what was going on with Jax and Phoebe.' She pointed a finger upstairs. 'That's all.'

'There's no time for that,' Helen argued. 'Jax, you'd better go and help carry food over from your mum's house. Phoebe will be fine with us and you can catch up with her later when you get back here.'

Knowing when there was no point arguing, Jax did as she asked, happy to be away from Piper and all her questions.

He stopped on the pavement and looked out to sea taking a deep, icy breath. Even here, next to the sea, the road was mostly covered in snow. He must make sure his mother was careful when carrying hot food along the icy pavement. Then, thinking of Margery, he turned and walked the few steps to her front door.

Jax knocked and, hearing her shouting that the door was unlocked, walked in. 'Merry Christmas, Margery,' he said, going up to her and giving her a hug and kissing her cheek.

'Merry Christmas to you, too.' She rubbed the side of her face and scowled at him. 'I think you should shave before doing that to anyone else, it wasn't pleasant.'

Unable to help himself, Jax grinned. 'I'm sorry, I wasn't thinking.'

Margery took a step back and looked him up and down. 'You look dreadful. Haven't you been to bed yet?'

'If you call some blankets under a table being to bed then I have, otherwise, no.'

'Then you need to go home and shower. Clean yourself up before lunchtime.'

Before he had a chance to agree, a man walked out of the kitchen. 'Alex? What are you doing here?' Jax asked, surprised to see Piper's boyfriend standing in front of him. 'I thought you were with your family in Poole. Didn't you take Fliss back with you then?' If Fliss was on the island he needed to tell Phoebe and give her the chance of deciding whether to spend the day with her friend.

'Give the boy a chance to answer one question before coming out with the next one, Jax,' Margery sighed.

'Sorry. I'm surprised to see you here, that's all.'

Alex walked up to him and shook his hand. 'Good to see you too, Jax. I'm in hiding.' Jax saw him exchange secretive smiles with Margery. 'I took Fliss home, swapped presents with my parents and asked if they were happy for me to return to the island to surprise Piper.' He frowned. 'You don't think she'll mind, do you?'

'Of course she won't. She'll probably think you being here is the best Christmas present she's had.'

'Good. Margery thought the same thing when I called her and asked if I could stay here for a few days.'

'Why are you staying here and not at the guest house?' Jax asked, unsure why Alex would not want one of the bedrooms at The Blue Haven.

'You really haven't had much sleep, have you?' Margery asked. 'He's staying here because he wants to surprise Piper. It won't be a surprise if he'd asked to stay next door, now would it?'

She had a point. 'Ah, right. No, it wouldn't.'

Jax felt Margery's hand on his elbow and let her lead him to the front door.

'You go and take a shower, shave, and if you get the chance maybe have a bit of a doze to catch up on some sleep. We'll see you later at lunch. Remember though, not a word about Alex being here to anyone.'

'There's certainly enough food to go round,' Jax said. 'Mum made Phoebe and I peel loads of potatoes this morning.'

'Phoebe's here?' Alex asked.

'No time for chit-chat,' Margery said, opening the door and pushing Jax gently in his back. 'You can tell each other everything you need to later.'

'Sure,' Jax said. 'See you then.' The door closed behind him and, remembering what he wanted to tell Margery about the slippery pavements, he turned and opened it again.

'What is it?' Margery glowered at him impatiently.

'The pavements are slippery so maybe ask Alex to help you walk next door.'

'Fine. Now, go.'

Jax walked carefully back to his home and couldn't help feeling excited that their usual quiet family Christmas looked as if it was going to be a lot of fun.

17

JAX

Jax loved it at the guest house, especially on days like these when the families got together. He felt much better now that he had showered, shaved and changed into clean jeans and a fresh sweat-shirt. He sat on the arm of the sofa next to Phoebe, listening to his parents teasing each other about past presents they had bought each other. Seamus was playing with the toy giraffe that he had been given and Piper was watching him, leaning forward and ruffling the fur on his head.

He had only been in the living room at the guest house for a few minutes when he spotted Piper get up and go to the hall. She was putting on her coat and he sensed where she was going. He leapt to his feet. 'Hey, where are you going? We'll be eating soon.'

She looked at him, clearly shocked by his reaction. 'Er, going to fetch Gran, of course. I don't want her slipping on her way here.'

Aware that Alex's surprise entrance would be ruined if Piper did as she was intending and knowing she wouldn't listen to him if he told her not to go, Jax took her arm.

'Hey, let go of me.' She pushed him away with her free hand. 'What's the matter with you?'

'I told Margery I'd go and fetch her,' he lied.

'I'm happy to,' she argued. 'You keep Phoebe company.'

Jax gritted his teeth. Then thinking quickly, said. 'You sit next to her. You've barely spoken to her yet and you don't want her to feel unwelcome, do you?'

Piper looked shocked by his question. 'I haven't done that, have I?'

'No,' he admitted guiltily. Piper would never do something like that to one of their guests and he felt bad for accusing her of such a thing, but it was all he had been able to think of to say in the time he had. 'But it's freezing out there.' He smiled to try and cheer her up. 'Let me go, I'd like to.'

'Fine. Go then, but I'm not sure what's got in to you today. You seem all odd and on edge.'

'Lack of sleep,' he said because that wasn't a complete lie. He took her coat from her and as Piper returned to the living room, Jax went to hang it on the clothes hooks by the door. As soon as he had let go of the coat the door opened and Margery walked in. She motioned for Jax to say nothing and waved Alex in behind her.

Jax went ahead of Margery and stood just inside the reception room. 'Look who's here,' he announced. 'After all that I didn't have to go and fetch her anyway.'

'Gran,' Piper said, standing and walking over to her grandmother and pulling her into a hug. 'We were just arguing about who was going to get you.'

'Never mind that,' Margery said. 'I've got a present for you, lovey.'

'What is it?' Piper asked, grinning happily.

Jax waited expectantly as Margery stepped to one side and, holding out her arm, said, 'This.'

Piper looked at the open doorway just as Alex stepped forward from the hallway and made his presence known.

Piper's mouth dropped open and Jax swapped happy glances with Phoebe as Piper ran to Alex. 'What are you doing here? I thought...'

'My parents understood that I wanted to come and spend Christmas with you.' He smiled at Margery. 'Your mum knows all about it and your gran kindly let me stay with her last night so that you didn't see me around the pier.'

'Oh, Alex.' Piper stepped into his arms and kissed him. 'I'm so happy you're here.'

'Me too.'

Jax saw the relief on Alex's face and knew that finally Christmas was properly underway. He turned to Phoebe and saw she was concerned, so went over to her and sat on the edge of the sofa where she was sitting. 'You OK?'

'Is Fliss here too?'

Glad that he was able to fill her in, Jax shook his head. 'No, she's back in Poole with her parents. Alex must be shattered.'

'He must be.' She looked over at the happy couple still standing by the door and stood. 'Margery, would you like to sit here?'

'That's kind of you, I would.'

Helen clapped her hands together. 'Right, now we're all here, maybe we should take our places at the table in the dining room. 'Piper, I've moved the settings so that there's a place for Alex.'

'Mum, you knew he was coming?'

'Of course I did. Now, I hope you'll stop looking so miserable and cheer up a bit.'

'I wasn't miserable,' Piper said, looking up at Alex. 'I was actually. In fact I was getting on my own nerves so I'm glad you're here.'

Alex laughed. 'Is there anything I can do to help, Helen?' he asked and then Jax noticed him spot Phoebe. 'It's good to see you, Phoebe,' Alex said. 'I was thinking that maybe don't tell Fliss you're here until after Christmas, otherwise she'll be bombarding me with angry messages and I've had enough of those from her recently. You know how she hates to feel left out.'

'I won't say a word. I've left my phone upstairs and have no intention of switching it on until at least tomorrow.'

'You're staying here, too?'

'I am.'

'Right, the food will get cold if we spend too long chatting,' Helen said. 'I want you all to sit down. Jax can help bring things to the table for me.'

He hoped he wouldn't spill anything. Serving food wasn't something he was very good at, but Piper was too wrapped up in her delight seeing Alex again and his mother deserved to sit down and enjoy her lunch. 'No problem at all, Aunty Helen.'

A short while later, everyone was seated and the food had been served. Seamus was eating from a small bowl of food that Helen had given Jax to put on the floor. She placed an old folded bath sheet in the corner of the room to give him somewhere soft to lie while the rest of them ate their meal.

'This all looks delicious,' Alex said. 'Thank you very much for including me today, I really appreciate it.'

'So do I,' Phoebe said.

'As do I,' Dilys added, smiling.

'Where's your grandfather today, Alex?' Jax asked. 'Is he on the island still?'

'Yes, Helen did invite him but he's decided not to risk slipping over. His leg is healed but he still has a few issues with it and thought it best to spend the day with Vivienne at her place.'

'Ah, that's nice,' Piper said. 'I'm glad he's all right. We can try and get to see him later if you like?'

'That would be lovely, if the roads have cleared a bit,' Alex replied. 'If not then we can wait until tomorrow.'

Jax sat and watched the people sitting around the large table that Helen and Piper had made by pushing two tables together. This was how he liked spending special family days, sitting around a table eating tasty food and everyone happy and chilled.

His phone rang and, concerned that it might be one of the Ecobichon sisters needing his help, he apologised and checked the screen. 'It's Beth,' he said standing. 'I'd better take this in case something is wrong.' He left the room quickly and when he was in the hall, answered the call.

'Everything all right?' he asked, hoping nothing was wrong with Billy.

'Wonderful,' Beth replied. 'Well, my parents made it here, but Vicki and Dan are stuck at home and couldn't get here. I have a sneaking suspicion that they're perfectly happy spending their first Christmas as a married couple alone, especially now she's pregnant.'

He hadn't realised. 'In that case, you're probably right.'

'Oh, sorry,' Beth said, obviously picking up on his discomfort. 'Did I interrupt your celebrations?'

'We were about to eat, but that's fine. Did you need me for something?'

'Sorry, Jax. No, but I have someone here who wanted to say something to you.'

He heard her whisper something and then Billy's voice. 'Jath, it'th me, Billy.'

'Hi, matey, how are you? Having fun?' Jax listened, a lump in his throat as the three-year-old told him all about the present Jax had given him, how it was his best present and how he and Mummy had made a snowman outside. 'That's so cool. Did you give it a carrot for a nose?'

'We did and Mummy put buttons for eyes.'

'Thanks for his present, Jax,' Beth said. 'He loved it. Are you having a fun day?'

'I am, thanks. You?'

'Yes.' There was a moment's silence and then Beth spoke. 'Well, I'd better let you get back to your meal, it won't taste nearly as good if it's cold.'

'It won't. Bye, Beth. Happy Christmas.'

'Happy Christmas to you too, Jax.'

18

JAX

Jax returned to the dining room to join the others.

'All OK with Beth and Billy?' Sheila asked.

'Yes, they're fine. Billy wanted to thank me for his present, which Phoebe kindly took me to drop off at their cottage last night.'

'Where's your jeep then?' Duncan asked. 'You've not crashed it again, have you?'

'Again?' Sheila exclaimed, her hand stilling with her fork halfway to her mouth.

Jax closed his eyes briefly before glaring at his father. 'Thanks, Dad.' He looked at his mother, wanting to reassure her. 'Someone reversed into my jeep at the beginning of the year. Broke a tail light but paid to have it fixed. It wasn't a big deal.' He turned his attention back to his father. 'And, no, Dad, I didn't crash my car. Someone blocked me in up at The Cabbage Patch and I had no choice but to leave it there.' Jax sighed, wishing his father didn't always seem to see the negative side of things, especially where he was concerned. 'I'll fetch it tomorrow, it'll be fine until then.'

'Maybe we should pop up later to check on the sisters?' Phoebe suggested.

'Or you could phone them first,' Helen suggested. 'To save you interrupting their day if they are all right.'

'That's a good point,' Jax said. It hadn't occurred to him that Meg and Amy might have had enough of people spending time in their home. 'I wonder if the others have managed to make their way home by now.'

'I presume so,' Piper said. 'Apart from maybe the older guests who wouldn't find it so easy walking long distances.'

'I'll give them a call after we finish eating.' Jax ate a mouthful of the tasty meal. He loved Christmas dinners and wondered why people rarely seemed to eat turkey during the rest of the year. And sprouts. He looked at the faces around the table, enjoying being a part of such a friendly, relaxed group. 'So, did everyone get what they had hoped for from Santa?'

'Your father bought me that pair of shoes with the wonderful memory soles.' Sheila smiled. 'I've been wanting a pair for so long and they're heavenly to wear.'

'They're just what you need to help your feet,' Helen said before popping a sprout into her mouth.

'That's what I thought.' Duncan winked at his wife. 'I'd had so many hints from Sheila though over the past few months that it wouldn't have been worth my while not buying the things.' He wrinkled his nose in distaste. 'They're not very attractive to look at though, are they?'

Sheila grumbled something under her breath and elbowed him in his side. 'That's not the point. If you spent hours standing all day like I do at the salon instead of sitting on your bottom at a desk then you might have an inkling how it feels to have sore feet and aching legs.'

'I'm teasing.' Duncan took her hand closest to him and kissed the back of it. 'If they're what you want and you're happy with them, then that's fine with me.' He focused his attention on Phoebe. 'It's been good to get to know you a bit, young lady.'

Phoebe finished eating her mouthful and lowered her cutlery on her plate, smiling. 'Thank you. I've enjoyed getting to know Jax and Piper's families. There's such a lovely sense of community here between everyone who lives on the pier.'

Margery mumbled something.

'What's that, Mum?' Helen asked, sounding irritated.

'I was just saying how sometimes a bit of space might be nice.'

'Rubbish, Gran.' Piper rolled her eyes at Phoebe. 'Gran moans about people knowing everyone's business here but would never dream of living anywhere else.' She turned to her grandmother again. 'Would you, Gran?'

Jax saw Margery's stern expression vanish and her mischievous grin return. 'She's right, lovey. I wouldn't ever leave this place.'

Jax caught Phoebe's eye and mouthed *You OK?*, happy when she beamed at him and nodded.

A thought occurred to him. Jax caught Piper's eye and wondered if she had had the same thought as him at that moment. He hated to think that all of them would be sitting in the living room after lunch and handing round their gifts when he didn't have anything to give to Phoebe. Blast, why hadn't he thought of that earlier. Then again, what good would it have done, he mused. It's not as if he had anything he could wrap for her back at their cottage. He saw Piper pull an odd expression. She was trying to convey something to him.

'Is there any more gravy in the kitchen, Mum?' she asked.

'Yes, lovey.'

Piper picked up a gravy boat from the table and went to leave the room. As she reached the door she turned. 'Jax, bring the other one, will you? I think we're going to need more than just this one filled.'

It dawned on him that she wanted to speak to him privately, so he picked up the other from the table and followed his cousin out to the kitchen.

'Quick,' Piper whispered. 'Give me that and shut the door.'

Jax pushed the door closed and placed the gravy boat onto the worktop. 'I need a gift for Phoebe. Do you have anything you think might be suitable for her that I can buy from you?'

'I thought we were thinking along the same lines and it seems that we were.' She began ladling gravy from a saucepan into the gravy boats. 'You don't need to pay me, Jax. I'm happy to let you have something for her.'

'No,' he argued. 'Thanks, but it wouldn't feel like a proper gift if I didn't pay for it.'

'What are you two doing in there?' Gran bellowed.

'We'd better go back in.' Jax picked up the two porcelain jugs. 'You open the door.'

'We can sneak upstairs when Mum is serving her chocolate log. She always makes a big production of doing that and hopefully no one will miss us for a few minutes.'

'Good idea,' Jax said, grateful to his cousin for her thoughtfulness. 'Just give me the nod.'

She opened the door and waited for him to walk through.

'Here we are,' Jax announced. 'Sorry for the delay, we were, er...' He tried to think of a plausible reason.

'Spilt some,' Piper said, always ready to have his back.

'Yes, and wanted to clear up the mess rather than leaving it.'

'Good,' Helen said. 'I don't need any more to clear up than there already is in that kitchen.'

'I'm happy to do the dishes for you,' Phoebe offered. 'It's the least I can do after you letting me join you here and giving me a room for the night.'

'I'll help you,' Jax said.

'And me,' Piper agreed. 'We'll have everything done in no time with the three of us at it.'

'And even quicker with four of us,' Alex added, raising his hand in the air.

Jax liked the idea of the clearing up being shared among the four of them. It would leave more time for sitting and relaxing later. He took his seat and, not wanting Phoebe to feel uncomfortable about anything, waited for her to finish a mouthful of her food. 'How are you doing?'

'Loving every minute,' she said quietly. 'It's such a treat spending time with your extended family, especially at this time of year. Our Christmases have always either been just the three of us or we've spent it at a hotel with a large group of people, most of whom I only vaguely knew.'

'I'm glad you're enjoying yourself.'

'I am. Very much.' She beamed up at him and Jax wished he could take her in his arms and hug her tightly to him. She had so much, yet at times seemed a little lost and he hated to think of her feeling that way. For all the material things that he supposed she had in her life, Phoebe seemed to fit in so well to his ordinary, if a little eccentric, family. He realised that the thought made him very happy indeed.

He noticed his aunt waiting for the last of them to finish the food on their plates and, amused, watched her trying not to show her impatience. It must be chocolate log time, he thought, enjoying how traditionally his family reacted to this particular day each year.

Phoebe finished her last mouthful and placed her knife and fork together on her plate. All eyes moved to Gran, who he always thought made a point of finishing her food last. Finally, she was finished and within a second Helen stood.

'Piper, Jax, you can clear the plates and bring them to the kitchen.'

Phoebe and Alex went to stand. 'No, Phoebe and Alex,' Helen said, raising a finger in the air. 'You're guests in this house and, apart from the washing up, you're to stay seated and relax until then.'

Jax could see Phoebe was happy to do as she was told and keep enjoying the chatter around her. He began collecting plates from one side of the table while Piper did the same on the other side.

They carried everything through to the kitchen.

'Mum, Jax and I need to pop upstairs for a minute,' Piper whispered.

Helen sighed. 'Whatever for? We're halfway through lunch for pity's sake.'

'I know, Aunty Helen,' Jax whispered apologetically. 'But Piper is finding something for me to give to Phoebe. I didn't expect to bring her to spend Christmas with us and need to give her a gift.'

'That's very thoughtful of you, well done. Hurry up though. You don't want everyone realising what you're doing.'

He and Piper tiptoed out of the kitchen and ran as quietly as possible up the stairs to Piper's room.

'What do you have in mind?' he asked, sitting on the end of her bed to keep out of the way while Piper opened a large cupboard.

'I'm not sure yet but I'll know it when I see it.' She peered forward and moved a couple of objects, taking them out and opening the bubble wrap to check what was inside. 'Do you have any idea what you'd like to give her?'

'None,' he admitted, irritated with himself for his lack of imagination.

'Come on, Jax,' she hissed. 'You know better than most what I sell. Try and picture some of the items and decide what you want?'

He gave her question some thought. He didn't know Phoebe well and it wasn't as if they were seeing each other or anything. They were barely just friends. 'I suppose it better be something fairly small. I don't want a grand gesture, it might make her feel odd, especially as she won't have anything to give in return,' he said thoughtfully.

'A small token then,' Piper suggested, reaching forward and taking a small package from a higher shelf.

Jax watched while she removed the protective covering and held it up.

'How about this?' Piper asked.

Jax looked at the mosaicked heart with red-coloured porcelain she had collected from her walks on the beach. 'A heart? Won't that give her the wrong idea?' Even if he liked the thought of them being more than friends, he thought miserably.

'You don't like her?' Piper seemed surprised.

'It's not that, it's just that we've only really started to get to know each other. I think a heart might give the wrong message.'

Piper wrapped the item carefully and placed it back onto the shelf before taking another. After unwrapping it, she held it up for him to inspect.

'That's better.' Jax stared at the blue and green seahorse with twine looped through a hole at the top. 'This doesn't look upcycled though?'

'It isn't. It's something new I'm trying out. I make the shapes and then add the scavenged pottery pieces. Do you like it?'

'Very much,' he said truthfully, taking it from her and holding it up. 'I think they'll sell really well.'

Piper frowned.

'What?'

'I'm glad to hear you like them, but do you think it's a suitable gift for Phoebe?'

'Yes, didn't I say?'

'No.'

'Sorry, I meant that I liked it for her, too.'

'I'll give you a little pouch for it to go inside, so you won't need to wrap it as well. Then we'd better hurry up and get back downstairs before Mum gets cross.'

He realised they had been a bit longer than Helen might have expected. 'Yes, let's go.' As they hurried down the stairs, Jax thanked his cousin. 'It's so cool that you have all this stock just when I need something.'

'It works both ways.'

'How? He stopped outside the dining room and waited for her to enlighten him.

Piper groaned. 'You're always bringing Mum, Gran and I mussels.'

'I see. I suppose so.' He placed the gift onto one of the branches of the Christmas tree and rushed back to follow Piper into the dining room.

He heard someone clearing their throat behind him and turned to see Helen widening her eyes at them as she carried a tray with a large plate displaying her chocolate log. 'There's a Christmas pudding in the kitchen. Pour a little brandy over it and light it then bring it through to everyone.'

'Will do,' Jax said, aware that his and Piper's time-wasting had irritated his aunt. 'Won't be a sec.'

He left them and went to the kitchen. He heard the delighted 'oohs' and 'ahhs' coming from the dining room. His aunt's chocolate cake was legendary but he much preferred the Christmas plum pudding that she also made each year.

'Where's the brandy?' he murmured to himself, searching the cupboards for it.

A hand produced a small bottle from next to him. 'I think this is it.'

He turned his head and smiled at Phoebe. 'You've snuck out?'

She pulled a cheeky face. 'I wasn't sure if you needed help with something.'

He cocked his head towards the kitchen door. 'You'll be in trouble if my aunt catches you, especially while she's showing off her baking skills.' He teased. 'You do know she only makes that log thing once a year and is very proud of it?'

'So I gather.'

'It is very chocolatey.'

'Then I'll make sure I try some.' She held up the bottle of brandy. 'Do you want this, or should I put it back on the shelf where I found it?'

'Jax! What are you doing in there for pity's sake?' his aunt bellowed.

He sighed heavily. 'Now you've got me into trouble too.' He grinned at her.

'Rubbish, I haven't been missing for fifteen minutes.' She gave him a searching look. 'Margery mentioned something about sending out a search party for you, but Helen said you wouldn't be long.'

He realised she was interested to know where he'd been but didn't like to ask. 'I needed to fetch something for you.'

Her mouth opened, then closed again. 'For me?'

He nodded, delighted that she seemed excited. 'Yes, and as soon as lunch is over I'll show you what it is, but right now I need you to pour that brandy over this pudding so we can light it and get back to the dining room before my aunt loses her temper.'

He watched as Phoebe pulled the cork out of the bottle and carefully poured the alcoholic liquid over the cake. He took a match from the box on the worktop and struck it, holding it near to the pudding. 'Yes,' he murmured when it lit instantly. 'Right, get the door for me will you?'

He entered the room to a round of applause and cheers.

'It's about flippin' time,' Margery grumbled. 'I thought you'd forgotten about us and gone home.'

Jax laughed. 'You know I wouldn't desert you, Margery.'

He placed the pudding on the table and went to Margery, giving her a kiss on her powdery cheek, wincing when she reached up and took his cheek between her thumb and forefinger and gave it a slight pinch. 'You're a charmer, you are. Now, go and sit back down again so we can sample these puddings Helen's spent hours baking for us.'

Jax sat and rested his hands on his thighs. He felt someone touching his right hand and looked down to see Phoebe's neatly manicured hand resting on his. Unsure what she meant by doing it, he reminded himself that she had said she was happy they were friends. Maybe she was trying to comfort him in case he had been concerned by Margery's criticism. He raised his eyes to look into hers. 'You OK?'

'I am,' she said quietly, shooting a glance to the others before turning her gaze back at him. 'I've had a lovely time here with your family today, Jax. It's very kind of you all to include me.'

'Nonsense,' Sheila said. 'We've thoroughly enjoyed having you here with us. Haven't we, everyone?'

Typical of his mum to have heard, Jax thought. His dad always teased that she could hear a pin drop at the other end of the pier if she wanted to.

'What?' Margery asked.

'I was saying how we've loved having Phoebe spend Christmas with us.'

Jax noticed Margery's perplexed expression. 'We have, but I don't know why you need to make an issue of it?'

'Mum.' Helen looked up from cutting slices of chocolate log for Duncan to eat. 'Sheila was only reassuring Phoebe that she's most welcome.'

'Oh, I see.' Margery's expression softened and Jax was relieved when she gave Phoebe a gentle smile. 'She is right, lovey. We're very happy to have you here with us today.'

'And tomorrow,' Jax said.

'Tomorrow?' Phoebe raised her eyebrows. 'I was intending to return home then.'

Jax realised he hadn't mentioned their Boxing Day tradition. 'Of course you must go home if you wish to,' he said, hoping to persuade her to delay her departure from the pier. 'But the rest of us will be going to lunch at The Bucket.'

'The Bucket?'

'The Bucket of Shells,' Duncan explained.

'Oh, right. Yes,' Phoebe said, smiling. 'I know that one.'

'It's a great place. And of course we also have the other pub here on the pier. The Dolphin at one end and The Bucket near the other.' He inclined his head at his wife. 'I like having a choice; it takes my wife a bit longer to find me when she wants me home to do jobs at the house.'

'Stop talking nonsense, Duncan.'

'It's lovely in there and the food is always great,' Piper said. 'It's a family tradition to meet up there on Boxing Day.'

Jax didn't miss her split second glance at him. His cousin knew him well enough to pick up that he was interested in Phoebe and wanted to spend more time with her. It dawned on him that Phoebe hadn't answered yet. He looked at her and saw she was trying to decide what to do.

'You don't have to make your mind up now,' Jax said, taking her hand and giving it a gentle squeeze. 'You have until tomorrow lunchtime. We have a couple of tables booked every year, so they always know to expect us and it won't be difficult to add another place setting.'

'Thank you,' she said looking grateful. 'I have loved it here today, but I'm aware that you're a close family unit. I'm not sure I should be involved in all your festivities, it doesn't really seem very fair to you.'

'We wouldn't invite you if we didn't want you to join us,' Margery said, pouring custard over her bowl of chocolate log.

'Don't feel that you have to,' Jax added, unsure if Phoebe wasn't wanting to join them and was too polite to say so. 'It really is up to you.'

Helen passed a plate of chocolate log to Phoebe and Jax let go of her hand so that she could take it. 'I look forward to hearing what you think,' Helen said, waiting expectantly for Phoebe to take a spoonful and give her opinion.

She ate a piece. 'Mmm, Jax said it would be delicious,' Phoebe said, smiling and pushing her spoon into the cake for a second time. 'He wasn't wrong.'

Helen gave a satisfied nod. 'Glad you like it. Eat up then. If you want cream or custard, Piper can pass it to you.'

'Not for me, thanks.'

Jax waited for his pudding to be served to him and sat silently eating it, amazed by the circumstances that had brought him and Phoebe together. He was surprised at how much he had enjoyed her company and wished that she did want to take their friendship further. But she seemed to have made up her mind and friendship was far better than nothing at all, he decided.

19

JAX

He would give Phoebe the gift Piper had found for him before the rest of his family exchanged gifts, he decided, as he put the final piece of cutlery away in the cutlery drawer. Piper was hanging up the damp tea towels that she and Phoebe had used to dry up to dry over the radiator. The rest of the family were still sitting around the table chatting and eating cheese and crackers.

'I've no idea how they can still be eating,' Piper said. 'I think they just aren't ready to leave the table yet.'

'I won't be a moment,' Jax said.

Piper gave him a knowing smile. 'I'll make us a cup of tea. Unless you'd like more wine, Phoebe?'

'I'd rather tea, please,' he heard Phoebe say as he reached for the small gift and hurried back to join them in the kitchen. 'I had rather a lot of wine last night.'

'You only had a couple of glasses,' Jax argued.

'That's more than I'm used to having.' She smiled. 'I hadn't had an alcoholic drink for the past two months and I think it probably went to my head a little last night.'

Jax wondered if she was making a point of saying this in front of him as an excuse for her snuggling back into him during the night. He decided not to react in case he was wrong. Happy to change the subject, he held out the pretty bag that Piper had given him for his gift.

'What's this?' Phoebe asked, eyes wide as she stared at it.

'Just that little something I mentioned earlier.' He looked at the bag. 'Well, take the bag.'

'I can't believe you've got me a present?'

He nodded. 'It's only a little one.' Not wishing her to feel awkward, he added, 'It's a family tradition that no one comes to ours for Christmas and leaves without at least one gift.'

'What a super idea.' Phoebe took the bag. Her smile slipped. 'But I haven't brought anything for you.'

Piper looked at Alex as he entered the room and saw Phoebe holding the gift. 'I haven't got you anything, Alex,' she said. 'I hadn't realised you would be here.'

He walked over to her, slipped his arm around her shoulders and kissed her. 'There, that's present enough for me.'

Jax had to resist from groaning. While he liked to see his cousin happy, he wasn't ready to spend time with two such loved-up people, especially when he and Phoebe were being slightly awkward with each other since waking so close together.

'I wasn't expecting you to,' Jax soothed. 'Anyway, it's not as if we had any of this planned, did we?'

'I suppose not.' Phoebe indicated the bag. 'May I open it now?'

'Of course.'

He caught Piper giving him an amused smile. No doubt she would tease him later for making up another tradition but it was all he could think of to say. He didn't want Phoebe to feel like she should have given him something, or that he had stronger feelings for her than he had intimated when they agreed that they were merely friends.

Phoebe withdrew the seahorse from the bag by its twine and held it up, inspecting it. 'Oh, it's adorable,' she said, lightly running her finger over the neatly arranged pieces of faded porcelain. She beamed at Jax. 'I love it so much. Thank you.'

'It was my pleasure,' Jax said. 'Actually, Piper found it for me in her stock upstairs.' He grinned. 'It's why we were missing for so long earlier.'

Phoebe held it against her chest. 'I'm very touched. Thank you both for being so kind, I really appreciate it.'

Jax heard the emotion in Phoebe's voice and hoped he hadn't upset her by giving her the gift. She was probably missing her parents regardless of what she said. Spending time with his eccentric, but close, family was probably more than enough for her to cope with without him giving her a present.

'No problem at all,' Piper said, stepping forward and giving Phoebe a hug.

When she moved back, Phoebe looked up at Jax expectantly and he wasn't sure whether to do the same as his cousin, or if it would be inappropriate.

Phoebe stepped forward and kissed him on his right cheek. 'Thank you, Jax. I love it.'

'I'm glad,' he said, resting his hand on her back briefly before she stepped back.

'Let's get these drinks then,' Piper said. 'I don't know about you two but I'm parched.' She finished making their teas and handed them out. After chatting for a bit in the kitchen, Piper picked up her mug. 'Shall we take these through to the living room,' she suggested. 'Now the cooker is off it's getting a bit chilly in here.'

'Good idea.' Jax opened the door and waited for Piper to lead

Alex and Phoebe from the room, then followed them into the reception area that was now more like a cosy sitting room.

'It's lovely in here,' Phoebe said, looking around at the bright coloured lights draped over the tree and decorating the reception desk.

'We usually register people in here,' Piper explained, indicating for Phoebe to take a seat next to Jax on the leather sofa. 'We've moved the furniture around a bit to make it more like a family space than a reception area.'

'It's always cosy in here with the fire lit though,' Jax said, feeling tired now that he had eaten and was settled in the comfortable room. 'Shall I add a couple of logs and really get this thing going?'

'Yes, why not,' Piper said. 'Mum will want to sit here for hours this evening, and we've still got the rest of the presents to open.'

'Tell me about the plans for Boxing Day,' Phoebe said, settling back in the seat and taking a sip of her tea. 'Is the pub you go to the one Fliss and I saw you at in the summer?'

Jax wondered if maybe she was planning to join them the following day after all. He hoped so. 'No, that's The Dolphin. We love that pub but this is one that's a little further along the pier. I'm not sure when the tradition started of us going there for our Boxing Day lunch, but I do know it's been that way for maybe fifteen years. Piper, what do you think? About that long?'

Piper shrugged. 'Possibly. It's not very big inside but it's very welcoming, the regulars are lovely and the food is delicious.' She thought for a moment. 'I think our families first went there when the old landlord took over the place.'

Jax recalled the old man well. 'He was jolly and some of us kids from round here thought he might be the real Santa.'

'He had a white beard then?' Phoebe joked.

'He did actually, and a balding head.' Jax replied. 'He had a really deep belly laugh too. Do you remember that, Piper?'

'I do.' Piper smiled. 'The new landlord is nothing like him but he, his wife and their son are lovely people. And the food is much better than it was before.'

'That's true,' Jax agreed.

'So how long has the new landlord and lady been there.'

Jax tried to work out the time the couple had been at the pub. He caught Piper's eye and they both laughed.

'What's so funny?' Phoebe laughed.

'We call them the new tenants of the place but I think they've been there about five years now,' Piper said thoughtfully.

'Maybe even six,' Jax said, shaking his head.

'So not that new then?' Phoebe said.

'No, not really.' Jax sighed. 'But if you do come, I'm confident that you'll enjoy yourself.'

'Then I will be there.'

Jax smiled at her, excited to have the next day to look forward to.

He heard voices and realised the rest of the family were on their way to join them in the reception area. 'Better move to a different chair,' he said, standing and reaching out to take Phoebe's hand. 'My mum, Gran and Helen usually make themselves comfortable on this sofa.'

Phoebe took his hand and stood. 'Where shall we go then?'

He wished he could take her somewhere quiet where they could sit and speak alone, but doubted that would be a possibility today. If only the weather wasn't so dreadful, then they could have taken a walk along the beach to his beach hut and spent time together. Maybe another time.

The reception room door opened and Seamus bounded into

the room. He leapt up into Jax's arms, causing Phoebe to shriek in surprise.

'Does he do that sort of thing often?'

Jax nodded. 'Yes, and usually when I'm least expecting it. I think it's his way of reminding me that he's there, not that I need any reminding.' He kissed the dog's fluffy head. 'Do I, you rascal?'

He lowered the dog to the floor. 'Why don't we sit down here?' he asked, indicating a coffee table with four chairs set around it under the window.

'Good idea,' Piper said.

Once they were all settled and Dilys had been helped to sit in one of the two armchairs and Duncan sat on the other, Jax offered to fetch them drinks. It gave him time to think. His mind raced. He hadn't expected to have feelings for Phoebe but as each hour passed he realised that he was liking her more.

Was this a brief attraction after spending an unusual evening with her the night before, or could there really be something between them? He had no idea but it unnerved him. He was happy with his life, or as happy as he could be so soon after his break-up with Beth. Either way he certainly wasn't looking for a girlfriend. He handed out the drinks and saw Phoebe laughing at something Piper was saying. She seemed so different to Fliss. So uncomplicated, kind and sweet. Was that really her, he wondered, or was she playing him like Fliss had done so easily in the summer before he had woken up to her cruel games? He had no idea. Maybe he just needed to spend a bit more time with her and find out.

20

PHOEBE

Having said goodnight to Jax, his family and Margery after an enjoyable day, Phoebe and Piper waited for Helen to take Dilys up to her room.

'Shall we go and find something for you to wear to lunch tomorrow now?' Piper asked.

'Thank you. It's very kind of you to offer to lend me a top of yours.'

'It's no problem at all. Right, let me see.' Phoebe waited for Piper to look through the clothes hanging in her wardrobe. 'How about this?' Piper held up a hot pink sweater. 'You can wear it over your jeans.'

Phoebe loved it. 'It looks brand new though,' she said, unsure. 'I'd rather borrow something older in case I spill food down it.'

'Don't be silly,' Piper argued. 'Try it on and see what you think. Unless the colour is too bright for you.'

'No. Not at all.' She pulled the sweater over her head and looked at her reflection in Piper's mirror. 'I love it,' she said, stroking the softness of the material.

'Then you can keep it.'

Phoebe was surprised. 'Don't be silly. I couldn't do that.'

'Why ever not? I've never worn it.'

'Exactly. It's new.'

Pipers shook her head. 'I think it looks great on you but the colour is much too bold for me. You can carry it off though. Please take it. I won't ever wear it and it's far too lovely to do nothing but take up space in my wardrobe. You'd be doing me a favour, honestly.'

Phoebe studied Piper's face and saw that she meant what she said. 'In that case, I'd love to keep it. Thank you.'

'It's my pleasure.'

'I wish I had something for you,' Phoebe said, feeling frustrated.

Piper closed her wardrobe and sat on the edge of her bed. 'There is something you could do for me if you didn't mind.'

Intrigued, Phoebe folded her arms. 'Whatever it is, you only have to ask me.'

She watched as Piper gave whatever it was some thought. 'It's just that I was wondering about how you feel about my cousin.'

Phoebe hadn't expected such a question. 'Jax?' she asked to give herself a little time to think.

'Yes. I hope you don't mind? I know it's a personal question.' Piper sighed. 'He's a strapping great chap and more than capable of looking out for himself physically, but I saw how Fliss messed him about in the summer and after Beth...' She hesitated. 'Well, finished things with him, I'd hate for him to get close to you if you're only interested in being friends with him.'

Phoebe wished that Alex and Jax were there and that she hadn't given Piper the opportunity to broach something she wasn't ready to answer. She didn't mind Piper asking about her feelings and liked that she was protective of her cousin, but she wasn't sure Jax would be happy to know they had been speaking about him in this way.

'I'm not sure what to say,' she replied honestly. She liked Piper but was under no illusion that her loyalties would lie with Jax and that Piper might tell him anything she said about him. 'I do like him but we are just friends.'

'I see,' Piper said, a thoughtful look on her face. 'I'm glad you like the top anyway. I know you'll look lovely in it tomorrow when we go to lunch.'

Phoebe thanked her, relieved their conversation was over.

* * *

The following morning after showering, eating breakfast and getting ready, Phoebe followed Helen and Margery, who each had linked arms with Dilys as they walked ahead of her and Piper, as they made their way to the pub. She was relieved to see that the snow had thawed a lot since the previous day and decided that whatever anyone said, she would make her way home after lunch. Everyone had been very kind and done all they could to make her time with them enjoyable but she dreaded outstaying her welcome.

She heard laughter and voices as they neared the pub and saw a small group of people standing outside, huddled together in the cold chatting as they smoked their cigarettes. Margery, Helen and Piper exchanged pleasantries with them and Phoebe waited until they walked inside.

The warmth of the pub seemed to envelop them and draw them inside. She looked around her at the dark heavy beams across the ceiling, the stone fireplace with polished horse brasses hanging on either side and cosy nooks with banquettes, window seats, and it seemed that all the tables had been taken.

Wondering where they might sit, Phoebe watched as the brunette behind the bar noticed them.

'Margery, Helen, girls,' she shouted, waving them over to the bar. 'We've kept your usual tables for you in the back. Jax and his parents are there already. Go through.'

'Thanks, lovey,' Margery answered before turning to Phoebe and Piper. 'Come along, girls, this way. You two are going to love this,' she said addressing Dilys and Phoebe.

Phoebe exchanged glances with Dilys. 'I'm looking forward to this,' she whispered.

'So am I.'

They followed Margery through to the back of the room and Phoebe wondered where on earth they could be going. The pub seemed rather small from the outside and she hadn't expected it to be this deep. Margery opened a door and they filed inside.

Phoebe realised they were in what looked like a smaller bar area and presumed it must be a lounge. It wasn't big enough to cater for many people but she supposed they kept this room for small functions or private parties. The decor was dark, as in the main bar, and there was a large table in the middle of the room with a window to the back and another large fireplace to the left of her.

'What do you both think?' Margery asked, looking pleased with herself for bringing them there.

'I can't believe I've never been inside this one before,' Dilys said as Margery showed her to a seat at the table.

'I think it's amazing,' Phoebe said. 'Like something from a forties movie.'

Jax laughed. 'Kevin, the landlord, likes to think that some sets on TV have been modelled on this place but I think he only says that to try and impress the customers and encourage them to get their mates to come here too.'

Phoebe didn't care either way, she just knew she'd never been anywhere like this before and rather liked it.

'You sit between Jax and Helen,' Sheila suggested.

Phoebe was happy to and walked over to take her place at the table just as Duncan entered the room. He stopped walking as he looked at her.

'Good grief, that top of yours is bright.' He grinned. 'If it gets foggy we'll still be able to find you.'

'Dad, that's not funny,' Jax said, scowling. 'Take no notice of him, Phoebe, he likes to think he's amusing when he's had a couple of drinks.'

'Yes, Duncan.' Sheila waved him over to her. 'Do sit down and stop being annoying. Sorry, Phoebe.'

Phoebe hadn't been offended, quite the opposite. 'It's fine,' she said to reassure them as she took her seat next to Jax. 'I love the colour, but your dad isn't wrong.' She smiled at Duncan, feeling sorry for him as he sat gloomily next to his irritated wife.

'Did you sleep well?' Jax asked quietly.

'I did, thanks.' She had been surprised to realise that she slept far better at the guest house than she ever did on her expensive mattress at home. 'I don't know what it is about that place but I really relaxed. Maybe it's the sound of the sea right outside my bedroom window?'

'Possibly. I know that I always sleep much better when I'm near the sea, though that could be because I've spent most of my life with it close to my home.' He leant closer to her. 'There isn't a menu today,' he said. 'We're being served seafood. I hope that's OK with you?'

Phoebe was relieved she liked most seafood. 'Yes, fine. I can eat everything apart from oysters or whelks.' She gave an involuntary shudder.

'That's fine,' Jax said, giving her a conspiratorial smile. 'I'll sneak yours onto my plate and eat them.'

It was only a small room and their chairs were placed close to each other. She presumed it was because they hadn't expected to include Dilys and herself when booking the meal but she was just grateful to them for including her at their lunch. Phoebe felt Jax's arm next to hers and the heat radiating from his leg as it almost touched hers under the table kept drawing her attention from what people were saying. She wondered why there was a spare chair with no one sitting on it and whether someone would remove it to give them a bit more room.

Phoebe looked around her at the happy faces and watched as several chatted to each other quietly while Margery explained to Dilys about an incident that had happened during her swim two days before.

The door to the snug-like room opened and a smart woman Phoebe presumed to be in her mid-thirties walked in. She had a cheery expression on her face and was laughing at something a younger man of about twenty was saying.

'Hey, you made it,' Jax said, standing and holding his arms open in welcome.

'Hi, Jax, good to see you, mate.' The blonde woman scanned the room. 'Is Mum...' She spotted Dilys and went over to her, tapping her on the shoulder to get her attention. Phoebe watched as Dilys broke off her chat with Margery and looked up, gasping in surprise and then beaming from ear to ear when she saw who it was.

'Simone! When did you get here?'

'About an hour ago,' she replied, bending down to give her a tight hug. 'Merry Christmas, Mum. You're looking good. Are you all right?'

'I am, sweetheart.'

'She's fine,' Margery said, looking delighted to see Simone.

'And she'll be even better now that you're here on the island.'

'I'm relieved. It's so good to be back.'

'You're sitting next to your mum,' Helen said, indicating the vacant seat. 'Now, if you'd rather stay the night at the guest house you just have to say.'

'Thanks, Helen,' she said. 'But I thought I'd take Mum home. Bradley and I will be staying at her place until the New Year, then if Mum's feeling up to it, we thought we'd take her back to France to stay with us for a bit.' She gave her mum a questioning look. 'Unless you'd rather stay one more night?'

Dilys patted her hand. 'No, I love that plan. Helen, Margery and Piper have looked after me splendidly,' she insisted. 'But I've been looking forward to having time with you again. We can make our way home after we've eaten lunch.' She looked around her. 'Where's Bradley?'

'He's at yours. I didn't think it was fair for both of us to impose on this poor family.'

'Nonsense,' Helen said.

Phoebe liked Dilys and thought her daughter seemed very pleasant too. She was glad to see the sweet lady had her family around her again. She was such a quiet and unassuming lady and she didn't think she had seen her looking nearly as happy as when Simone had arrived. When everyone began chatting again she decided to ask Jax about her.

'Is that not Simone's husband then?' she asked as the man who had accompanied the newest member of their group left the room.

'No, he's Paul, the landlord and lady's son.'

'Right. Does Dilys just have the one child?'

Jax nodded. 'Yes. She adores her and the feeling is mutual.' He glanced at the pair of them and Phoebe waited for him to continue, aware that he had something to add. 'She adopted

Simone when she was nine, having fostered her for a few years. It was a happy ending to a difficult early life, or so my mum tells me.'

Phoebe looked at Simone when she knew the woman was deep in conversation. How sad that some people were faced with difficult childhoods while others like herself had everything they could possibly want. She watched Simone and Dilys interacting. Dilys's hand resting on the back of Simone's and Phoebe couldn't miss the affection in the woman's eyes. Whatever she might have been given growing up, Phoebe thought, she doubted she had ever seen either of her parents looking at her in such an adoring way. Then again, she mused, it was satisfying to know that even the worst starts in life could be turned around.

She felt Jax watching her and turned her attention to him to see he was smiling down at her. 'Sorry, did you say something?'

He shook his head. 'No, I was watching you. Deep in thought?'

'I've really enjoyed spending time with you all,' she admitted. 'I'll be sad to go home and leave all this behind me.'

Jax thought for a moment and she wondered what he was going to say. 'We could go out for a walk later, just the two of us, if you'd like?'

Phoebe couldn't help smiling. 'I would like that, thanks.' She waited while the landlady and her son served their meals, thanking them both with the others as four enormous platters laden with fruits de mer were placed onto the table.

'Wow, look at this lot,' she said, stunned at the elaborate display of food. 'I don't think I've seen anything like this since I was in the South of France with my parents several years ago.'

Jax laughed. 'Then you need to come out with my extended family more often.'

'I'd like that,' she said honestly, wondering if he would

remember to take her when they did this sort of thing again.

Jax picked up her plate and began serving mussels, prawns, langoustine and other tasty-looking bits from the enormous platter nearest to them. 'Just put anything onto my plate that you don't want,' he reminded her.

Phoebe thanked him and picked up a piece of bread and some butter for her side plate.

Drinks were served and Jax offered Phoebe some wine.

'No thanks,' she said, raising a hand. 'I'll be driving home later, so I'll just stick to water.'

He reached for the bottle of water and poured some into her glass.

She ate a langoustine, relishing the sweet, delicious taste. Keen to keep him talking, she said, 'Where shall we go walking later then?' It was still very cold outside but she had her jacket and thought that she could always ask Piper to lend her a woolly hat.

'Depending on what you prefer, we could either walk along the beach, or the promenade to my beach hut. Stop for a chat there, or just come straight back. The tide shouldn't be too far out when we've finished here and I always think it's the perfect way to help digest a meal. What do you think? Too cold for you maybe?'

Phoebe liked the idea. She had spent a lot of time inside over the past few days and the weather, although cold, was sunny. It would be refreshing to spend some time outside again. 'I'd like that.'

His expression brightened. 'Great. Then that's what we'll do. We'll pop home and fetch Seamus, if that's all right with you? He loves his walks.'

How could she refuse the funny little dog anything? Phoebe loved that Jax never left his dog out of anything if possible. 'Of course he must come with us,' she said, amused.

21

JAX

Jax found it almost impossible to hide his delight that Phoebe had agreed to go out for a walk with him. She might just wish for them to be friends but at least she wasn't opposed to spending time with him. And Seamus. He focused on eating his food so that she wouldn't see how happy she had made him and was glad when Dilys and Simone drew Phoebe into a conversation asking her what she did for a living.

'Nothing much really,' Phoebe said, after a moment's thought.

'I don't understand, dear,' Dilys said.

Jax heard Simone murmur something to her mother and supposed she might be trying to get her to change the subject. He looked sideways at Phoebe to see if she was all right and saw that she seemed a little uncomfortable.

'Are you OK?'

'Yes,' she said. 'Just not sure what to say.'

Now he was confused. Either she had a job or she didn't, surely? 'It's no one's business what you do,' he said, hoping to reassure her. He presumed she didn't need to earn a living but couldn't imagine what she did with herself all day. Maybe she had a hobby that kept her busy, he thought.

'Are you into crafts, like Piper and her friends?' Helen asked, pushing her glasses up onto the bridge of her nose. 'That seems to be so popular nowadays.'

'Er, no.'

'You must do something,' Margery said, looking baffled.

'I'm an influencer,' Phoebe replied quietly, shifting awkwardly in her seat when most of the people around the table stopped talking and focused their attention on her.

'What's that?' Margery asked, placing her fork down onto her plate. 'I'm not sure I understand what that means.'

'She's an influencer, Gran,' Piper explained. 'On social media.'

The rest of them stilled, forks halfway to mouths, conversations stopped and everyone was staring at Phoebe, Jax noticed.

'I think you'd better explain a little further,' he suggested quietly.

Margery peered at Phoebe. 'What do you influence?'

'People, Gran,' Piper said. 'Phoebe influences people to buy things.' She raised her eyebrows at Phoebe. 'That's right, isn't it?'

'It is.' Phoebe cleared her throat. 'Basically I promote companies' products and places online.'

Margery and Dilys swapped confused glances.

'Mostly on Instagram but now also on TikTok. They're social media sites online.'

Jax saw his father take an interest. 'And you make a living doing this sort of thing?'

'I do.'

'Well,' Dilys sighed. 'It all sounds very futuristic, if you ask me.'

Jax wasn't sure how Phoebe could answer that comment. 'I

think you have to be on social media to understand this a bit better.'

'Probably,' Phoebe agreed. She focused on her food and Jax sensed Phoebe wanted everyone to divert their attention from her and onto something else.

He tried to think of something to say to help her. 'Do you think we'll have any more snow?'

'What?' Margery, Dilys and his mother all asked in unison.

Jax laughed, aware that any conversation about the weather always grabbed their attention. 'It was just a question,' he said, wanting to keep their attention away from Phoebe and give her a chance to eat something. When the conversation didn't continue and people still sat staring at Phoebe as if she was an exhibit on display, he knew he needed to divert them. 'How's everyone's food? Mine is delicious.'

That did the trick. The conversation went on to what each was enjoying the most and then his parents began bickering when Duncan said that he thought last year's Boxing Day meal was better and that there was more choice.

'Nonsense,' Sheila argued. Then Margery agreed with Sheila. Dilys added that at least their family arranged something like this on Boxing Day and Simone suggested her mother might be better to keep out of the argument and then Jax felt they were all distracted enough and gave Phoebe a gentle nudge.

'You OK?'

Phoebe finished chewing her mouthful and swallowed before nodding. 'Yes. Thanks for that.'

'My pleasure.'

'I'm not used to being part of such a large family gathering,' she said. 'It's a little alarming when they all focus their attention on you at the same time, isn't it?'

'I suppose it must be. I'm used to it, so don't really notice it too much if they do it to me.' Jax bent his head closer to hers. 'You did very well though.'

'You think so?'

'I do.' He wanted to know more about her and her life. 'Tell me a bit about your work.'

'All right. What would you like to know?'

He thought for a moment. 'Well, I suppose I don't understand how you make money from your photos. Are you paid by a modelling agency?' He hoped it wasn't an intrusive, or stupid, question.

Phoebe smiled. 'No. I'm approached by brands wanting to sell products they feel I might be able to incorporate into my photos.' Jax tried to work out what she meant. 'You know, lifestyle choices, that sort of thing.'

Jax struggled to work out exactly what she meant. 'Like lamps and cushions, you mean?'

'Maybe. Mostly clothes, handbags, or make-up sometimes, or skin lotions. All sorts of products that companies feel my followers might be encouraged to use if they think that I do. They pay me to have photos taken with them and post those photos online.'

He looked into her beautiful eyes and a wave of affection swept over him. Phoebe's lifestyle might be the antithesis of his own but as far as he was concerned their differences could only make them more interesting to each other and give them more to learn about each other. And surely that could only be a good thing. *Couldn't it?*

* * *

Jax always enjoyed family get-togethers but today he was relieved when lunch was over and he could be alone with Phoebe. Or, he thought, rescue her from any more questions from his family. His mother had suggested he leave Seamus at home, as it would be too cold for him to walk so far in the snow and Jax eventually agreed that she might be right.

'I love this strange sort of eerie peace that descends onto a place in heavy snow,' he said. 'Not that I've experienced it many times in my life, living here.'

'It is a bit other-worldly, isn't it?'

'It is.' He tried to imprint the sights and sounds of the pier area, aware that he probably wouldn't experience the sensations again any time soon, if ever.

They walked across the parking area to the sea wall to begin their trek to his beach hut. He zipped his jacket as high as it would go and pulled a beanie from his jacket pocket. He held it out to her. 'Here, do you want to wear this?'

'Won't you be cold then?'

He shook his head. 'I'm a tough old beach bum.'

She laughed and gave him a relieved smile, then took the hat from him, immediately pulling it on her head and dragging it down over her ears. 'That's better. It's freezing out here.'

'We don't have to stay out. We can go back to my place if you'd rather do that.' He put his arm out for her to link hers through, which she did straight away. 'It would be warmer at home.'

'No, it's fine. I like being out here with you.'

She was probably exhausted from spending time under so much scrutiny, he thought. 'You do?'

She looked up at him and his stomach clenched as her mouth drew back into a smile.

'Yes.' She giggled. 'I've been skiing many times but it never feels this cold for some reason and when we ski it's always up some mountain or other.'

'It's because it's also damp here, being so near to the sea.'

'Yes, I hadn't thought of that.'

'Sorry, I forget you've lived here for years too.'

Realising he wasn't sure exactly when her parents might return to the island, he asked, 'When are your parents coming back, do you know?'

'Probably after the New Year. I doubt it'll be before then.'

He hated to think of her all alone for the next week. 'Don't you have anyone who can come and stay to keep you company while they're away?'

'Not really.' Her face reddened slightly. 'Most of my friends live in England. My fault really for never bothering to make friends here. I do have our housekeeper, Beryl, but my parents gave her time off over the festive holidays. She will be back on the second of January, so it's only a few days.'

'It's a week.' Feeling her shivering, he withdrew his arm from hers and put it around her shoulders, hugging her closer to him as they walked.

'That's better,' she said, slipping her arm around his waist.

'Good. We're almost there,' he said, wishing his beach hut was closer than another ten minutes' walk away. 'I'm not sure why I thought this was such a good idea now. I suppose it was because I thought of it when I was in a warm place.'

Phoebe laughed. 'Yes, I can see how that might make things seem a little better. But we're on our way now, so we may as well keep going. Hopefully if we quicken our stride a bit we might warm up slightly.'

'We do have to walk back again, unfortunately.' It really had been the most stupid suggestion to make he decided.

'This is one of those experiences that we'll laugh about in the future.'

Jax liked the thought of them having some sort of future together but noticed her cheeks reddening. Although he wasn't sure if it was the cold making them go that shade, he suspected it might be because she realised what she had just intimated.

'Yes, you're probably right.'

They reached the lane to the beach hut and trudged through the virgin snow along the track until they reached the ramshackle shed. Jax retrieved the key and opened the door, closing it as soon as they were inside to block out the freezing wind.

'You find us two chairs and I'll light the gas fire, we'll soon have this place warmed up. Although I'll need to open the window a fraction to let some fresh air circulate.'

'Won't that defeat the object?' Phoebe asked through chattering teeth.

'A bit, but we have to do it with this gas fire, unfortunately.'

Once the fire was lit, Jax shook a picnic rug to make sure there were no insects in it, although how anything would have survived the cold he couldn't imagine. Then he sat next to her and covered them both with the rug. 'Better?'

She rubbed her hands together to warm them and then slipped them under the plaid cloth and nodded. 'Getting there.'

He watched as she looked around the hut. 'It's rather pleasant in here, isn't it?'

'I'm glad you think so.'

'It could look amazing.'

Jax laughed, amused at her forthright comment. 'Are you telling me you don't approve of my messy decor?'

'I am.' She sighed theatrically. 'If you ever decide to tidy this place up and do something creative with it I'd love to help you.'

He hadn't expected her to offer her time. 'You'd do that?'

'Of course I would. I'd love it.'

'Then when the weather warms up a bit you can come and help me give this place a...' Jax tried to think what to call whatever it was that his beach hut was lacking.

'A makeover?'

'Is that what it is?'

'Yes,' she laughed.

'Fine. Then that's what we'll do.'

'When was the last time you did anything to this hut?'

He looked around him, seeing the dust, flaking paint on the walls and cobwebs at the corners of the window. It did look a mess, he realised. 'I've never done anything to it,' he admitted.

'Never?'

He shook his head. 'It was my grandad's and I wasn't ready to change things, I suppose. Keeping everything as he'd left it before he died helped keep him closer to me.' He wondered if she thought him silly for thinking that way. 'Does that sound odd?' he asked looking at her and seeing her eyes shining and looking suspiciously as if she was trying not to cry.

She cleared her throat and shook her head. 'Absolutely not. You keep it this way forever, if you prefer. Maybe it's supposed to stay this way. It does have a certain charm about it.'

Jax realised she was trying to be kind and sighed. 'I think that's a bit of an exaggeration but thank you all the same.'

'Maybe, but it's your special place and it should be exactly as you want it.'

He found her hand under the blanket, took it in his and gave it a gentle squeeze. 'Thank you.' Then, letting go of her hand, asked, 'But if you were to change it, what would you do?'

They chatted for a little longer about how Phoebe imagined his hut to look after working her magic and Jax realised he didn't want there to be too drastic a change. 'That does sound great, but

I don't think I'm ready yet to change anything much,' he explained. 'I love being able to come and spend time sitting here where my grandad used to mend his lobster pots, fixing odds and ends from his and my gran's home, which was down the lane there,' he said, pointing to their right. 'The house isn't there any more unfortunately. It was sold when he died and Gran wanted to move into sheltered accommodation.'

'That must have been upsetting for you?'

He remembered the feeling of loss only too well. 'I was heartbroken. He probably knew I would be and maybe that's why he left me this place in his will. I used to come here with him at every opportunity when I wasn't at school and loved being here with him.'

'You're lucky to have such cherished memories of your grandad,' Phoebe said wistfully. 'I never knew mine.'

'What, on either side?'

'That's right.' She took her hands from under the cloth and held them out in front of the fire. 'My mum's parents died when she was young and she was brought up by her aunt and my dad fell out with his parents when he dropped out of university.'

'Really? That sounds a little extreme, don't you think?'

'Maybe. Apparently they had high hopes for him. He was the first person in their family to go to university and they felt he was throwing away his future by leaving.'

'How wrong they were.'

'I know. Silly devils.' She pushed her hands back under the cloth again. 'Anyway, I think they're both dead now too. Sad really.'

It was, Jax thought. The choices people made and the time wasted was tragic.

'I meant it when I said that you could come and stay with us until your parents are back.' He thought of their tiny cottage. 'Or I could ask my Aunt Helen to put you up. You must know now that she would happily have you to stay with her and Piper.'

'I couldn't impose.'

He thought he noticed a suggestion of regret in Phoebe's voice. 'Just think about it,' he said, hoping she would.

22

JAX

Jax was about to try and encourage her to stay for at least another night when Phoebe raised her left hand and tilted her head to one side. 'Did you hear that?'

He listened but couldn't hear anything. 'No. What was it?'

'I thought I heard someone calling out.' She lifted the rug from her legs and stood. 'They sounded elderly.'

Aware that the temperature outside was probably below freezing and recalling how he and Piper had found Dilys when she had become dizzy and collapsed, Jax didn't waste any time going to check. He stood and dropped the rug onto his chair, then heard the voice he assumed Phoebe had heard a moment before.

'I heard it that time,' he said. Not wishing to put his beach hut at risk, he switched off the gas heater and closed the window. 'We'd better lock this up in case we don't come back here for a while.'

'You do that and I'll go and find out what's happened.' Phoebe had only run a couple of steps when they heard the voice again. 'It's coming from over there.' Jax pointed to the lane further up from where they had walked earlier. 'It's OK,' he shouted to whoever was in a state. 'We're on our way. Try to hang on.'

He caught up with Phoebe as they rushed through the thick snow past a row of pine trees. They turned a corner and saw that a vintage Morris Minor was part way into a ditch. An elderly man, whose overcoat came almost to his ankles, was bending down struggling to reach a small dog that seemed unable to scramble out of the ditch. The old man was in obvious distress.

'Hi, I'm Jax and that's Phoebe,' Jax explained as he took in the reason for the man's cries for help. He took his arm and helped the man stand upright.

'I can't quite reach him,' the man explained. 'Each time he tries to climb out he slips back down again.'

'If you move back and stand next to Phoebe, I'll fetch him out for you.'

'Would you?' the man asked, sighing with relief. 'That's very kind.' He peered down at his dog. 'Calm down now, Fred, this kind man is going to rescue you.' He moved out of the way, giving Jax the space he needed to kneel down. 'He followed me out here when I came back to the car to put up a hazard board to warn other lane users about it being partially in the way. Silly chap ran to the bottom and then couldn't climb back out. We've been here for almost half an hour now.'

Jax reached down, unsure whether the dog would cower back from him, but after sniffing his hand for a moment he stilled and allowed Jax to grab him and lift him to safety.

'There you go,' Jax said, wrapping one side of his jacket around the shivering dog.

'What kind people you are.' He extended a gloved hand. 'I'm Helier Le Cras. I was silly to let Fred come out with me but he doesn't like being left at home without me since the wife passed early this year.'

'I'm so sorry,' Phoebe said, stroking Fred's head. 'What happened with your car?'

'I was coming home last night in the dark and misjudged the corner. How, I don't know. I've lived here for fifty-four years, so should know this place well enough by now.'

Jax could sense the man's annoyance with himself and wanted to put him at his ease. 'It's difficult to know exactly where you are in these conditions sometimes.'

'I shouldn't think you'll be the only one who's done this last night,' Phoebe said. 'Are you all right though?'

'I am. A little shaken because of being unable to rescue Fred, but that's all.'

Jax didn't expect others to use the lane under the circumstances, there was still a thick covering of snow on the ground so you couldn't tell what was the lane and where it met the grass verge. Even the trees were covered in white. He was beginning to hope that it would all begin to defrost soon so that people like Mr Le Cras could move about safely without hurting himself or damaging his car.

'The wife would be furious if she could see what I've done to her precious car. She loved this vehicle and even when she gave up driving refused to part with it.' He thought for a few seconds. 'In the end I sold my car because it didn't make sense to have two of them in our short driveway but this is a tough thing for me to drive, no power steering and I'm too old for all that heavy work now I'm ninety-three.'

'You're ninety-three?' Phoebe shrieked. 'You certainly don't look it.'

Helier laughed. 'Well, that's very kind of you to say, but I have to admit that after the fright I gave myself this morning I feel about a hundred and ten now.'

Jax wasn't sure how long the man had been outside in the

cold. 'Look, why don't you show us where you live, then you and Fred can get back to the warmth. The poor little chap is shivering in my arms. Then I'll go with Phoebe to get my jeep. We'll come back and I'll tow your vehicle out of the ditch with a tow rope and push it back to your home. Does that sound good to you?'

'It does. Thanks, Jax.' Helier looked anxiously towards the corner of the lane. 'Should I maybe move the hazard board further round the corner to warn anyone sooner if they do come this way.'

'Good idea,' Phoebe said. 'I doubt anyone should come but just in case they do, it'll warn them. I'll fetch it and go and place it somewhere where others will see it.'

They waited for her to do as she had suggested, then Jax carried Fred and walked with Helier and Phoebe along the lane until they came to an entrance way with an open metal gate.

'We're the bungalow in here,' Helier said.

Fred immediately began wagging his tail frantically in Jax's arms and as soon as they reached the door Jax lowered the excited dog to the ground.

Once inside, Jax noticed there was a small Christmas tree about a metre tall with lights and tinsel and a worn-looking angel on top.

'It's not much,' Helier said, embarrassing Jax for being caught staring at it. 'But my late wife would have wanted me to make the effort for Fred and me.'

'It looks very festive,' Jax said.

'Not nearly as beautiful as she would have had it though,' he replied, his voice cracking with emotion.

Not wishing Helier to become upset and wanting to take the chill from the room, Jax offered to light the fire for him, noticing that there wasn't enough coal or wood to keep the fire going for more than a few hours.

Helier must have noticed him looking at the sparse coal bucket and scant pile of chopped wood. 'I had intended buying more today if I found a shop around here that was open.'

'Don't worry,' Jax said. 'I can ask up at the farm if they have any when I go to fetch my jeep.' He wondered if there might be anything further that Helier needed and asked him.

'I think I have enough to keep me going until tomorrow. I can walk down to the nearest shop then for my essentials.'

'Or I can fetch them for you if you need me to,' Jax said.

'Yes,' agreed Phoebe. 'Or I can. May I use this?'

Helier nodded and Jax watched as she wrote down her phone number. 'Jax, you write yours underneath it and then we know Helier can call one of us if he needs to.'

'That's terribly kind of you,' Helier said, stroking Fred's head as the dog nuzzled into his leg.

'Right,' Jax said. 'You stay here and keep warm and we'll go and try to sort out your car.'

'Would you like me to make you something to eat or drink before we go?' Phoebe asked.

'Thanks, dear, but I'm used to taking care of myself. Fred and I'll be fine. In fact, I'd better hurry up and feed him, it's getting late.'

Jax and Phoebe left Helier's home and walked back to the promenade. 'I think this is the safest way to make our way back to the pier,' Jax said. 'At least no cars can skid into us along here.'

It took them less time to get back to the pier and as soon as Phoebe had collected her keys from the guest house she drove the two of them to the farm.

'I'm glad I have this car,' she said, concentrating on the road ahead. 'It must have been frightening for Helier to come off the lane like he did.'

'Poor chap. You could see he was still shaken.' Jax knew that whatever it took he would find a way to drag the Morris Minor from the ditch so that Helier could relax.

Phoebe had to slow down as they turned off the main road onto the lane that would take them to the farm. 'This snow is still very deep here. Whoops!'

Jax grabbed hold of the door handle as the car slipped sideways before righting itself. 'That was a bit close,' he said, seeing the granite wall they had only just missed.

'Urgh, I don't want to do that again.'

They finally reached The Cabbage Patch and parked. Jax willed the car that had been blocking his vehicle to have moved.

'It's gone,' he cheered when he walked around the Range Rover and saw his car parked with several others, none of which were blocking him in. 'Finally!'

He didn't want to be too long getting back to Helier's car, so hurried with Phoebe into the farmhouse after knocking on the door. They found a group of people sitting around the dining table laughing and eating what looked very much like a Christmas lunch. He recognised some of them from the other night but didn't know them personally.

'You're back,' Meg said, waving for Jax and Phoebe to sit with them.

'We'd love to but we can't, I'm afraid,' Jax said and then explained about Helier and his car. 'I need to get back to him as soon as I can, I don't want him worrying unnecessarily.'

'You're a good boy, Jax.' Amy said. 'Always willing to help others when they need you. Are you sure you don't want anything to eat or drink before you get going?'

Jax glanced at Phoebe to check she didn't want something. She shook her head and smiled. 'I'm fine, thanks. We had a massive lunch a little earlier and I'm still rather full.'

'Me, too.' Jax recalled the logs he was going to ask about. 'Mr

Le Cras was a bit low on coal and logs for his fire,' he explained. 'I was wondering if you wouldn't mind me taking a bag of wood to him, if you have any spare.'

The sisters laughed loudly, amused at his suggestion that they might not have enough. 'If you go to the outbuilding closest to this house,' Meg said, 'you'll find a mountain of wood. There are sacks there too, if you need them.'

'Take whatever you need,' Amy said. 'There's more than enough for everyone.' She addressed the others sitting around the table. 'And any of you, if you need wood for your fires, please help yourself before you leave to go home.'

There was a chorus of 'thank yous' and Jax added his own. 'That's very kind of you. If you're sure you don't need us for anything.' He shrugged. 'Anyone need a lift somewhere, that sort of thing? If you do, we'll need you to come with us now so that Mr Le Cras isn't waiting for us for too long.'

'We're fine, thanks,' a man said, indicating the woman next to him.

'I think we all are,' another replied.

Happy to know that the sisters and their guests were comfortable and not needing his help, Jax led Phoebe to the outbuilding and opened the door. 'Look at this lot,' he said, stunned to see the stack of wood from floor to ceiling taking up two-thirds of the room. 'They'll be fine for years with so much wood.'

Phoebe peered inside next to him. 'You're not kidding.'

Jax picked up a sack and held it while Phoebe loaded it with logs. Then after leaning it against the wall, he picked up a second one. 'If Mr Le Cras doesn't want all of this we can pass it on to Piper's gran.'

'Good idea.'

Once they had what they needed, Jax carried the sacks to his jeep and placed them on the back seat. 'Shall I follow you?'

'No,' Phoebe said. 'I'll let you go first.'

'Fine. We'll take it easy and pop by the pier first. I think I'm going to need Alex's help with that Morris.'

'And maybe the landlord's son,' Phoebe suggested. 'What's his name again?'

'That's Paul. Yes, good idea. We'll ask him, if he's finished his shift at the pub.' Jax walked Phoebe to her car and opened the door for her, then just as she moved forward to get in, he leant closer to her and gave her a peck on the lips, surprising himself as well as her, he realised, as he saw shock register on her face.

'I'm sorry about that,' he said taken aback. 'I'm not sure what came over me.'

'It's fine.' Phoebe frowned, looking uncertain. 'I also feel a bit like this is some sort of adventure.' She took a deep breath. 'Shall we get going?'

'Er, yes, we better do so.' He waited for her to step up into the driver's seat and closed the door for her, unsure what to do next. Then remembering that he was leading the way back to the pier, he gave himself a mental shake and went over to his jeep. *What the hell had he been thinking?* Jax turned over the ignition, relieved when the vehicle started immediately and mortified for kissing Phoebe when they had agreed they'd remain as friends. He groaned and put the jeep in gear.

23

PHOEBE

Phoebe followed Jax's vehicle, unable to shake off the tingling sensation that Jax kissing her had sparked. If only he had meant that kiss, she thought as she focused her attention on the road ahead and not just been consumed by the excitement of the moment. He was such a lovely man, the nicest and most handsome she had ever met. Yes, there was something about him that caused her alarm. What was it though?

She was still wondering what that might be when she saw Jax pointing to a parking space at the beginning of the pier and carefully drew her father's car up alongside it. Phoebe locked the car and went to join Jax at the guest house.

'Will you go and find Alex for me while I turn my jeep round at the bottom of the pier.' He gave her a wry smile and Phoebe nodded.

'Will do.'

Shortly after, she walked outside with Alex and Piper following.

'I'll go and speak to Paul at the pub,' Alex said. 'Ask Jax to drive to the other end of the pier when he's turned and I'll meet you all there.'

* * *

As Jax drove the five of them to Helier's home, Phoebe was glad that she had been the one to drive the previous evening. The jeep seats were horribly uncomfortable and wind blasted in through the small vents under the windscreen that were rusted open. Then again, it seemed like a very old vehicle, so that probably wasn't surprising. And she now knew Jax well enough to know that he wasn't one to worry about creature comforts unless it was for his dog or someone else. The thought made her feel all warm inside and she looked at the back of his messy blond hair as he drove and chatted to Alex and Piper, explaining about what had happened to the Morris Minor and what he hoped to do when they reached the lane.

They drove up to where the car was sloping down in the ditch and parked, then Phoebe and Piper carried the sacks of logs up to Helier's bungalow.

'You are kind,' the old man said.

'We'll unpack some here,' Phoebe explained, taking several loads from the sack and heaping them on top of each other neatly. 'Do you have somewhere you'd like us to store the rest, so you can get to them easily.'

He nodded. 'There's a small utility room off the kitchen. They could go there by the back door.'

'No problem.' Phoebe followed Piper and once they had placed the sacks by the wall, ensuring that the back door could open fully, they returned to the living room.

'Jax and two friends are with your car now,' Piper said, having introduced herself. 'If they can't pull the car out with his jeep then I know a farmer who will happily bring his tractor for us to use instead.'

'Should we make the lads something to drink?' Helier asked, standing in the middle of the living room and looking as if he needed to keep busy.

'I'm sure they'd love one,' Phoebe answered. 'I know I wouldn't mind a hot drink.'

Piper swapped glances with her. 'Me, too.'

Phoebe hated to be hovered over when she was working on anything so thought that she and Piper should leave Helier to do the drinks. 'We'll go and see if the guys need any help and will bring them back here for the teas.'

Helier smiled, looking happy with her suggestion. 'I'll fetch a tin of biscuits from the cupboard and you can all join me for some of them,' he said cheerfully.

As she and Piper made their way back along the lane, Phoebe couldn't help thinking of Helier mentioning about losing his wife earlier in the year. 'His wife died not that long ago,' she explained to Piper, feeling very sorry for the elderly man. 'I didn't see any recent photos of family, so maybe he doesn't have children.'

'Or grandchildren,' Piper added. 'Do you get the impression that he is a bit lonely?'

'I do,' Phoebe said, feeling sad to think that such a lovely man might not have anyone close to him.

'Yes, me too. Especially when he seemed to cheer up so much at the thought of sharing his biscuits with us.'

Phoebe had to clear her throat to stop from crying. What was the matter with her? She didn't know Mr Le Cras' personal situation, so why was she feeling so emotional?

'Hey,' Piper said, stopping and resting a hand on Phoebe's back. 'Are you OK?'

Phoebe pulled a tissue from her jeans pocket and blew her nose. 'I am. I don't know what's wrong with me.'

'I always get a bit emotional at this time of year for some reason,' Piper said. 'I think a lot of people do even if they don't admit it, but I have been thinking…'

'What about?'

'Mr Le Cras. I'm going to invite him to join my family for our New Year's Eve drinks. He can bring Fred along with him. The only other dog there will be Seamus and he always wants to be everyone's new best friend.'

Phoebe cheered up at the thought of Helier having an invitation for a get-together. 'That's so kind of you, Piper.'

'Not really. I know that Gran will want to meet him. She hates to think of anyone being alone if they'd rather have company. I know that if I introduce him to her she'll soon have him involved in some of her hobbies and meet-ups.'

'I do hope so.' Phoebe heard Jax instructing one of the others to reverse his jeep and Alex shouting, 'Steady!' 'We'd better go and see what we can do to help.'

As they rounded the corner, Phoebe was thrown by the sight of Jax, his jacket removed and his sleeves rolled up past his elbows revealing tanned, muscular forearms. That tingling sensation ran through her again and she had to take a deep breath to calm herself. She watched him working, oblivious to his audience and then, realising that Piper had gone ahead to help, quickly ran after her to catch up.

Paul was in the driver's seat of the jeep and slowly edging it backwards while Jax and Alex held onto either side of the Morris Minor as the tow rope pulled it slowly backwards. She thought they had succeeded until the jeep slipped and the vintage car dropped back into the ditch again.

'Damn thing,' Alex shouted. 'We almost had it there.'

Jax groaned. 'I think more of the old car is deeper in the ditch now than it was when we first tried to pull it out.' He closed his eyes, looking as if he was trying to calm his frustration and then opening them again, rested his hands on his hips. 'Right. Let's try something a little different.'

Phoebe was getting so cold that her teeth began to chatter as they had done earlier. She folded her arms across her chest to try and keep as warm as possible and moved from foot to foot. If only she had thought to bring warmer clothes with her the previous evening.

'Do you need us for anything?' Piper asked, cupping her hands over her mouth and blowing on them. 'Or can we fetch something for you?'

'No, thanks,' Jax said. 'You two may as well go and keep Helier company.'

'Yes,' Alex agreed. 'There's no point in us all freezing to death out here.'

Paul laughed. 'You lot are such wimps. When I worked a season on the ski slopes in Austria it was far colder than this and I never heard anyone complaining this much.'

Piper and Phoebe looked at each other and, amused by how right Paul was, laughed.

'He's right,' Phoebe said, recalling how cold she had been at times in the past when skiing off-piste. 'Though I wish I'd thought to bring my ski wear today.'

'Go back to the house,' Jax suggested.

'We will do,' Phoebe said. 'Thanks. Oh, and Helier is making us all cups of tea and has some fancy biscuits he's going to share with us.'

Her words seemed to spark something in Jax. He raised his eyebrows, looking inspired by the thought of a sugary treat and rubbed his hands together. 'Tell him we won't be long.'

'You don't know that,' Alex argued.

'I do. Now listen to me, this is what we're going to do.'

Phoebe had heard enough. She was desperate to get back to the bungalow and linked arms with Piper to encourage her to hurry. 'Come along, let's go.'

Jax had been right, she thought, amused as the three men appeared at the front door when she and Piper were drinking their second cup of tea and finishing another delicious, buttery shortbread biscuit from the plaid tin that Helier had explained had been sent to him in a small Christmas hamper from his niece.

'You three look very comfortable and cosy,' Jax teased after washing his hands in the kitchen sink and appearing in the warm living room. 'I see the fire's going well.' He motioned for Alex and Paul to enter the room next to him. 'The Morris is fine and now safely inside your garage.'

'That's splendid,' Helier cheered, clapping his hands together gleefully. 'You are a first rate bunch of youngsters. Thank you for all your help. I've no idea what I would have done if you hadn't found me on the lane earlier.'

'It's our pleasure,' Jax said.

They all agreed that it was.

'Sit yourselves down, lads,' Helier said. 'I'll pour your drinks.' He pushed the open tin of shortbread towards the three of them sitting close to each other on the floral sofa. 'Help yourselves.'

Everyone sat chatting and listening to Helier explaining how pleasant it was to have company. 'I don't recall the last time I had so many people in my living room.'

It occurred to Phoebe how relieved she was to have had her earlier conversation with Piper and know that he wouldn't be as lonely for much longer.

'I've been thinking, Helier,' Piper said, interrupting her

thoughts. 'I would love for you to meet my gran and wondered if you might consider joining our families for drinks on New Year's Eve. She'll be there. I think you two will get along well. Her name is Margery and she has lots of friends I'm sure she'll want to introduce you to.'

The man's lined eyes seemed shiny suddenly. 'What do you think of that then, Fred?' he asked, looking down at his dog and making Phoebe suspect that he was trying to control his emotions. She closed her eyes for a moment, desperate not to give in to hers. Helier took something from his pocket and she saw it was a bone-shaped treat for Fred. He held it out to the little dog who wagged his tail in appreciation before taking it gently from Helier's fingers.

'Fred thinks it's an excellent idea. Don't you, Fred?'

The little terrier barked and everyone laughed.

Phoebe sighed, feeling happier than she had done in months. This Christmas was turning out much better than she could have imagined and certainly more heart-warming.

24

JAX

None of them spoke as Jax drove everyone back to the pier a little later. He imagined it was because they were all tired, or maybe, he mused as he slowed to wait for a car in front of him to turn off the road, it was because they were all emotionally drained like he seemed to be. What was it about this time of year that did this to people and certainly to him? And this year the intensity of it all seemed to have increased ten-fold.

He would be glad to get back to his daily workload and spend time with Seamus. Life with Seamus was uncomplicated, as long as he was fed twice a day, given a couple of walks, lots of cuddles and various treats throughout the day then his dog was happy and so was he.

'It was lovely of you to invite Helier to meet your gran,' Phoebe said, breaking the silence in the jeep. 'I think he was probably very touched by your kindness.'

'I just couldn't bear to think of him spending so much time alone,' Piper said, causing the others to murmur their agreement. 'He seems such a sweet man, don't you think?'

'I do.'

Jax glanced quickly at Phoebe sitting to his left in the middle of the front seat with Paul by the passenger door. He wondered if she had been so aware of Helier's loneliness because of her own. He supposed it must be why. The realisation saddened him. He loved spending time alone, he mused, not considering Seamus to be anything other than an extension of himself. Then again, he chose to be by himself so much of the time and imagined it must be very different to make that choice as opposed to having loneliness forced upon you.

'You're looking very thoughtful,' Phoebe said quietly when Piper and Alex began chatting with Paul about their plans for the following few days as they sat in the back of the vehicle. 'Is everything all right?'

'Fine, thanks,' he reassured her. Why did people always say they were fine when asked how they were? he wondered. Was it because they didn't wish to open up about their true feelings, like he had just done? Or, maybe they were being honest.

He looked sideways at her and caught her watching him thoughtfully. 'I can see you don't believe me.'

'It's just that you had a sad look on your face and I was going to ask if there was anything I could do to help.' She watched him, her beautiful eyes tired from the previous few days but still the prettiest eyes he had ever looked into.

'Watch out!' Paul shouted, leaning across Phoebe and grabbing the steering wheel to straighten it. 'You nearly hit that wall, Jax. Are you all right, mate?'

Shocked to have almost caused a crash daydreaming over Phoebe, he shook his head. 'Hell, sorry about that, everyone. I think I must need to catch up on some sleep.'

'I'm not surprised,' Alex said. 'You can't have had much over the last couple of days, what with the excitement at the farm the other night and it being Christmas yesterday. I think we're all a bit shattered.'

'Yes,' Paul agreed. 'I know I am. It's nightmarishly busy at the pub at this time of year and my parents always want to make the most of it to make up for any quiet periods over the next couple of months.'

'We're nearly there now though,' Jax said, trying to hide his embarrassment. He daren't look at Phoebe. What was he thinking, staring at her like some love-sick teenager. Maybe it would be for the best if she returned to her home. At least then he wouldn't make such a prat of himself and could catch up with some sleep.

He dropped Paul off in front of the pub. 'Thanks again for your help,' Jax said. 'I really appreciate you coming out when you've got so much on.'

Paul closed the car door. 'I was happy for an excuse to get some fresh air, so don't be too grateful.' He grinned at Jax and waved at the others. 'Maybe I'll see you all later in the pub for a drink?'

'We'll certainly catch up with you over the next few days,' Jax promised, not wanting to agree to something and then let Paul down. 'I think that today will be taken up by family stuff.'

'Of course.' Paul nodded. 'No problem.'

Jax drove on and, relieved to find a parking space in front of the guest house, parked the vehicle and then helped the others out of it before locking it. 'Thanks again, you lot.'

'You coming to the guest house with us three?' Piper asked, having presumed that Phoebe would be going with her and Alex.

Unsure whether to or not, Jax shook his head. 'I'll just go and check on them at home first.' He looked at Phoebe, not wishing to be rude. 'I'll pop by shortly though to see you off.'

'Why?' Piper asked. 'Where are you going, Phoebe?'

When Phoebe seemed at a loss Jax realised how his words must have sounded. Damn. Now he'd almost discouraged her and after spending time earlier trying to persuade her to stay for another couple of nights. What a rotten way to behave. Having embarrassed himself for the second time in five minutes, he rested a hand on Phoebe's shoulders. 'I'm sorry. I don't mean to sound like an idiot. I don't even know if you are staying here for longer.'

Phoebe stared at him silently and he could see by the hurt look in her eyes that his comment had stung. Why hadn't he thought before speaking?

A smile appeared on Phoebe's face but Jax could tell it was forced and hated himself even more for putting her in a position where she had to act as if she was fine.

'Jax is right,' Phoebe said. 'I had intended returning home later today all along. I really shouldn't leave the house empty for too long, especially in these cold temperatures.'

'That's true,' Alex said thoughtfully. 'I remember when I was in my teens going away for a sunny holiday in Africa with my family and my dad received a call from whoever it was he had asked to check up on the house during our holiday. The pipes from the water tank in the roof had burst and water had been coursing through most of the house for a couple of days.'

'That sounds nasty,' Jax said, feeling slightly less guilty.

'It was,' Alex agreed. 'The worst bit was that my parents had only just paid for twelve months' worth of renovations to the place.'

'What happened then?' Piper asked.

'We could only return to the house to collect certain bits, the rest was put in storage or dumped and my parents had to rent another house for us to stay in while the renovations were redone.'

Jax noticed Phoebe shudder. 'I can't let that happen to our

house, Dad would never forgive me.' She frowned thoughtfully. 'In fact, I think I'll grab my bits and leave right away.'

'Stay for a little while, can't you?' Piper asked.

'No, I'd feel better getting home. I know it's when the thaw comes that any problems make themselves known.'

'You're not kidding,' Alex said. 'Would you like me to come with you to check everything is as it should be?'

Not wanting Alex to go instead of him, Jax stepped forward. 'It's OK, you stay here with Piper. I'll follow you back to your place, Phoebe,' he insisted. 'Once I'm confident you're happy, I'll leave you in peace.'

Phoebe looked up at him and he saw she was struggling with conflicting thoughts. 'I'm not sure.'

She looked as if she would rather not spend time with him. Jax decided that even if he had been a fool he still wanted to make sure she was OK. 'I promise I won't stay any longer than you're happy for me to,' he added in an effort to persuade her.

She stared at him, her upset gone and now replaced by annoyance. 'Fine. If you're happy to.'

'I am.'

'All right then. How long do you need to get ready?'

'I just need to fetch Seamus.' He saw that she didn't understand why he had to take his dog along with him. 'I'll take him for a walk on the way back from seeing you home.'

'I see. Then shall we say we'll meet out here in ten minutes?'

'Sounds good to me.'

'Thank heavens for that,' Margery grumbled, alerting Jax to her presence at the open front door to the guest house. 'What a load of nonsense you youngsters speak sometimes.'

Jax stepped back at the same time the others did to let Margery pass.

Piper linked arms with her grandmother but Margery tried to

shrug her off. 'No, Gran, I'm helping you home. I won't stand by and watch you slip over.'

'For pity's sake, I'm capable of walking a dozen steps without tumbling,' she snapped, shaking her head as she walked to her door with Piper still holding on to her.

Jax watched as Piper returned as soon as Margery was inside her cottage and joined them. 'It's freezing out here, I'm going inside. You coming, Phoebe?'

Phoebe nodded and followed Piper into the guest house. Alex patted Jax's arm. 'It'll be fine, you'll see.'

Jax wasn't sure what he meant and had no time to ask when Alex followed the women into the guest house and closed the door behind them. He stared at the door for a moment trying to make sense of what had happened then, aware that Phoebe would be leaving soon, returned home.

'Come along, Seamus,' he said, picking up his little dog. 'You're coming with me.'

'You going back out, love?' Sheila called.

'Yes. I'm taking this little guy with me and we'll both see you later.'

He went back outside and placed Seamus on the passenger seat, took his harness from the footwell in the back of the jeep and fastened it to him and then to the seat so that the dog was safely strapped in. Jax had no intention of taking any chances with his beloved dog and certainly not when the road conditions were so appalling.

He saw Phoebe coming out of the guest house and waved, not surprised when she returned his cheerfulness with a slight nod.

Jax waited for her to get into her dad's car and turn it so that it was facing the right way. He then followed her, intrigued to see where she lived.

25

PHOEBE

Phoebe tried to focus on driving as carefully as possible but seeing Jax's jeep behind her irritated her and inflamed her already bad mood. Why did she like him so much? He wasn't her usual type. They didn't really have anything in common either. What did she know, or want to know about his work or lifestyle? Nothing, that's what.

'Bloody infuriating man, that's what he is,' she grumbled, glaring at him in the rear view mirror and screeching when he spotted her and mistook her look for gratitude that he was coming home with her and gave her the thumbs up. 'Urgh.'

It was her own fault really, she decided. She had fallen for his good looks and it served her right that she had been so shallow doing that. She now knew her feelings for him to be stronger than his must be for her and that she had clearly outstayed her welcome as far as he was concerned. It was probably for the best, she reasoned. What would they ever hope to spend their days doing if they had got together, she wondered. 'We'd probably spend them bickering like we almost did this afternoon.'

She didn't know whether she was more angry with herself for

harbouring hopes of a future with Jax, or with him for proving her to be silly enough not to see through his charm and good looks. She had to swerve to miss a red squirrel and realised she needed to concentrate on driving and forget about Jax if she was to ever reach her home with the car unscathed.

Relieved to reach their driveway, Phoebe indicated and slowed the car, waiting for the electric gates to open after she pressed the fob attached to her car keys for that very reason. She drove the car slowly through the thick snow up the driveway and pressed another button on the fob for the garage doors to open. She drove inside and closed it after her. Let Jax wait for her to walk through the house and open the front door for him, it would give her a couple of minutes to gather herself.

She unlocked and pulled back the large front door and, seeing him watching her from inside the jeep, waved him in.

'Is it all right if I bring Seamus?' He looked concerned and Phoebe assumed he hadn't considered what to do with his dog while he checked her parents' home.

She knew they would be horrified to think that a dog had been into the house but didn't have the heart to expect Seamus to stay outside in the cold.

'Of course. Hurry up though, we're letting all the cold in the hallway and it's cool enough in here already.' She hated the cavernous hallway with its tiled floor and floor-to-ceiling windows. Even at the height of summer this place felt cold, although, she reminded herself, she was happy for it to be that way at that point in the year.

'Sorry about that,' Jax said, walking up the steps to the front door, Seamus snuggled under his jacket. 'I should have left him at home but he usually has a walk around now and I didn't want either of my parents to feel like they had to take him.'

'It's fine,' she said honestly. She closed the door after them and walked through the hall. 'Follow me.'

'Would you like me to remove my shoes?'

'No, it's fine.' Her parents would be horrified to see him wearing his boots through the house but they weren't here now, Phoebe mused and with the tiled floors it wouldn't be a problem cleaning up any dirt that might come off Jax's boots.

Phoebe showed him through to the kitchen, hearing his footsteps and Seamus's paws as his nails occasionally tapped along the flooring. She was intensely aware of Jax's presence and forced herself to push aside any feelings of attraction for him.

They reached the large, ridiculously expensive kitchen that her mother had insisted needed to be installed despite not using it to make anything more elaborate than a bowl of soup for herself once or twice.

'This is amazing,' Jax said.

'Do you really think so?'

'I do.'

Did he mean it, she wondered, or was he just being polite? 'I think it looks more like an expensive aircraft hangar.'

Jax laughed. 'I wouldn't say that.' He looked around him. 'Well, maybe a little.'

Unable to help herself, Phoebe laughed. 'I much prefer the galley kitchen at the guest house,' she admitted, yearning for a home that felt like a hug rather than a showpiece.

'Really? It's almost impossible to sit in there.'

'I don't care. Even a kitchen that much smaller than this room is somewhere for the family to congregate.'

'Yours don't do that here?'

She shook her head miserably. 'It would be nice if we did, but that never happens.'

Jax stared at her thoughtfully and she wished she hadn't opened up to him, yet again. 'Where do you all sit.'

'Sit?'

'You know,' he said. 'When you and your parents are watching a movie together in the evenings, or reading, that sort of thing.'

She studied his face, aware that he really had no idea how different her life was to his. 'We don't do those sorts of things,' she admitted, aware that she needed to be honest with him. There was little point in pretending her family life was better than it truly was.

The look of sympathy that exuded from his face made her want to run from him. 'Don't look at me like that, Jax,' she snapped. 'I didn't tell you that so that you could feel sorry for me, so please don't. There's really no need.'

'But, Phoebe...'

'No,' she said shaking her head. 'Don't forget that I've never lived any other way. This is normal for me and I'm fine with it.' She was lying and she saw by the questioning look on his face that he knew it.

He walked over to her and opened his arms.

'What are you doing?' she asked defensively, stepping away from him.

He seemed nonplussed. 'I only wanted to give you a hug.'

'Why?' she asked, annoyed. Pity was the one thing she couldn't abide others feeling for her, not when she had so much that others didn't.

He seemed unsure. 'I... er... Forget it.' His arms lowered.

Desperate to change the subject, Phoebe indicated the back door. 'You can let Seamus out through that door,' she said. 'It's a big garden so you'll need to look out for him.'

'I will,' Jax said, still seeming stunned by what had happened between them. 'Thanks.'

She watched Jax take his dog outside and folded her arms thoughtfully. Why was she being so unfriendly towards him, taking what had happened earlier between them so much to heart? They weren't well suited. Maybe Jax had more sense than her and had worked out as much, or it could be that he simply wasn't attracted to her and was awkwardly trying to make sure she knew where they stood with each other? Yes, she decided that must be it. She needed to be less sensitive to what he said, especially as she had decided that she didn't want to be with someone so different to herself anyway.

She watched them in the garden. The little dog's legs appearing every few seconds as he leapt out of the snow. He really was the cutest dog and she wished her parents had allowed her to keep a pet. She knew why they hadn't, it had been some sort of odd punishment for not wanting to join her mother riding horses when she was younger. Her mother insisted that horses were the most magnificent creatures and liked that they lived in stables with stable hands to look after them.

'A dog,' she recalled her mother telling her, 'has to live inside the home and unless we have staff to feed and water them at all times, then it will be left for us to do it instead.'

Phoebe had pleaded for her mother to change her mind and promised to take care of any pet they allowed her to keep but it was to no avail and she eventually gave up.

Jax was coming back inside and she spotted the snow accumulated on Seamus's furry legs and belly. She needed to find a towel for Jax to dry him or the poor dog wouldn't warm up. She went to the airing cupboard and grabbed the nearest towel she could find, returning to the kitchen just in time for Jax to carry Seamus inside.

'Here you go,' she said handing it to him.

Jax thanked her quietly but didn't look at her and Phoebe

could see she had hurt him somehow. Why had she let him follow her home? All she wanted to do now was change and sit in front of the fire and read one of the many books she had filling the two large bookcases in her bedroom.

'I'll fetch him a bowl of water,' she said, going to take a metal bowl from the pantry. She poured some water into it and placed it on the floor near the dog.

'Thanks.'

Jax finished drying him and stood. Then, turning, he went to hand her the towel. His eyes fell on hers and Phoebe's breath caught in her throat at the intensity emanating from them.

'Phoebe, I...'

Without another thought, she stepped forward, reached up and slipped her hands behind his neck, stood on tiptoe and kissed him.

26

JAX

What the hell was happening? Jax wondered, shocked by Phoebe taking hold of him and kissing him. For a moment he didn't react, too stunned to even think. Then, not wishing her to stop, he let go of the towel, took her in his arms and kissed her back.

Seamus growled but Jax tried to ignore him, aware that his dog sometimes thought that people who hugged Jax might be hurting him. Phoebe kissing him did not hurt, in fact it had the opposite effect and seemed like the most natural kiss ever.

Jax felt Seamus's two front paws slam into the back of his knees. 'Stop that!' He moved back from Phoebe, wondering what was wrong with his dog. 'Sorry about him,' he said, dropping his arms from around her and turning to check on Seamus.

As soon as he did, the dog ran over to the window and began batting at the glass with one of his paws.

'Maybe he needs to go outside for a wee?' Phoebe suggested.

Jax doubted it because Seamus had already done that when they had been out in the garden a few minutes earlier but not wishing there to be an embarrassing incident in the immaculate kitchen, opened the door to let him out. 'I'd better go with him,' he said frustrated for their kiss being interrupted but not wishing his dog to get lost or in any bother.

'What is it, boy?' he asked as the dog stopped and sniffed the cold air. He'd never seen Seamus act this way before and couldn't understand what had caused it. Maybe it was the unfamiliar territory, or it could be simply that he had sniffed a rabbit, or another dog from somewhere across the fields bordering the large garden.

'Come along,' he said aware that it was now dusk and would soon be dark. His mind raced. She had kissed him and it had been amazing. He couldn't wait to kiss her again. 'Let's get inside before we get too cold.' He patted his thigh and Seamus followed him back into the house.

'Anything?' Phoebe asked frowning.

'Nothing.' Jax was perplexed by Seamus's uncharacteristic behaviour.

'He seems fine now though, doesn't he?'

Jax bent to stroke his dog. He wasn't trembling as he usually did when there were fireworks or thunder and seemed calm enough. 'He does.' Jax sighed and when Seamus went to lie down by the glass kitchen door watching outside, he turned to Phoebe wanting to kiss her again.

'I'm sorry about before,' she said, turning her back to him and lifting the kettle and filling it with water from the tap. 'I don't know what came over me.'

Struggling to hide his disappointment, Jax wasn't sure how to react. He didn't want her to feel bad and wondered if maybe her kissing him had been a momentary lapse of... what? He had no idea.

'It's fine,' he said eventually as she placed the kettle back onto its stand. 'I liked it.' He smiled when she looked over her shoulder at him. 'I don't mind you doing it again, if you decided to.'

Instead of her being amused by his comment, Phoebe scowled at him. What had he said to cause that reaction? he wondered.

'I thought we talked about us remaining as friends?'

'We did.' He didn't like to add that her kiss had made him hope that she might have changed her mind. Her reaction hurt and confused him, but maybe that was a good thing, Jax thought. They really were very different after all. 'I should probably take Seamus home now. He'll be wanting his food soon and if you thought he was a pain then wait until he gets hungry.' He attempted a smile to show he was making light of the situation. 'Unless you'd like me to stay for a bit longer? I'm happy to do that.'

She shook her head. 'No, that's fine. I think I'll just take a long soak in the bath and then have an early night. I'm rather tired after the fun and games of the last few days.'

'Sounds like a good way to spend a wintery evening.' He smiled at her, wishing she had let him stay for a tea, but understanding that she wanted to relax. 'Come along, Seamus.'

Seamus got to his feet, tail wagging and followed Jax to the door. Phoebe went to follow but Jax shook his head. 'No need to follow us out.'

'Thanks again then, Jax. It was kind of you to see me back home.'

'No problem,' he said. 'Call me if you need anything, I can be here in ten minutes.'

'I will, but I'm sure it won't be necessary.'

He left the house wishing he didn't have to go back out into the cold weather. Picking Seamus up, Jax carried him to the car, stunned when the little dog growled and wriggled almost causing Jax to drop him. 'Hey, that's enough.'

Whatever it was that was upsetting him must be nearby, he

thought, opening the jeep passenger door and struggling with Seamus to get his harness back on. Seamus growled again and Jax stopped trying to clip on the harness. Concerned his dog had hurt himself, Jax ran his hands lightly over the little dog's head, body and legs expecting that if he was sore that he would flinch and let him know. But there was nothing. Jax was confused, his concern increasing.

'What's the matter with you, little guy?' Jax held Seamus's head lightly in his hands and bent to kiss the top of it. 'You're OK.'

Satisfied that Seamus was fine, if a little spooked by something, Jax closed the passenger door and walked around the front of his jeep intending to get inside when he noticed footprints in the snow to his left. He stopped and peered at them. They were too small for his feet and far too big for Phoebe's he presumed. Anyway, he thought, recalling the boots that she had been wearing, the footprints couldn't have come from the same footwear.

He tried to think back and picture if he had seen them on his arrival, but couldn't remember looking this way. Would he have noticed them anyway? He was used to looking out for unexpected signs and things that shouldn't be somewhere. He realised that if these footprints had been there when he and Phoebe arrived at the property, he would definitely have noticed.

Unsure what to do next, he thought for a few seconds. This was Jersey and most of the time people were completely safe, but Phoebe had mentioned that the housekeeper was away for a few days. What if someone had known that her parents were away and that she would be in the house alone? All it would take, Jax mused, was one of them to mention it to a friend in a public place and for some unsavoury person to overhear them speaking. Or the housekeeper could have done just that. Whatever it was, he decided he had to check the property to be certain she was safe before he left her alone. He would rather risk Phoebe being angry with him than for her to be hurt, or frightened.

He thought of Seamus and although he would rather leave him in the vehicle, it was too cold to do so without leaving the engine running and the heater on and he had no intention of doing something that dangerous. Jax walked back to the passenger door and quietly unclipped Seamus.

'Is this why you've been so upset?' he whispered, as it dawned on him that Seamus might have been attempting to alert him to some sort of danger. He lifted the dog down from the car seat. It would make perfect sense. 'Right, little guy, let's go and have a look around this place.'

He let Seamus go and, not wishing to tip off anyone who might be nearby, lightly tapped the side of his thigh for his dog to keep close to him. They had covered the length of the side pathway to the back garden and Jax was beginning to worry that Phoebe might see them and think he was stalking her or something. Then, they turned the corner and Jax spotted a hooded man standing outside what he assumed must be the kitchen door, with one hand resting on the door handle.

'Oi,' Jax bellowed, breaking into a run with Seamus almost managing to keep up with him. The person's head immediately jerked up. He then pulled the top of his hoodie to cover the upper half of his face at the same time as turning and running away from Jax.

The kitchen door opened and Phoebe stepped out, causing Jax to take evasive action so that he didn't slam into her. He swerved around her, slipping on the icy terrace and lost his footing. Unable to help himself, Jax fell down the three granite steps onto the pathway below the terraced area running the length of the house.

'Get him, Seamus,' he yelled, standing as quickly as he could and pointing at Phoebe. 'Get back into the house. Lock the doors.'

'What's going on?'

'Now, Phoebe!'

Determined to do his best to catch whoever had entered the garden, Jax chased after his dog. At least it wasn't completely dark yet, he thought, becoming aware of a stinging pain in his right calf. Not caring about the pain, Jax focused on not losing sight of Seamus. His dog meant more to him than anything else.

The man ran off through some trees at the opposite end of the garden and, not knowing the area well, Jax had no idea where his route would take him. His leg was hurting badly now and he could see Seamus struggling in the deeper snow and decided it was time to call him back.

'Seamus, here boy!'

The little dog ran on for a another metre before stopping. Jax hobbled up to him and lifted him up out of the snow. Hugging Seamus close to him, Jax brushed off the excess snow from his paws.

'Good boy,' he soothed the panting dog, feeling the little heart beating rapidly under his furry chest. He stared out into the darkness to the trees on the edge of the property looking for any movement. Not seeing any, Jax supposed that the man was now far away.

'Come along,' he said taking first Seamus's front paws in his free palm to try and warm them and then his rear paws. 'Let's go and tell Phoebe why we're racing around in her garden when we were supposed to have left.'

* * *

'A man?' Phoebe asked, placing a folded towel down on the floor in front of the living room fireplace for Seamus and handing Jax a second towel with which to dry the dog.

'Yes, I noticed footprints at the side of the house, at the beginning of the pathway next to where I'd parked my jeep.'

'Do you suppose that's why Seamus was barking and wanted to go out earlier?'

Jax nodded. He rubbed his dog with the towel and, satisfied that he had managed to dry him as well as possible, encouraged Seamus to lie down in front of the fire and knelt next to him. 'Could it be anyone you know?' He knew it was an odd question to ask but didn't want to immediately speculate about his thoughts and frighten her.

Phoebe shrugged. 'Who would come to the back of the house though? If anyone wanted to visit me they'd come to the front door surely?'

'Yes, that's true.'

'Anyway,' Phoebe said, leaning against the mantelpiece. 'If it was a friend why would they run away. That makes no sense at all.'

'It doesn't, does it?'

He saw Phoebe narrow her eyes and peer downwards at his shin. She stepped forward and reached down. 'You're bleeding.'

Jax felt the pain in his leg once more now that he had been reminded of it. He went to stand, wincing as the pain caught his breath. Then reaching down, he touched where it hurt and felt dampness on his fingertips.

'Damn, your mother's beautiful rug – I think I've bled on it.'

Phoebe frowned. 'Come and sit over here and let me look at it.'

Presuming she meant to inspect the damage to the expensive rug, he did as she asked and sat on the chair she had indicated.

But instead of going to the rug she knelt in front of him and took the hem of his jeans and lifted one leg.

'What are you doing?' Jax asked, feeling awkward.

'Checking what you've done to yourself, of course,' she said, shaking her head.

He waited for her to lift the material. Phoebe sucked in air between her teeth and grimaced.

'What's the damage?' Jax asked. 'I must have done it when I fell over,' he said, aware he was stating the obvious as soon as the words were out of his mouth.

'It's mostly grazed but there's a nasty groove gouged out of the skin.' She shuddered. 'Probably from catching the edge of the steps as you fell.' She sat back on her heels. 'I'm sorry, Jax.'

Confused, he frowned. 'What for? You haven't done anything.'

'If I hadn't come out of the house at the same time as you were passing then this wouldn't have happened.'

It was true, but he couldn't let her feel guilty over something that was an accident. 'It couldn't be helped. Anyway, I'm more concerned about who this person was and what they were doing here.'

'It's shaken me up a bit too,' she said and for the first time he saw her hands were trembling.

Jax leant forward and took her hands in his. 'Try not to worry. I'm sure we'll be able to see more in daylight. I can stay here for tonight, if it'll make you feel better.'

'You wouldn't mind?'

'Not at all.' He was relieved she had agreed, though wasn't sure what he might have done if she hadn't. Slept in his jeep probably. Jax knew he couldn't in all good conscience leave her here without keeping an eye on the house to make sure the stranger didn't return during the night.

'But what about Seamus?'

'Do you have a problem with him staying too?'

'No, how could I when he was the one trying to warn us about an intruder in the first place.'

Jax sighed. 'He did his best to try and tell us, didn't he?'

'He did.' She looked at the little dog curled up in front of the fire. 'What can I feed him? He must be hungry if he hasn't been fed yet.'

Jax realised he had been intending to feed Seamus when he returned home. 'A tin of tuna will make him very happy. If you have any?'

'Plenty of them.'

Jax smiled. 'Then I can give him half a tin tonight and the other half in the morning. He'll be delighted. He and I can make up a bed in the kitchen and keep an eye on the place while you sleep.'

'You will not,' she argued. 'We have enough rooms here for you to spend the night comfortably. I'll make one up for you.'

Jax shook his head. 'No, Phoebe. If your mother doesn't like having dogs in the house it wouldn't be fair of us to let Seamus go upstairs into one of her bedrooms. If you don't want us sleeping in the kitchen then we can make ourselves very comfortable in here.' He looked around the living room and decided it would be a very pleasant place to stay warm and get some sleep overnight.

'If you're sure you don't mind.'

'I'm one hundred per cent certain,' he assured her.

'Thank you,' she said. 'I will feel much safer knowing my two heroes are downstairs looking out for me.'

'I'm not so sure about us being heroes, after all we didn't catch him,' he laughed. 'But it's no problem at all. I'll give my mum a quick call to let her know I won't be back tonight, so she doesn't worry where we've got to. Then if you show me where your food is kept and what bowls I might use for Seamus's food, that would be great.'

'I'll leave you to call Sheila while I fetch some bedding for you both.'

Jax returned Phoebe's smile and saw that she was shaken by what had happened. He wasn't surprised. The thought of him not noticing the footsteps and what could potentially have happened to Phoebe all alone in this enormous house troubled him. His phone pinged, reminding him that he was supposed to be phoning his mum.

With Seamus's brilliant hearing and him being alert there was little chance of the intruder getting into the house without one of them noticing.

27

PHOEBE

Phoebe went upstairs and closed her curtains and those of the other bedrooms just in case the would-be intruder returned and tried to work out which room she was sleeping in. Then, after putting on nightlights in three of them, went to the landing and opened the door to the airing cupboard. She closed the door behind her, needing to feel secure and wanting a moment to herself to try and process what had happened.

It wasn't only the shock of Jax finding someone in the garden but also the thought that he might have done as she insisted and left her alone here. She hugged herself, feeling sick at the thought that someone could have forced their way into the house and... And, what? Phoebe shuddered. It didn't bear thinking about. She needed to gather herself. The intruder had been chased away by Jax and he was still here with his trusty little dog. That's what she needed to focus on, not what-ifs.

Phoebe felt overwhelmed by her gratitude towards the kind man who pushed her aside when *she* had kissed him but put her safety before any annoyance she might have stirred in him. Jax really was a good man and she was grateful that he had agreed to stay the night so that she could sleep feeling safe. If only she could stop thinking about them kissing and that he had kissed her back. She pushed thoughts of him away.

Who was the person that had come into the garden? It unnerved her not knowing. Who could have known she wasn't intending staying the night? Phoebe thought if she might have told anyone. She probably mentioned it to Piper, Alex and Paul, the pub landlord's son, maybe while they were driving home from helping Helier. But why would any of them come to her home? Or, more troubling, who might have known she would be here alone this week?

She remembered sending a text to their housekeeper, Mrs McDonald, asking if there was enough bread in the freezer so that she could take out a loaf instead of trying to find an open store to buy some on her way home from staying with friends, but Jax had insisted the intruder had been a man, so it couldn't be her. There must be some explanation for what had happened, but what?

Phoebe hoped that either she, or Jax, would work it out before she had to spend another night in the house by herself. If not, she would have to ask Piper and Helen if she could spend another couple of nights at their guest house after all. Or at least until either Mrs McDonald or her parents returned from their holidays.

Yes, she decided, that's what she would do. Feeling slightly better now that she had a vague plan, Phoebe began looking for blankets, pillows and a duvet for Jax and a couple of older blankets for Seamus to sleep on.

28

JAX

Jax wondered where Phoebe might have got to and considered going to find her but he wanted to give her some time to herself after everything that had happened. He needed some himself, he decided, still surprised by Phoebe's unexpected kiss earlier. It had been filled with a passion he never would have expected from her, although he had no idea why he would think of her in that way. Maybe it was because she always seemed to be so self-contained and in control. It wasn't just her behaviour but even the level of her voice was understated.

There was nothing loud, overstated, or demanding about Phoebe. She seemed shy rather than confident and in his experience, always erred on the side of caution, so to kiss him out of the blue as she had done was surprising. Pleasant, he thought. No, more than pleasant, incredible. In fact, now he was thinking about it, he wished she would do it again. He would like to kiss her but it was hardly the right time after the earlier drama. No one whose house had almost been invaded would feel the compulsion to kiss someone, surely? No, he decided. If anything,

Phoebe would want to feel safe and it was up to him to make her feel that way.

He went to stand, groaning when his leg stung and reminded him that he had hurt himself. He looked down at his leg and seeing the blood on his jeans decided that he needed to clean himself up.

Deciding that the best place to find a first aid kit would be the kitchen, Jax walked down the hallway and into the large immaculate space. One wall of the kitchen seemed to be mostly constructed of huge glass windows but there were no curtains or blinds. He looked out of them at the garden now shrouded in darkness and wondered why anyone would want to feel this exposed at night. Then again, he mused, the kitchen might overlook the garden but it was a large walled-in space, or at least that's what he had imagined it to be. This was also a safe island and not somewhere that you would need to concern yourself too much with strangers breaking in. What had almost happened unnerved him and left a sour taste in his mouth.

Seamus nudged his bad leg and Jax winced. 'Steady on, little guy,' he said, picking him up and hugging him. Jax noticed the time was a little after six and it was now almost half an hour after Seamus's usual supper time.

'Phoebe will be back soon and I'll feed you something then.'

He heard footsteps coming along the hallway.

'Sorry to have taken so long,' Phoebe said. 'I've left some bedding in the living room for you.' She stopped in the doorway, looking at Jax with Seamus in his arms. 'This is becoming a habit.'

'What is?'

'You sleeping on people's floors. Are you sure you don't want to sleep in one of the spare rooms. Mum would never need to know and I'm sure Seamus wouldn't do anything he shouldn't.'

Jax looked at her sincere expression and was tempted for a couple of seconds, then shook his head. 'No, I'll sleep too deeply if I'm in a bed. All sorts could happen and I might not wake up until first light tomorrow morning.'

He saw her shoulders lower slightly and knew that he had said the right thing.

'That's very kind of you,' she said. 'Now, I think we need to start cleaning up your leg.'

'Can we feed this little one first?' Jax raised Seamus slightly.

Phoebe smiled at his dog. 'Does he always pull that face?'

'You mean the one that says "I'll starve if I'm not fed immediately"?'

Phoebe laughed. 'That's the one.'

'His nickname at home is Larry.'

She frowned. 'Larry? Why?'

Enjoying Phoebe seeming calmer, Jax smiled. 'After Sir Laurence Olivier. Dad is always saying that this dog deserves an Oscar and he's right. He's a proper little actor with a speciality in pretending to be hard done by.'

Phoebe started to laugh. The sound tickled Jax and soon they were laughing together. But without warning Phoebe's laugh became high pitched and he realised it was bordering on the hysterical. Shocked, he wasn't sure how to react. Then, aware that she needed to be comforted, he stepped forward and opened his arms. She stepped into them and wrapped her arms around his waist as he enveloped her, holding her against his chest.

'It's fine, Phoebe,' he soothed. 'I promise you. You're safe. I'm not going to let any harm come to you. You mustn't worry.'

He heard strange gulping sounds and realised she was sobbing. 'I-I'm so s-sorry, J-Jax. I d-don't know wh-what's come over m-me.'

He held her tighter against him. 'There's nothing to apologise for,' he said, desperate to comfort her, yet angry with whoever was responsible for the shock she had suffered. He was going to stop at nothing to discover who had been at the house.

It took a little longer than he had imagined for Phoebe to calm down and for a moment he was worried that he might need to call Piper and ask her to come to the house and help him. When Phoebe did relax slightly and her trembling subsided a bit, she took a deep breath and pushed away from him.

'I'm so sorry about that,' she said taking a piece of kitchen roll and wiping her eyes, then blowing her nose. 'I'm not usually given to crying.'

'It was the shock, I imagine,' he said. 'It's better to let it out than to keep it bottled up inside.'

She poured half a glass of water from the tap and drank it. 'There, that's better. Now, let me find some bowls and food for poor Seamus. If it wasn't for him barking earlier and making such a fuss you might not have noticed the footprints in the snow and come back.' Jax saw her shudder and then force a smile. 'He needs a treat as a reward.'

Jax nodded his agreement. 'He will be delighted. He hates being hungry.' He bent and patted Seamus who was sitting patiently. He must sense there was something wrong, Jax thought, because Seamus rarely behaved so well.

'Will this do?' Phoebe asked from the open pantry door holding up a can of tuna.

'Perfect.'

She handed Jax the tin and then went to another cupboard and took out a plastic takeaway bowl. 'How about this for his food? Do you think it's big enough?'

'That's just right,' Jax said.

She pulled open a drawer and handed Jax a fork, as he opened and spooned half the tin of tuna into the bowl for

Seamus. Jax set the bowl down on the floor to the side of the back door. They watched in silence, leaning against the granite worktop, as the dog quickly ate his food.

'He's really sweet,' she said, breaking the silence. 'He must be a great companion for you.'

'He is.'

'Have you always had a dog?'

Jax nodded. 'Always. They were family pets when I was little but then I heard a dog had been rescued and that it desperately needed a home when I was about seventeen and begged my parents to let me have him.'

'Seamus?'

'Yes, him. So I've had him almost ten years now and I can't imagine life without him in it.' He wondered if maybe Phoebe might enjoy living with a dog. 'Are you certain your parents won't consider you having a dog?'

She shook her head. 'I know they won't.' She frowned thoughtfully. 'Maybe it's time for me to move out and find my own place though,' she said. 'Then I can have a dog, or anything else I might choose.'

'It's expensive even renting a place over here now though,' Jax said. 'It's why I still live at home. That and because my parents' cottage is right by the water and I have no commute to work.'

Phoebe smiled. 'I don't have much of a commute either. I only need my computer and everything that goes with my online job.'

'Could you afford to have your own place?' he asked, unsure if he wasn't being too indiscreet in doing so.

'I could. I only live here because, well, why not? It's a lovely home and garden and at least here I have company a lot of the time.'

How lonely her life must be? Jax thought sadly. He enjoyed his own company but that was mostly when he was foraging. He supposed Phoebe's influencer life must also be spent with mostly her and her camera recording outings. He wondered who took the photos of her.

'Do you work with someone?'

'Pardon?'

'I was thinking you must need another person to take photos of you for your online accounts?'

'Some I can do for myself and other times I use a friend who's a photographer, Dave. He comes to the island from London if I need him to and we take quite a few different pictures over a couple of days. I change clothes and my hairstyle and try to take enough to cover at least a couple of weeks. I intersperse those with the ones I take for myself. It seems to work well enough.'

'I see,' Jax said, wondering how close she and this Dave chap might be. It was none of his business and would be intrusive to ask, he decided.

She indicated Jax's leg. 'Right, Seamus has been fed, now it's your turn.'

'For food?' he asked realising he was rather hungry.

'Maybe in a bit,' Phoebe answered, amused. 'No, I meant it's time for your leg to be looked at and cleaned up.'

Jax groaned. 'I can do it.'

'No, you sit down on that chair and I'll clean it up.'

Feeling a bit awkward that Phoebe was insisting on cleaning up his leg, Jax didn't like to argue. She was already upset from what had happened earlier and he didn't want to be the cause of an argument or anything that might upset her further, so he did as she asked.

'I really can do this myself,' he said, giving it one more try.

'It's fine. I have first aid training.'

Unsure whether she was joking, Jax asked, 'Why do you have that?' It wasn't as if she had a job where she might need it, like he and Dan did with the boat charters. He recalled the two of them carrying out three days of first aid training before starting their tours.

'I can see that you're confused about why I have my certificate,' she said, amused.

'A bit.'

'I saw a feature on breakfast television once when a doctor suggested that people should consider having some training because they never knew when it might come in useful. I had nothing much to do that week, so booked a course for myself. I enjoyed it.'

'Well done you. I'm impressed.'

She took the first aid kit from a cupboard, ran warm water into a small china bowl and then, taking some pads, knelt at his feet. 'Um, I think it might be better if you take your jeans off. I can wash them and then at least you won't arrive home and give Sheila a fright.'

She had a point. His mum would only panic if she saw blood on his trouser leg.

'Thank you.'

He stood, unfastened his jeans, dropped them to the floor and stepped out of them. Then, pushing them to the side with his right foot, sat back down onto the chair. It felt a little odd having Phoebe kneeling in front of him, especially now that he was only wearing his pants but he wasn't in a position to do much about it.

Phoebe smiled up at him. 'Ready for me to begin?'

He cleared his throat, wishing she would hurry up and the whole thing would be over. 'Um, yes. Go ahead.'

Phoebe talked about Seamus and asked why Jax had chosen his name as she dipped the first couple of gauze pads into the warm water and carefully washed the drying blood on his calf. 'Tell me if this hurts too much so I know to stop.'

'It's fine,' Jax said, gritting his teeth and not wishing to cause her any reason to delay finishing what she was doing. Her light touch on the other side of his leg as she held it in place and cleaned the cut made him clench his stomach.

She seemed confident administering first aid to him and he wondered if she hadn't missed her calling as a nurse.

Finally, after cleaning the wound and then washing it with saline solution, she looked up at him. 'Do you want to have a look before I apply the dressing?'

May as well, he thought, supposing that he should really know what damage he had done to himself. Jax leant down and studied the jagged cut. 'That looks worse than it feels. Thanks, Phoebe, you've done a good job there.'

'My pleasure.'

'Have you ever thought about being a nurse?'

'Only when I was about four or five and wanted a nurse's outfit for my birthday.'

'Did you ever get one?'

She laughed. 'I did. My mother used to get very angry when I didn't want to take it off to change for bed.' She covered the cleaned wound with a gauze pad and stuck it to his leg with medical tape. 'There. All done.'

'That's great. Thanks.'

'Time for food,' she said getting to her feet. 'Should I make us something to eat right now?'

'I can do that while you put my jeans in the wash,' he suggested in case she had forgotten she was going to do that.

'That's agreed then. You'll find everything you need either in the pantry, in the freezer in that room at the back of the kitchen, or in the fridge over there.'

Jax watched as she pointed to all of the places where he needed to look. 'Any preference to what you want to eat?'

'Nope,' she said picking up his jeans. 'I'll leave that up to you.' He watched her carrying his jeans out of the kitchen and presumed she must be taking them to a utility room. This house was so well equipped that he understood her reasons for not moving out.

'Right,' he said to himself, rubbing his chin. *What to cook for their supper?* He felt a little self-conscious cooking half-naked in her home, but supposed Phoebe mustn't mind or she would have suggested bringing him a pair of her father's trousers if she wanted him to cover up.

As he cooked for them, he told Phoebe to go and make herself comfortable in the living room.

'Why?' she asked. 'What are you making us?'

'It's a surprise.'

She laughed. 'Fine, if you insist. Shall I take us through some drinks?' Jax nodded. 'Beer? Or something else?'

'Beer would be perfect,' he said.

Finally, he carried a tray with their two plates through to the living room.

Phoebe watched, amused as he set out the tray onto the small table in front of her. He waited for her reaction to his cooking and when she clapped her hands together knew he had made the right decision. She clearly was a girl after his own heart.

'Fish fingers, mash and peas,' she laughed. 'How did you know this was my favourite meal when I was a child?'

'It was a lucky guess.'

'It's my favourite comfort food.' Phoebe's smile vanished and she stared at him. 'I really appreciate you staying with me tonight, Jax.'

'It's fine. I'm happy to do this,' Jax assured her, sitting down with the tray holding his plate.

'I don't mean the food, although that's amazing. I mean for

trying to make me feel better. This is perfect for how I feel right now.'

'It's what I cook for myself when I'm down,' he admitted, surprised when he heard himself saying as much. Piper was the only one other than his mum who knew that this was what he treated himself to whenever he was miserable. And now he had shared it with Phoebe.

'Who'd have thought in the summer that we would be sitting here like this now,' she said thoughtfully. 'I know I could never have imagined this happening.'

He thought about what she had said. 'No, me neither.'

Phoebe sighed and Jax sensed she was starting to think about earlier that evening. 'Don't you dare let my delicious food go cold.'

She laughed and pulled a shocked face. 'Ooh, I'd never do that.' Then, after cutting a piece of fish finger, she placed a dollop of mash and a couple of peas onto it and ate it. She closed her eyes in delight. 'That is perfect, Chef.'

'I aim to please.'

Jax ate his food and watched Phoebe, wondering about his first impressions of her when they had met months earlier. He hadn't given her much thought then but if he had he would have presumed she had all that she could possibly want in life. It seemed now that he knew her slightly that she had all she needed materially but that she missed out on the most important things that he took for granted. Being loved and having those loved ones enjoying spending time with her and enjoying making her happy.

It occurred to him that he wanted to be the person to do that for her. The thought stunned him. What was happening to him? Is this what it felt like to actually fall in love with someone?

29
PHOEBE

After Jax helped Phoebe clear away the plates they returned to the living room to sit in front of the fire.

She stood at the doorway staring at his toned physique hoping he didn't notice how attracted to him she was. Jax seemed to sense her standing there and turned his head suddenly towards her. 'Everything all right?'

Phoebe cleared her throat, embarrassed to have been caught watching him. 'Yes, fine. I was wondering if you were warm enough, or if you'd like me to find something of Dad's for you to put on.' She hoped he didn't take her up on the offer and watched him give it some thought.

'I'm all right, thanks. Unless you'd rather I put something on.'

'No.' Damn, why had she answered so adamantly. 'That is to say, I don't mind if you don't.' She gritted her teeth. Why was she being so tongue-tied around him?

Jax turned away from her. 'No need to bother.' He waved for her to join him. 'Come and sit by the fire, then you can show me some of your influencer photos.' Jax looked hesitant. 'I don't really understand what an influencer is. Maybe it's because I only really go on social media to promote our sea tours and my foraging business. Other than that though, I'm not really on there.'

Phoebe wasn't surprised. From what she knew of Jax he spent more time out on a beach or on a blustery clifftop than sitting looking at his phone. 'I wish I didn't have to bother with it so much, if I'm honest,' she admitted. 'But it's what I've chosen to do and I can't let my followers down now.'

'You have a lot of them then?'

Phoebe felt awkward having the conversation with someone so clearly unaware of what she did. 'About eight hundred thousand.'

He looked astonished. 'Seriously?'

Phoebe nodded. 'You're probably wondering why they want to see pictures of me, aren't you?'

'No, I just didn't realise there would be so many.' He puffed out his cheeks. 'Now I really do need to see what this is all about.'

Why did she feel so embarrassed? Phoebe wondered. Normally she would be delighted to introduce someone new to her Instagram page, but showing Jax made what she did seem silly and unimportant in some way. Probably, she mused, because his foraging helped teach youngsters something useful and worthwhile, whereas her work, although promoting useful products, was mostly to make herself money and give her an independent income from her parents.

Not wanting to keep him waiting, she picked up her mobile, found the app and opened her profile page.

'There,' she said, handing him the phone. 'You can scroll down if you want to and ask me whatever you like.'

He took the phone, concentrating on the screen as he looked through several of the photos. 'Where was this one taken?' he asked, pointing to a photo of Phoebe dressed in a green-and-azure-blue bikini holding a large straw hat as she stood on the water's edge of a beach.

'Bali, I was there a couple of weeks ago for a few days promoting bikinis and other beach wear.'

'A few days? Did you go just to take the photo then?' Phoebe couldn't miss the look of disbelief on his face and, thinking how it must look to someone so personally invested in sustainability, cringed.

'Yes.' She closed her eyes briefly. 'I know it's wrong to fly all that way for a few photos but I was sponsored by one of their hotels to do it and you'll see the next photo is taken of me being greeted at the front door.'

'I see.'

He didn't sound convinced and, seeing what she did from a different light, was beginning to weigh heavily on her. 'Maybe I should start having photos taken closer to home,' she suggested thoughtfully. 'This is a beautiful island and there are many settings that would be perfect for my page.'

Jax's mouth slowly drew back in a smile. 'It is a lovely island with a lot of spectacular views. We could go for a walk in the morning, if you like. I could try and take some relatively decent photos of you then.'

Phoebe wasn't sure how good his photography skills might be but liked the idea of going out walking with him again. 'Why not? It might be fun, especially if I dress properly for the occasion this time.'

Jax laughed. 'That would make it far more enjoyable for you. Your teeth were chattering so much when we were making our way to Helier's that I was beginning to worry that you might chip them.'

Phoebe turned to him, surprised. Had she been that cold? She noticed the twinkle in his eyes and realised he was teasing, so nudged him in his side.

'Ouch.'

'That's for taking the mickey out of me.'

He rubbed his side. 'Ouch, you're tougher than you look.'

'I am?' Phoebe laughed. 'Well it serves you right, making fun of me like that.'

Jax looked at her phone again. 'You look far more confident in these photos than I would imagine you to be.'

'Do I?'

He looked at her, an anxious expression on his face. 'You don't mind me saying that, do you?'

'No, of course not. I like people to be honest with me.' She took the phone from his hand and studied the photo, then others. 'I suppose I do look comfortable posing in front of the camera.' She wished she had a photo of him and had an idea. 'Maybe we can take a few selfies tomorrow when we're out?'

Jax didn't seem enamoured with the idea. 'Only if you don't share them on this page of yours.'

She would have loved to share a photo of her standing next to Jax, but would never do anything he didn't want her to. 'I promise I won't.'

'Then I'm happy to take a few.' He handed her phone back to her. 'These really are very good. Colourful, and I'm sure they make people want to go on holiday and see parts of the world they haven't visited yet.' He stopped at one of the photos. 'What is this photo for?'

'That was to promote ski attire.'

'Clothes? So like modelling then?'

'Yes, I suppose they're all modelling for some reason.'

'Do you get to keep the clothes if you want to?'

He seemed intrigued and it felt good to be spending time with someone who seemed interested in her work. 'Yes, if I wish to.'

'You kept these?'

She nodded. 'Yes, and another couple of outfits that you'll see on the next two pages if you swipe the picture to the left.'

She watched Jax as he slowly did as she suggested and studied the photos. 'Do you find it difficult?'

He really was interested, Phoebe thought happily. 'Most of the time. Sometimes, if I'm tired or not feeling too well then it can be a bit of a struggle, but mostly it's fun.'

'So why the clothes instead of the locations you're promoting?'

'Because my followers ask what I'm wearing and where they can buy them, that sort of thing. They ask who designed my bikini, or where I stayed, or what make-up I used in the photo, if I used a self-tanning product, that sort of thing.'

Jax looked bemused. 'It's another world to the one I inhabit,' he said thoughtfully.

'I suppose it is, but sometimes it's the differences in people that make them interesting.'

'Yes, I agree.' He looked at her and Phoebe wished she had the courage to kiss him again but wasn't sure if she should. Kissing him once unexpectedly was one thing, but doing it again when she wasn't certain he wanted to be with her was too risky. She didn't want to humiliate herself.

She liked Jax despite what she had said before about wanting to be friends. That had only been because she hadn't ever imagined he might be attracted to her in a serious way. Now though, having kissed him, she knew that regardless of their differences she was going to have a battle on her hands if she was to keep her attraction to this gorgeous man at bay.

Jax was staring into the flames and seemed deep in thought. What was he thinking? Could he be trying to work out what his feelings might be towards her? She doubted it. He might have returned her kiss in the kitchen but it had taken a second or two for him to react after she had flung her arms around his neck and planted a kiss on his perfect lips. Urgh, why had she acted so impulsively? If only she knew how he really felt towards her. Especially now that they were here, spending yet another night together, albeit under unusual circumstances.

'Please don't worry about whoever was outside,' he said. 'I'm sure we'll find out more about the person in the morning and I'm not going to leave you here unless you're feeling safe.'

So that's what he had been thinking about. Phoebe was relieved that he was focusing on her concern. 'Thank you, I know you won't.'

'Should we maybe get some sleep now?' Jax suggested. 'I can check your room before you go up there if it makes you feel any better.'

Phoebe shook her head. 'No, it's fine. I've checked all the doors and windows. I'm not sure though why the outside security lights didn't come on when the intruder was out there. They're usually very sensitive to movement, it's why Dad had them installed.'

Jax stood and Phoebe wondered why. 'Would you like a drink or something?'

'No, I thought I should go out and check to see if there's snow covering the sensors. Maybe that's why the security lights didn't work.'

Why hadn't she thought of that? 'Good idea.' She looked at his bare legs. 'Let me find some of Dad's tracksuit bottoms for you to put on. You can't go outside wearing just your underwear, you'll freeze your...'

Jax laughed. 'I'm used to the cold. And I won't be long.'

'Fine, then I'll come with you.'

Jax shook his head. 'No, you'd better stay inside with the doors locked. I don't think the intruder is still there, but you never know and I wouldn't forgive myself if he got in when my attention was elsewhere.'

Phoebe shuddered at the thought. 'Fine, then I'll stay inside with Seamus. He can guard me.' She pointed to the snoring dog to lighten the mood.

Jax smiled and shook his head. 'Typical. Although if he heard movement that he didn't recognise he'd be up and out that door to find whatever it was in a split second.'

'Now, that does make me feel better.' She stood. 'Let me come through to the kitchen with you and I'll lock you out.' She grinned at him. 'Don't worry, I promise to let you back in again as soon as you want me to, I don't want you getting hyperthermia.'

He carried the tray through to the kitchen. Jax slipped his feet into his boots, took his jacket from the back of one of the chairs where he must have left it and put it on and zipped it up. 'I won't be long.'

She watched him go and quickly closed the door and locked it. Hearing tapping behind her she turned to see Seamus trotting across the tiled floor. He whimpered as Jax walked away from the kitchen door, clearly upset to have been left behind.

Phoebe bent to comfort him and stroked his head. 'Jax will be back soon,' she soothed, crouching next to him. 'Your daddy is a lovely man, isn't he?' It felt good to speak openly about Jax even though it was to his dog. 'You're very lucky to have him.'

Seamus looked up at her and gave her a searching look. Surely the dog didn't understand what she had said? She shook her head, amused at her silliness. Of course he didn't. It was probably his recognition of her mentioning Jax's name and nothing more.

She saw movement and the next second light flared up across part of the garden, then another one and she could tell Jax was succeeding in sorting out the security light issue.

Standing up, Phoebe stared out of the window at the garden with Seamus. At least it didn't look as if it had been snowing again. She hoped the thaw might start in the morning so that the island's roads could be cleared and everyone could begin to get back to some sense of normality.

Her thoughts were interrupted by Jax striding across the terrace to the back door. Phoebe unlocked it and opened the door as soon as he reached it, closing it as soon as he was inside.

'It's freezing out there still,' he said, rubbing his hands together, 'but I think I managed to find all the light sensors and clear them of the snow that had been sticking to them.'

They both looked out at the brightly lit garden. 'I can't imagine anyone getting close to the house now,' Phoebe said, feeling an enormous sense of relief. 'Thanks for doing that, Jax, I really appreciate your thoughtfulness.'

'No need to thank me, I'd do that for any of my friends,' he said, staring at her for a moment before taking off his coat. 'Now, I think we should try and get some sleep.'

Phoebe agreed, turning away from him so that he didn't see her disappointment. 'Help yourself to anything either you or Seamus need and I'll see you both in the morning.'

Without waiting for him to reply, she left the room and walked miserably upstairs. She was overtired, but Jax's pointed reaction proved to her that he really did only see her as a friend. She wished she was as confident with Jax as she always was in front of the camera but that girl on her social media platforms didn't have to think of the right thing to say, know how to behave around people who she wanted to impress, like Jax. She supposed her main reason for spending so much time with someone as outgoing as Fliss growing up had been how she had managed to mask being socially awkward in one-to-one situations.

30

JAX

Why had he mentioned them being friends again, he wondered, irritated with himself. He was so determined not to let Phoebe see he had feelings for her that he was risking offending her. He didn't wish to do that and wondered if tiredness was the reason behind his lack of tact.

'Come along, Seamus,' he said switching off the kitchen light before leaving the room and making his way to the warm living room. The past few days had been like living through an emotional roller coaster and he looked forward to getting back to work and not having to double guess his reactions to this attractive woman, who seemed to have affected him in a way that he wasn't used to experiencing.

He settled down and pulled the blankets she had left for him over the lower half of his body and patted those that she had folded and placed on the floor next to him for Seamus to lie down.

'Let's see if we can get some shut-eye, shall we?'

* * *

The following morning, Jax woke to the sound of humming. He opened his eyes and gazed around the large bright room, taking a moment to familiarise himself. Then, getting up, he folded his bedding and placed it neatly on the sofa. He also folded Seamus's but left that on the floor. Phoebe's mother wouldn't be impressed if blankets that had been used for a dog were mixed with her better fabrics, he was certain of that.

He made his way into the kitchen. 'Sleep well?'

'I did, thanks,' she said. 'I thought I'd make us some breakfast.' She indicated the stairs. 'I've left a new toothbrush, towels and a few toiletries for you in the bathroom at the top of the stairs. You'll find your clean jeans in there too on the towel rail. Second door to your left.'

'That's kind of you,' he said gratefully. 'Thanks, I'll go and freshen up after I've let Seamus out for his ablutions.'

'Leave him to me,' she said. 'You go and shower and I'll see you back down here when you're ready.'

Jax wondered if she was in a rush to get rid of him or to go out for their walk. 'You seem all bright and chirpy this morning. I'm glad.'

'I think I need a bodyguard sleeping downstairs in this house every night,' she laughed.

Relieved to know that Phoebe had slept well, Jax asked, 'By bodyguard are you referring to me, or Seamus?'

Phoebe giggled. 'Why, Seamus of course.'

'I thought so.' He was enjoying their banter. It was good to see Phoebe happy and carefree like this.

'I barely recall getting into my bed. As soon as my head hit my pillow I must have fallen into a deep sleep. I haven't slept that well in months.'

'Glad we were able to be of service, milady,' he said giving her a bow.

Happy to have started the day off so cheerfully, Jax went up to the bathroom. Standing under the power shower, he washed his hair, showering and thinking how much he wouldn't mind having such an impressive bathroom as this one in his own house. He reminded himself that he needed to actually get a home of his own before being able to even plan doing such a thing.

'I'm back and starving,' he said a few minutes later, announcing his arrival in the kitchen.

Phoebe smiled at him and pointed to Seamus who was happily scoffing his breakfast from a bowl. 'I hope he doesn't mind tuna again.'

Jax laughed and saw Seamus give him a self-satisfied look. 'He seems to be loving every mouthful.'

'That's a relief,' she said, picking up a pair of tongs and turning over several rashers of bacon. 'I thought I'd make us eggs and bacon?'

'Perfect,' Jax said, his stomach rumbling.

'There's a coffee machine in the wall there,' she said. 'Although don't ask me how to use it because I've no idea. It's Dad's favourite thing in the house.'

Jax was impressed. 'I feel very spoilt today. I'd better not get used to this treatment.' Not wishing to get into an awkward conversation, he looked for a cup in the cupboards.

'Over there.' Phoebe pointed to the right cupboard and Jax pulled open the door and took out two mugs. 'Shall I lay the table for us?'

'That would be great,' she said. 'You'll find everything you need in the cutlery drawer over there. Napkins are in that one. I have the plates out already.' She splashed hot fat over the eggs with a spatula.

'Anything else I can do to help?'

'If you can work the coffee machine, you can make one for me too, and maybe do some toast for us?'

'Will do. Coffee and toast coming up.' Jax busied himself, surprised at how relaxed he felt in the smart house. Then again, he reminded himself, he never would have expected to spend the night in a place as impressive as this one before now. It made him think how normal and unaffected Phoebe seemed by all this wealth and luxury. She was a kind, thoughtful woman and he was glad he had been given a chance to get to know her a little better. He wondered if they could be more. Dare he try to push things between them a bit further? She had kissed him, after all. Surely she had acted impulsively like that because she liked him? He hoped so.

'How's that toast coming along?' Phoebe asked.

'Here it is,' he said, cutting the pieces in half like his Aunt Helen did at her guest house and standing each piece in a silver toast rack he had found on one of the worktops.

'Great, you take that and our coffees to the table and I'll serve this lot.'

Jax carried the drinks to the exquisite almost black marble table and sat down. 'Maybe we should go outside together and see if we can trace the intruder's footprints after we've eaten?' He waited for her to consider her answer but as she still had her back to him while she cooked he couldn't make out what she made of his suggestion. Believing it to be the best way to help Phoebe come to terms with the drama of the previous evening, he added, 'It might not seem quite so upsetting to you in daylight.'

'I'm not so sure about that,' she said, serving the eggs onto a plate and bringing them over to the table. 'It does feel as if my sanctuary here has been breached.'

'I'm sure it does, but I'll do all I can to resolve the mystery of who was here.'

'Thanks, Jax, I appreciate that.'

Once seated, she took a tentative sip of her coffee. 'That's good, thanks.'

'Pure fluke. I had no idea what I was doing with that machine and I think it has a mind of its own.' He drank some from his cup, needing something to help clear his head from his long restless night's sleep. 'So, what do you think? If you'd rather not check outside then that's fine too. I'll still go out there with Seamus.'

Phoebe took a bite from a piece of her toast and ate it. 'No, it's fine. I think I'd like to come with you.' She looked out of the nearby window. 'At least it doesn't seem to have snowed any more in the night and the footprints should still be clear.'

'Good point.'

* * *

'That was delicious,' Jax said when he'd finished eating. His stomach was relatively full and it had helped him wake up fully; he felt more willing to take on whatever the day threw at him. 'After we've checked the garden we can go for that walk and take some photos of you for your social media.'

'I'd like that.'

'Good,' he said, determined to take her mind off what had happened. He stood and carried their plates, cups and cutlery over to the sink, then turned on the hot tap to wash up.

'Please don't worry about that,' Phoebe said. 'Leave them there and I'll stack them in the dishwasher later when we get back.'

'OK, then I'm going to go and clean my teeth and put on my boots and jacket. It's still very cold out there.'

'I'll do the same,' she said, smiling and looking, Jax thought, much more relaxed than she had the previous evening. He was relieved. It had been upsetting to see Phoebe so unnerved by whoever had thought it acceptable to come to the house. Jax only hoped that he might discover somehow who the perpetrator was so that he could put an end to it for Phoebe's sake.

Having cleaned her teeth, Phoebe went back downstairs to the kitchen. She opened the door and Seamus pushed past her to get outside to run about in the deep snow.

'Hey, that was rude of you,' Jax shouted giving Phoebe an apologetic grimace. 'He has no manners sometimes. He'll be back in a few seconds when it dawns on him how deep the snow still is.'

Phoebe pulled on a woolly hat and laughed as she stepped outside.

Jax followed, closing the door behind them. He took in a slow deep breath of the clear, cold air and the chill hit the back of his throat making him cough. 'Blimey, it never gets this cold here.'

Phoebe stood on the terrace and gazed out at the white expanse of garden. 'Doesn't it look beautiful though? Like a magical setting.'

'I can't imagine anyone being able to replicate this,' Jax said, trying to picture what this place looked like in the height of the summer. He spotted a rectangular shape further down the garden. 'Is that a swimming pool under there?'

'It is. I find it difficult to imagine that only four months ago I was lying on a sunlounger moaning about it being too hot and needing to jump in the pool to cool down.'

'I love the different seasons here though, don't you?'

'I do,' she replied, her voice wistful. 'In fact I can't imagine ever being truly happy living anywhere else.'

The discovery that Phoebe loved this place as much as he did delighted Jax. Most people who grew up here couldn't wait to leave and see the rest of the world. Not that most of those didn't return at some point. Although he had travelled extensively, it had never been for long and he had always yearned to be back on the island and doing what he loved best.

'Right, let's start following those footsteps and see if we can find where they lead us.'

'Good idea,' Phoebe said, looking a little anxious at the prospect.

'Lead the way, Seamus.'

31

PHOEBE

Phoebe would much rather not have to go with Jax but didn't want him to think she was being a coward. This was her home and she needed to show that she wasn't scared by any stranger, even though the experience had shaken her badly. She suspected that Jax was determined to solve the mystery for her and was a little overwhelmed by his thoughtfulness towards her. It was his Christmas too and he should be spending the time having fun with his family, not protecting her.

The warm feeling she'd had when Jax insisted on spending the night so that she could feel safer still bolstered her. She followed him as he walked next to the line of footsteps and her mind wandered back to their kiss. Phoebe smiled. No one had ever kissed her like that before. She had been elated by the chemistry she and Jax had shared in that kiss. Maybe he hadn't felt the same spark between them that she had. Could that be why he didn't seem interested in her?

He walked down the steps from the terrace onto the snow-covered lawn and pointed ahead. 'The footprints go towards those trees in the far corner.'

He had said as much the previous night. 'At least there don't seem to be any more of them,' she said.

'I was thinking the same thing. Whoever it was had sense not to return last night, but that doesn't mean that they won't decide to when this snow thaws and they can come here without leaving a trace behind them.'

Phoebe stopped walking, horrified at the thought.

Jax seemed to realise she had stopped and turned to her. 'Hell, I'm sorry. I should think before speaking. That was tactless of me.'

She struggled to hide her fear by forcing a smile onto her face but wasn't sure she had managed it. She knew she hadn't when Jax walked back to her and took her in his arms, hugging her tightly to his chest.

'That really was bloody stupid of me, Phoebe. I'm so sorry.' He leant back and Phoebe knew he was waiting for her to look up at him. 'I promise I won't leave you here alone until either your parents return or we figure out who the intruder was.'

'Really?' she asked, stunned that he would make such a promise, and intensely relieved. 'You would do that for me?'

He didn't speak for a moment and the next thing Phoebe knew Jax was kissing her. This time his kiss was gentle but held no less passion. She returned his kiss, her arms reaching around his back and holding him tightly. She relished the romance of being kissed so perfectly in the snow and knew that in any other circumstance this would be a magical moment. Slowly, her fear diminished.

'In case I forgot to answer your question,' he said his expression serious. 'I would do almost anything for you, Phoebe. I'm beginning to realise just how special you are to me.'

Phoebe doubted there would ever be another moment to

surpass this one in her life and gazed up into the still-tanned, handsome face of the man she was falling very deeply in love with. It dawned on her that Jax had the power to break her heart. She had never felt so safe in someone's arms while at the same time being aware how vulnerable he made her feel. It dawned on Phoebe that this was another level of emotion entirely to any she had ever experienced before. She would need to find a way to trust her own instincts thoroughly though before allowing herself to fall for him completely.

Seamus barked and then a couple more times before running into the trees.

'Damn, I'd better go after him.' Jax groaned, his arms dropping from around her.

Phoebe watched Jax running across the lawn, her mind racing. He had kissed her and unable to help herself, his words had made her wonder if they might be about to start a relationship. She'd had a crush on him for so long and now that he had kissed her she couldn't help hoping this was the start of something exciting. Aware she should follow him, Phoebe began running, making a point of following the anonymous person's footprints as she went. Clearly whoever it was had come this way and it occurred to her that maybe the person was still in the garden hiding. A shiver shot through her. Thank heavens Jax was still here with her.

As she reached the edge of the trees, it occurred to her that the person couldn't have spent the night out here without freezing unless they had set up some sort of camp with warm bedding. Surely the intruder hadn't been that organised? She preferred to think that the invasion into the garden had been an opportunistic event. Something more calculated frightened her terribly.

She saw movement ahead and realised she'd fallen behind Jax. She rushed to catch up.

'Seamus, here, boy!' Jax shouted. Phoebe couldn't miss the concern in his voice and hurried her pace in an effort to catch up with him. Finding the little dog was far more important than any intruder.

'Seamus!' She called out to the little dog hoping they could locate him before his feet got too cold. He only had short legs and she noticed the groove in the snow that must have been made by Seamus's belly.

'Got him!' Jax bellowed.

Phoebe hoped he meant Seamus, but couldn't be certain. She ran as best she could in the deep snow and soon reached him. Jax was holding Seamus against his chest and had wrapped his jacket around his beloved dog.

'Silly boy,' he said kissing the top of the dog's head. 'When will you learn not to run off?' He looked at Phoebe. 'His paws are frozen. I'm going to have to take him back inside then we can come out here and keep looking.'

'You go in,' she said. 'I'll stay here and keep looking.'

'Are you sure?' Jax asked frowning. 'I don't want you to do anything that makes you uncomfortable.'

'Perfectly sure,' she said, deciding that it was her home and her fear was now morphing into anger. How dare anyone make her feel unsafe here? she brooded. She gave Jax a determined smile. 'It's broad daylight, so I'm sure I'll be fine. Don't be too long though, will you? I'm not sure how long I can keep this bravado up for.'

He nodded. 'Come inside if you feel at all uneasy. I won't be long though. I just want to dry his belly and paws and then I'll be right back.'

Phoebe didn't watch Jax return to the house, but decided to

keep following the footsteps. It was a little difficult at first because Seamus's groove and Jax's steps coming back on themselves had obliterated some of the other person's prints, but after a couple of minutes she saw the footprints she was following turn and go slightly to the right. Phoebe followed them until they stopped right before an old wooden gate. She had no recollection of ever using this entrance to her home and wondered where it led to, aware that by the drag marks in the snow this gate had been used recently.

She stood and waited for Jax to return, unsure if she should venture out from the property without him knowing where she had gone. Then, she reasoned that if she had followed the other footsteps this way then Jax would be able to do the same thing.

Phoebe lifted the handle to open the catch at the top of the gate and pulled it open with a little difficulty. She stepped forward and looked out to an expanse of fields. It was difficult with everything covered in snow to determine where there were any pathways, or lanes, but when she looked to the right, Phoebe noticed a row of several small bungalows. She presumed that they had been built sometime in the thirties or late forties but had no idea who lived there. Other than those properties, there didn't seem much else nearby.

'What have you discovered?' Jax asked, his voice giving her a shock.

'I didn't hear you coming back,' she said, her hand resting on her chest to calm her racing heart. 'Whoever was here last night came out this way and I presume this was his way in too.'

'Do you know the area at all?'

She shook her head. 'No, but I wondered if maybe the person lives in one of those houses?'

'It's a possibility,' Jax agreed. 'Shall we go and ring on some doorbells and try to find out?'

Phoebe's boldness began to evaporate and she wanted to say no, but if she did that then she would possibly never discover who had come uninvited the previous evening, and she had no intention of letting someone make her feel scared long term in her own home.

'Yes, why not?'

32

JAX

Jax held out his hand for Phoebe to take. He was glad he had taken the opportunity to kiss her earlier and was relieved she had reacted well. He hadn't missed her conflicted thoughts about going to the bungalows though, he reasoned, dragging his mind back to the present. He would have preferred to go alone to speak to the residents of this row of properties himself but sensed that the best way for Phoebe to find closure was for her to witness all that was about to happen. If, indeed, anything did result from him knocking on the front doors of these places and asking a few questions. He hoped he was doing the right thing.

She took his hand and he could feel it trembling despite the thick ski gloves she was wearing.

'It's going to be fine, Phoebe,' he soothed. 'Speak if you feel you want to, but otherwise you can leave the talking to me. Whatever makes you feel comfortable.'

'Thanks, Jax.'

They walked up the snow-covered pathway to the first front door and Jax raised the door knocker and hammered it against the wooden door a couple of times. He heard footsteps and gave Phoebe a reassuring smile.

The door opened and an elderly lady gave him a quizzical look. 'Good morning,' she said, looking first Jax and then Phoebe up and down. 'Have you broken down near here?'

They shook their heads. 'No,' Jax said. 'We, um, Phoebe lives nearby and we wanted to check up on the people living along this way to see if there was anything we might do for you.'

The lady's face broke into a smile. 'What a kind thing to do.' She shook her head. 'I'm here alone but my daughter and her husband are on their way with a few bits for me. Thank you though.'

'No problem.' Jax smiled. 'We'll leave you in peace then.'

'Happy Christmas,' Phoebe said before they turned and walked away. 'That was quick thinking,' she said quietly when they reached the bottom of the pathway and began walking along the road to the next place.

'It occurred to me that having two strangers pitching up on their doorsteps might be troubling to these people, so thought I should have a reason for us being there.'

'You really are a very thoughtful person, do you know that?' she said, smiling up at him.

Jax gave her hand a gentle squeeze. 'I like to feel useful.' He cocked his head to the left. 'House number two. Let's see what happens here then, shall we?'

They walked up the pathway and knocked on the front door. Jax could hear whispered arguing and wondered what was about to happen. He saw someone through the mottled glass coming towards the front door and then it was opened and a middle-aged lady stood there looking shocked to see Phoebe standing next to him.

'Phoebe? What are you doing here, dear?' The woman peered at Jax. 'And who might this be?'

'Mrs McDonald? I didn't know you lived here?'

Jax saw the woman's face soften. 'Why ever would you know that?' She looked up at Jax. 'Is something the matter at the house?'

'You know Phoebe's house?' Jax asked, intrigued.

The woman laughed. 'I should hope so,' she said. 'I've been housekeeper there these past eleven years.'

Jax glanced at Phoebe. 'Really?'

'Yes,' Phoebe said, smiling. 'Mrs McDonald has the week off. I thought you were going to spend Christmas with your sister?'

Mrs McDonald shook her head. 'I was but she was needed elsewhere. Her daughter was due to have her second baby in a couple of weeks but went into labour two days before Christmas. My sister had to go to her place and look after the older child.' She stepped back. 'It was a shame but couldn't be helped. Look, it's freezing chatting on the doorstep, why don't you both come in and I'll make you a quick cup of tea?'

Jax was about to tell her it wasn't necessary, when a man stepped into the hallway from one of the rooms looking shifty.

'I think they're here to see me, Blanche,' he said without looking his wife in the eye. 'You'd better bring them into the living room.'

Jax looked at Phoebe and saw the surprise register on her face.

'What are you talking about, Syd?' Mrs McDonald asked, moving back to give Phoebe and Jax space to enter the house. 'No idea what he's on about,' she said quietly as she closed the front door. 'Better do as he asks though, and if we're lucky we might find out.'

Jax followed Phoebe through to where the man was now waiting.

'You may as well sit down,' Syd said. 'I suspect you're looking for the person who came to the house last night, aren't you?'

Phoebe gasped. 'You?'

'Syd! What have you been doing?' Blanche sat down heavily on an armchair.

Jax saw the man give his wife an embarrassed roll of his eyes. 'Sorry, Blanche. You're not going to like what you're about to hear, I'm afraid. I've done something rather silly.'

Jax sat next to Phoebe, aware that she was now clutching his hand in both of hers. 'Go on,' Jax said. 'You may as well tell us what happened.'

'Blanche told me that your folks were away for Christmas and New Year,' Syd began. 'But she never mentioned you being there by yourself, Miss.'

'What's that got to do with anything?' Blanche grumbled, glaring at him, clearly mortified to be shown up in front of her employers' daughter.

He ignored her and focused his attention on Phoebe. 'I'm sorry, miss. I know I gave you a fright, but when this enormous brute ran after me with his dog hurtling towards me, I was petrified.'

'You're the intruder?'

'Intruder! Syd, what the ruddy hell have you done?'

He turned to face the window. 'Blanche, if you wait a moment I'll tell you.'

'Hurry up then,' Blanche snapped, turning to look at Phoebe and mouthing an apology.

Syd faced them once more, pushing his hands deep into his baggy trouser pockets. 'You told me Phoebe had called to say she would be staying with friends over Christmas, didn't you, Blanche?'

'Yes, so?' Blanche said before narrowing her eyes thoughtfully. 'Ah.'

'What is it?' Syd asked, glaring at her. 'You've remembered something, haven't you?'

Jax saw the woman give Phoebe an embarrassed look. 'I seem to have forgotten to mention your text to Syd.'

'Text?' He stared at her angrily. 'What text might this be?'

Blanche explained that Phoebe had messaged her to ask about a loaf of bread in the freezer.

'It never occurred to me to mention it.' Blanche said quietly.

'Well, maybe you should then I would have known someone was there and wouldn't have gone to investigate when I took my walk before going to bed last night and saw lights on in the house.'

'How?' Jax asked, unsure whether the man could see lights from the other side of the fence if the only lights on had been downstairs.

'Sorry?' Blanche shook her head.

'The lights,' Jax repeated. 'How did you see them?'

Syd shook his head. 'What? You don't believe me?'

'Which lights did you see?' Phoebe asked. 'I think Jax is trying to understand how you could see the downstairs lights on from the other side of the fence.'

'It was two upstairs lights I saw,' Syd said. 'I only saw the downstairs ones on when I went into the garden to check on the place.'

'He's right,' Phoebe said quietly. 'I did go upstairs to my room and the other light must have been the hall light shining into one of the other bedrooms up there.'

'Carry on,' Jax said, satisfied with Phoebe's explanation.

'I walked through the trees and saw movement.' He gave a pleading look to his wife. 'You'd want me to check on the place if I thought something was amiss, wouldn't you?'

Jax saw Blanche consider her husband's question before nodding.

'You're right, I would, Syd.'

Seemingly reassured by her agreement, Syd looked a little bolder. 'As I explained, I saw movement and, wanting to be sure what explanation to give to the police when I called to report someone had broken into the place, I crept up to the kitchen door to have a proper look inside.'

'And that's when we saw you,' Phoebe said sounding much calmer. 'But why didn't you just tell me who you were. You scared me half to death last night, Mr McDonald. We thought you were an intruder.'

He hung his head looking embarrassed. 'I'm sorry, lass. I didn't mean to frighten you.' He looked at Jax, 'Or you, lad.'

'Silly fool,' Blanche said.

'Me?' Syd snapped. 'I wasn't to know who he was and it's not my fault he chased after me.'

'But why did you run away when I called out to you?' Jax asked, confused.

The man looked at Jax as if he couldn't believe he had asked such a silly question. 'What would you do if you were outside some posh house you thought had been broken into and you heard a dog bark and a man more than twice your size was running towards you, shouting?'

'He has a point, Jax,' Phoebe said thoughtfully.

He did, Jax reasoned, looking at the slight man who must have been no more than five feet five in height. 'Didn't you think that to run away might look worse than stopping though?'

The man stared at him, bemused. After a moment's hesitation, he sighed heavily. 'Do you imagine I would have done that before or after the huge man hurtling after me caught me and beat me up.'

'I had no intention of doing anything of the sort.' Jax looked at Phoebe to reassure her.

'I know that,' she said. 'But Mr McDonald didn't, did he?'

Jax thought about it and had to agree that the man had a point. 'I suppose we're both a bit to blame for the outcome, aren't we?'

Mr McDonald nodded. 'Yes, we probably are.' He looked at his wife. 'You see? My intentions were good.'

Blanche glanced at Jax then back at her husband. 'Maybe, but I wouldn't have been foolish enough to do what you did in the first place.' She shook her head. 'You should have come here and told me then I could have told you it was probably young Phoebe in the house and then phoned her to check if it was before reporting anything to the police. Surely it's simple enough to work that out?'

'I think none of us know how we'd react on the spur of the moment in a crisis, do we?'

Mrs McDonald looked from her husband to Jax. 'Probably not, but some people obviously react more foolishly than others.'

Jax could see the couple were about to descend into a row and didn't want to put Phoebe in another upsetting situation. 'Shall we go now you know who it was?' he whispered.

'Yes, please.'

They stood and when Blanche took a breath from shouting at her husband, Phoebe spoke. 'We're going now.'

'I'm so sorry for all the trouble he's caused you, Phoebe.'

'It's fine,' Phoebe said. 'We're just happy to know that there was no malice involved.' She looked at Syd. 'And despite how it turned out, I want to thank you for caring enough to check on the house.'

Jax noticed Blanche calm slightly and hoped that the upset between the couple might now be resolved. Syd seemed much happier too.

'Thanks, lass. I appreciate that.'

'We'll see ourselves out,' Jax said in a hurry to get back to check that Seamus was all right in the strange house and hadn't resorted to tearing up the towels he had left him sitting on.

'Well, that's a relief,' Phoebe sighed once they were outside. 'I never would have suspected Syd of being the intruder,' she said before starting to laugh. 'Honestly, such a drama.'

Jax put his arm around her shoulder as they walked the short distance back to the house. 'I'm glad you thanked him,' he said. 'I thought his wife was about to cause him some damage if you hadn't done.'

'Yes, she can be quite formidable. I'm just glad we know who it was and that I can relax now.' She looked up at Jax and he bent to kiss her.

'Does that mean you don't need me to stay at your house tonight then?'

'Er, no.'

Jax laughed, happy to think he would be spending more time alone with her.

'I might not need a bodyguard but I do enjoy your company,' she said, stopping as they arrived at the terrace outside the kitchen and reaching up to slip her hands around his neck. 'I also rather like spending time kissing you,' she added pulling his head down so that their lips met in a kiss.

Excitement flared through Jax. She was kissing him again. Her earlier impulsive kiss hadn't been a one-off. That had to be a good sign, didn't it? 'Look at him,' Jax said, spotting his dog's fury as he saw them through the glass back door. He pointed at his lovable dog jumping up and down inside the kitchen. 'Seamus has spotted us.'

He felt Phoebe's hand take hold of his. 'I think we'd better hurry up and get to him, don't you? We don't want Seamus being put out and taking against me.'

'He'd never do that,' Jax assured her as they hurried inside.

As soon as Phoebe opened the back door, Seamus launched himself into Jax's arms.

'Hello, boy,' Jax said, hugging his dog's warm body to him. 'I hope you've been good while I've been gone.'

'I can't imagine he could do much damage with the amount of marble we have in this room,' Phoebe remarked as Jax set Seamus down onto the floor.

Jax quickly scanned the room to satisfy himself that there was nothing untoward he needed to clean up on Seamus's behalf. Seeing that everything looked as neat as it had done when they left, he refilled the dog's water bowl and placed it near to where they had made him a bed.

'There you go.'

He took off his jacket and draped it over the back of one of the chairs, then waited for Phoebe to remove her hat, gloves and coat. She looked even prettier than usual with her cheeks and the tip of her nose pink from cold. Feeling a compulsion to kiss her again, he took her hand in his and pulled her back into his arms. She gave an excited squeal and wrapped her arms around his neck, kissing him before he had the chance to kiss her.

'Well, this looks cosy.'

Jax's blood froze on hearing the familiar voice with its mocking tone.

Phoebe tensed immediately and dropped her arms from around him. 'Fliss? What are you doing here?'

33

JAX

Jax wasn't sure who was more surprised to see Fliss standing by the back door, himself or Phoebe. By the look of astonishment on Phoebe's face, he suspected it might be her.

Fliss had her hands resting on her hips and was shaking her head slowly, an amused expression on her face. 'Enjoying my cast-offs, Phoebe?'

'What?'

Jax clenched his teeth together to stop from retaliating to Fliss's nasty jibes.

Fliss laughed. 'Look what happens when I turn my back for five minutes,' she mocked. 'My best friend in the entire world takes up with my ex-boyfriend.'

'I'm not your ex anything,' Jax argued, hoping to make the point before Phoebe thought there was more between him and Fliss than she had imagined. He looked sideways at Phoebe to try and gauge her thoughts but her face was impassive and it was impossible to tell what was going through her mind.

'I'm only teasing,' Fliss said, giving Jax a look that he presumed was supposed to make him feel embarrassed. Turning her attention back to Phoebe, she added, 'I'm here for you, Phoebe.'

Phoebe stepped closer to Fliss. 'But I thought you weren't supposed to come here until after the Christmas and New Year holidays,' she said, her voice gentle and not showing any hint of the annoyance Jax was feeling.

'I wasn't supposed to be but I spoke to Alex and he mentioned your parents were away over the Christmas holidays. My mum was very upset to hear you were here all alone and agreed to have a word with Dad about me coming to stay with you. He gave in and let me come back to Jersey.'

Jax watched Phoebe's reaction. He thought he spotted a hint of disappointment.

'There's no need for you to stay here any longer, Jax,' Fliss said. 'You can go back to your family. I'm here for Phoebe now.'

Jax knew that however Phoebe was feeling right now, it was nothing to the crashing disappointment that he was no longer needed at her home.

Their eyes met. 'I suppose Fliss is right, I'll be fine with her in the house now she's come to stay,' Phoebe said her voice flat. 'Thank you for everything you've done though.' She looked away from him when he couldn't find the words to convey how he felt. 'And thank you too, Seamus. I've loved having you both here with me.'

Jax tore his eyes from Phoebe and looked at Fliss to discover her watching him, a smug smile on her face. Determined not to give her any satisfaction, he lifted his jacket from the back of the chair where he had only left it moments before and put it on, trying desperately to find the right words to say to Phoebe before leaving.

'We've both enjoyed being here.' He grinned at Seamus with forced jollity. 'Haven't we, little guy?' Seamus leapt up into Jax's open arms and Jax felt soothed by the warmth of his beloved dog's body. 'We'll go and leave you both in peace,' he said, not wishing to drag out his departure for a moment longer than was necessary.

'I'll see you out,' Phoebe said.

Jax shook his head not wishing to make things any more awkward for her than they already were. 'There's no need. Give me a call if you need anything though, won't you?'

'I will,' she said, looking utterly miserable and exactly how he was feeling at that moment. 'Maybe we can take that walk after New Year,' Phoebe said as Jax reached the back door and Fliss moved to one side to give him space to leave.

Hearing the hope in her voice and not wishing to depart on bad terms, he reached out and took her hand briefly in his free one. 'I'd like that very much.'

Her face broke into a smile. 'Good. Then that's what we'll do.'

'Bye, Jax,' Fliss said sounding friendly and he would have thought she was being pleasant if he didn't know any better. But he did and knew without any doubt that he had been dismissed.

He left the house and walked to his car in silence. Once Seamus was safely strapped into his harness, Jax got into his jeep and drove from Phoebe's home. How had he ever imagined that there was anything likeable about Fliss? Probably because Alex seemed like such a decent bloke, Jax thought, and he had presumed they must be similar in character. He didn't have any siblings, nor did his cousin, Piper, so he had little experience of what it must be like to have a brother or sister. But one thing meeting the Coopers had taught him was that siblings could be extremely different to each other.

Once back at the pier, he parked and carried Seamus to their cottage passing neighbours' cheerfully lit Christmas trees, their lights casting coloured shapes through windows onto the melting snow. Jax stopped and looked around him at the familiar pier that he loved so much. Everywhere locals laughed and swapped stories about their Christmas Day disasters caused by the power failure, while others wished friends a Merry Christmas. He knew it was supposed to be a happy time and he wondered if maybe he felt a lot worse simply because he had expected to be cheerful right now. Damn it, he thought, falling in love is not the rose-tinted experience conveyed in films. What if Fliss came between him and Phoebe? She was certainly manipulative and determined to get what she wanted and he doubted she would be happy to see the two of them in a relationship, especially after he had turned her down.

'Come on, boy,' he said kissing the top of Seamus's head. 'Let's get inside.'

'You're back,' his mum said, drying her hands as she stepped out from the kitchen into the hallway to see who had arrived. 'We weren't expecting you so soon.'

'You've not had a row with Phoebe, have you?' his father yelled from the living room where Jax presumed he was watching reruns of his favourite war films on television.

'No, I haven't.' He put Seamus down onto the floor, took off his jacket and hung it up on one of the coat hooks behind the front door. 'Her friend, Fliss, arrived unexpectedly. She's come to stay with her so they didn't need me any more.'

He followed his mother into the kitchen.

Sheila stopped drying her hands and studied his face.

'What is it, Mum?' he asked, knowing from experience that she had picked up on the emotions he was trying hard to hide.

'I know something has happened between you and Phoebe. She seems such a pleasant girl. I hope you two haven't fallen out.'

He shook his head. 'No.'

'Then why do you look so miserable?'

'I hadn't thought I did.' He sighed, aware that his mother wasn't about to give up so easily. 'It really is as I said. Her friend arrived at the house and there was no point me staying where I wasn't needed.'

'I suppose not,' she said not looking convinced. 'It was nice seeing you getting along with her on Christmas Day at lunch and then on Boxing Day, especially after Beth finished with you like she did.'

He wasn't sure what his mother was getting at. 'Mum, I understood Beth's reasoning and, to be honest with you, as much as I did like her, I think I enjoyed spending time with Billy as much as I did with her.'

His mother's face seemed to crumple slightly.

'Now what have I said.'

She reached up and took the gold pendant she always wore around her neck between her thumb and forefinger, rubbing the gold between her fingers thoughtfully.

'What is it, Mum?' He hated it when his mother went all melancholy. She was tough and very straight talking most of the time but occasionally she became thoughtful and sad and he had noticed that it only ever seemed to be over something that had happened to him. 'Mum?'

She shook her head and let go of the pendant, reaching out to stroke his upper arm with her right hand. 'It's nothing, sweetheart.'

'I can see that there's something bothering you. Tell me what it is, or I'll worry.'

'Bless you, Jax.' She sighed heavily. 'I just hate to think that you're ready to settle down and have a family of your own when you don't have a partner to do it with.'

Jax groaned. 'Mum, I'm fine. I promise you. I only felt that way with Beth because that was her situation. I like Phoebe, but haven't thought once about settling down and having children with her.'

'Because you don't like her that much?' his mother asked, a quizzical look on her face.

'No, Mum,' he replied, exasperated. 'Because I'm only just getting to know her. I'm not desperate to settle down, whatever you might believe, but if the time comes when I do feel inclined to set up a home with someone, or marry, or whatever, then I'll think about it then. Right now, I'm fine. I promise you.'

'Are you sure?'

Jax closed his eyes briefly. 'Yes. I am. I'm also very tired because I had another late night last night. So, I might just go and have a bit of a kip now, if you don't mind.'

'That sounds like a good idea,' she said, seeming satisfied now she knew that he'd had little sleep the previous night. 'I'm sure you'll feel much better afterwards.'

He hugged his mum, loving that she cared about him so much, but also finding it a little tedious having to explain himself when she got this way.

As he walked out of the kitchen and up the stairs to his bedroom, Jax wondered if maybe now was the right time to find somewhere of his own to move into.

34

JAX

Jax woke three hours later, surprised to discover it was lunch-time already. He could tell by the brightness of the wintery light coming through his bedroom curtains that the sun was out, so got out of bed and decided to take Seamus for a walk on the beach.

The beach, its fresh air and familiar scents always cheered him up. And with his mother so sensitive to his mood the last thing Jax wanted was to worry her. It was Christmas and he needed to get into the right frame of mind and add to people's cheerfulness, not lower everyone's mood. No, he needed to buck up and stop being such a misery. He liked Phoebe, very much, but she had been friends with Fliss for much longer than she had known him and he had no right to expect her to choose his company over her long-time friend's.

He freshened up and went downstairs. Going into the living room he saw Seamus snuggled up on his father's lap. 'Want to...' Jax didn't have the chance to finish his sentence before Seamus launched himself off his father, causing his dad to grimace in pain.

'That dog of yours is a menace,' he grumbled.

'Sorry, Dad. My fault.'

His father shook his head and began watching his programme again.

'Come along,' Jax said quietly as he tapped his thigh. He went into the hallway and was doing up his jacket when his mother appeared from the kitchen.

'Feeling better, lovey?'

'Yes thanks, Mum,' he said, walking over to her and giving her a hug. 'I had a doze and now I'm taking this little guy out for a bit of fresh air.'

'Mind you both don't get too cold out there. I popped over to see Margery an hour ago and take her some leftover turkey for her supper and it was perishing.'

'Don't worry, Mum, we'll be fine.'

He put on his boots and left the cottage with Seamus. It wasn't surprising that few people were outside. People needed waterproof footwear to walk through the slushy snow that was now melting in the watery winter sunshine although he knew that later on after sunset, the temperature would drop again and the pavements were going to be treacherous with ice.

Jax noticed Paul, the landlord's son, walking their black Labrador, Dexter, down the slipway. Jax didn't shout out to him in case Paul lost his footing and slipped on the wet cobbles. He reached the beach and threw Seamus's ball as far as he could. 'Go on, Seamus, get it,' he bellowed.

He heard a voice calling out to him and saw Paul retracing his steps to join him. 'Hey, mate,' Paul shouted, throwing his ball for Dexter to race after. 'How's it going?'

They fell into step and Jax was pleased to have someone to chat to. 'Fine thanks. We all had a brilliant time at the pub yesterday. The food was delicious, as always.'

'Thanks. I'll tell Mum and Dad, they're always happy to hear positive reports. I was wondering how Phoebe is. She seemed really lovely.'

'Phoebe's fine, thanks,' Jax said, feeling his stomach ache at the thought of missing her.

'She's not local, is she? I don't think I've seen her around before.'

Jax nodded. 'She is, but tends to work away a lot.'

'You seeing her then?'

I wish I knew, Jax thought. He shook his head. He decided to be vague. 'She's Piper's boyfriend, Alex's sister's best friend.'

Paul stared at him thoughtfully for a few seconds, then threw his head back and laughed. 'I'm too shattered to try and work that out right now. She seemed really nice.'

'She is.' Jax bent down when Seamus ran back to him, took the ball from his mouth after a bit of a tussle and then threw it for him again.

'You might not be seeing her, but I can tell by your reaction that you'd like to.'

Jax sighed. 'I would.'

'So, why don't you go and see her after this walk then?'

'Because her friend has just arrived from the mainland to stay with her and it doesn't feel right to hang about while they catch up.'

'Fair enough.' His attention was taken by Dexter bounding into the sea. 'Hey, Dexter, get out of there now!' He turned to Jax. 'He's such a water baby that dog. Now he's going to drip all through the pub to our flat upstairs before I can dry him off. Mum is going to go mad. She hates the smell of wet dog.'

Jax laughed. 'It isn't the most pleasant scent but I suppose she's more worried about the people relaxing with their drinks in the pub.'

'She will be.' He sighed heavily. 'Dexter! Out, now!' Paul

shook his head. 'I'd better go and fetch him, he's ignoring me again. Will I see you and your folks at the pub early on New Year's Eve?'

'Maybe,' Jax said unsure what they would be doing. 'Er, Dexter is swimming. Do you need me to come and help get him out of the sea?'

'No, we don't need both of us getting soaked. Damn dog.'

Jax watched Paul race off down to the sea relieved that Seamus was more interested in fetching his ball than the water. He decided to keep going and take a longer walk along the beach to try and clear his head further. He still needed to check up on Helier at some point, but didn't want the poor man feeling like his privacy was being imposed upon.

Jax recalled Piper inviting Helier to join their families for drinks on New Year's Eve where he would meet her grandmother and felt sure that Margery would invite him to join her friends in one of her pursuits. Margery, with all her directness, had a kind heart and he was very fond of the woman he had known and been told off by his entire life. He felt certain that Helier and she would get along well.

As he and Seamus reached the next slipway, Jax spotted a couple walking down the slip holding hands. He couldn't make out if he knew them at first because both wore puffy jackets and hats but as they neared each other he saw that it was Matteo and Casey.

'Hi there,' Jax said picking up Seamus's ball and throwing it for him to keep him busy. 'I hope you both had a good Christmas in the end.'

'In the end?' Casey asked. Then nodding. 'Ah, yes. The Cabbage Patch party and power cut. It was touch and go for a while,' she explained. 'Mum was beside herself when she thought she wouldn't be able to cook the turkey in the morning but on

Christmas Eve Matteo invited us all to the cottage where he's staying to have lunch.'

'There wasn't a power cut there then?' Jax asked surprised to learn that it hadn't been an island-wide issue after all.

'There was but the cottage is part of a luxury hotel and they have a generator,' Matteo explained. 'The electricity had come back in the morning but by that time Casey's mum decided she liked the idea of being served her Christmas lunch so we kept to the plan and enjoyed our Christmas lunch that was cooked in the kitchens at the hotel and brought over for us to eat at the cottage.'

'It was very Christmassy,' Casey said. 'We spent the evening with all the candles lit and ate a light supper in front of the roaring fire in the cottage. Mum, my sister, Jordi, and I loved every moment. Dad did too, apart from his panic first thing in the morning before the power came back on that he might not be able to watch his usual programme on the telly.'

'My dad would be the same,' Jax agreed.

'Casey's dad did have to admit he enjoyed himself in the end though,' Matteo said.

'Yes, now Mum has cooked our turkey and I have a feeling we're going to be eating slices of it in sandwiches, salads and working our way through turkey curries for a couple of days. We're going to be sick of it soon.'

Jax laughed. 'Thankfully we ate ours on Christmas Day, otherwise I'd be facing the same thing.' Jax couldn't help thinking how happy Casey and Matteo seemed and wondered what would happen with him and Phoebe. Deciding not to dwell on his own emotions, Jax asked, 'Your tour over now then?'

Matteo nodded. 'Yes, and the song has been released and made it to Number One on Christmas Day, so my manager, Martha, is ecstatic and I can relax for a little while.'

'Congratulations,' Jax said, giving Matteo a pat on the back. 'That's brilliant. Are you here for a bit longer?'

'Until the second of January. I'm looking forward to spending some quality time with this lady here.' He lifted Casey's hand and kissed the back of her glove.

Seamus returned with his ball as if on cue and Jax smiled. 'I hope you have a relaxed few days and will probably see you both sometime.'

'I'd like that,' Matteo said. 'Bye, Jax.'

He said his goodbyes to Casey and whistled for Seamus to follow him, deciding to walk along the beach and go to check up on his beach hut. There wasn't much else he could do with his day and Jax didn't fancy sitting in front of the television for hours on end like his father seemed to enjoy doing.

He carried Seamus up the steps to the promenade and had just checked on his beach hut and found everything was in order when he recalled how close to Helier's home he was and decided that maybe Helier wouldn't mind him popping in quickly. 'Do you want to meet a new friend, Seamus?' he asked.

He walked up to Helier's front door, still carrying Seamus so that his dog didn't jump up and knock over the frail old man.

He wasn't sure if he should knock again when nobody answered. Could Helier be having a snooze or maybe he was out somewhere? Jax doubted he would have gone out, but it was a possibility.

Eventually, he heard movement behind the front door and it opened. Helier gave him a questioning look for a second and then beamed at him. 'Jax, dear boy. It's grand to see you again. Come in out of the cold.'

'I hope you don't mind me bringing my dog, Seamus,' Jax said. 'But we were out walking and decided to pop in to see how you were.'

'That's very kind of you. I haven't taken Fred out for a couple of days now. I was concerned about slipping over in the snow and the poor lad has had to be satisfied with wandering around in the back garden.'

'Then Seamus and I will take him for a walk today.'

'You don't mind doing that for me?'

Jax shook his head. 'Of course not. Why don't I take him now and then we'll come back and have a nice cup of tea with you? If that suits you?'

'I'd like that very much.' Helier beamed at him and Jax wondered if he was the man's only visitor since he and his friends had been to help him with his car. 'I'll just fetch his lead.' He looked at Seamus and, seeing he wasn't wearing one, added, 'I like him to be kept on lead so that he doesn't run off. I'd hate to lose him.'

'That's fine.'

As Jax walked the dogs on the beach a while later, he looked out across the beach at the small groups of people enjoying the sunshine and fresh air and decided that when the weather warmed up and the walkways were less slippery he would make sure to invite Helier and Fred to go for a few walks with him and Seamus. Maybe he could invite them to the beach hut for some drinks and a chat sometimes. Yes, he thought, that's what I'll do.

35

PHOEBE

Fliss had been staying with her for four days and Phoebe had long ago grown tired of the mess her friend left in each room and her insensitive behaviour. She tried not to resent Fliss ruining the time she could have been spending with Jax, aware that it was her own fault for not speaking up, or contacting Jax and asking to see him. Knowing Jax as she now did, she suspected he hadn't called her because he didn't want to interrupt her time with Fliss. Urgh, it was all a mess and it was her own fault for letting things, or Fliss's behaviour, get out of hand. But with Alex staying on the pier, she could hardly ask Fliss to leave. No, she had to stick it out and hope that Fliss would return home soon.

Phoebe decided that if she wanted to see Jax again, then it was up to her to find something to keep her friend busy and give him a call.

But how to go about it without being rude?

She decided to message Piper. Since staying at the guest house Phoebe had become fairly close to Piper and realised that she would be happy to help. Piper replied within minutes, telling Phoebe that she would ask Alex to call Fliss and invite her out with him and Piper for a drink somewhere. Then, Phoebe could give Jax a call and arrange to see him. It was worth a try, although she knew that Fliss wasn't always willing to do what others hoped she might.

She heard Fliss's phone ping and watched as her friend picked up her phone from the kitchen counter and looked at the screen. 'It's Piper,' she said. 'I wonder what she wants?'

'Read it and see,' Phoebe said with a smile, trying her best not to sound desperate and tip her friend off that she had anything to do with Piper making contact.

Fliss frowned and looked at Phoebe. 'She wants to pick me up and take me out for lunch somewhere with her and my brother.' Fliss pulled a face. 'Don't worry, I'll make up an excuse and tell her we're busy.'

'Don't do that,' Phoebe said, aware as soon as the words had left her mouth that she had reacted in the wrong way.

'What's wrong with you?' Fliss asked suspiciously.

'Nothing. I just think it would be nice for you to see your brother. You didn't see him over Christmas and haven't spent any time with him since returning to the island.'

'Whose fault is that?'

Phoebe concentrated on keeping her voice calm. She couldn't recall Fliss ever willingly taking responsibility for anything, always believing that any mishap, or argument, was the other person's fault. 'No one's,' she replied. 'But don't you think it would be a nice thing to do? Also,' she said, coming up with what she believed to be a clever thought, 'your parents will no doubt expect you to see Alex while you're here, won't they?'

'I suppose they will,' Fliss agreed grumpily. 'You're right. I may as well see them for lunch. I'll tell them you're coming too.'

'No. Don't do that.'

'Why not?' Fliss asked suspiciously.

Phoebe wracked her brains to come up with a plausible excuse. Noticing magazines strewn across the kitchen table, she pointed at them. 'I'll need to tidy up this place,' she said. 'Unless you want to stay here and help me do it?'

'No chance.'

Phoebe barely managed to hold back the grin Fliss's expected reaction had caused. 'Then I'll get on with it once you're gone.'

She watched Fliss replying to Piper and then race upstairs to change before Piper and Alex collected her, then quickly sent a message thanking Piper and asking if she knew where Jax might be.

He's taken Helier shopping before delivering a few bits to the Ecobichon sisters, then dropping Helier home. He shouldn't be too long. You'll probably find him stopping by his beach hut maybe sometime soon. Good luck. x

'Good,' Phoebe said. It would give her a little time to tidy up the mess. After a lifetime living with a mother who abhorred an untidy home, Phoebe knew how to tidy a place in no time at all.

A few minutes later she said goodbye to Fliss and returned to her cleaning. Then, half an hour after that was on her way to Jax's beach hut, hoping to catch him there. She needed to let him know how much she had missed him. And if she didn't feel his arms around her soon and those perfect lips of his on her own she wasn't sure what she might be liable to do.

36

JAX

Jax was glad he had decided to leave Seamus at home, aware that he would be happy to doze in the living room after his early walk. It was one thing taking Seamus out with him to go walking but another entirely expecting him to spend hours in the jeep when he took Helier shopping and then ran errands for other people.

With Helier dropped off and the old man's shopping unpacked, Jax decided to go and spend a little time at his beach hut. He needed time to think and where better to do it than in the solitude at his favourite place. He wasn't sure if his low mood was due to missing Phoebe, having now not seen or heard from her for a few days. He had been tempted to call or message her several times but knowing Fliss as he did, did not want to chance Fliss being with Phoebe when she heard from him, so had thought better of it.

He drove the short way to his beachside hut and parked his car, spotting a vehicle he didn't recognise parked near the trees just off the road. He supposed someone was visiting a friend nearby. Jax walked across the grass and spotted someone standing by the sea wall looking out to sea. He decided not to disturb them but when he reached the door to his hut, it dawned on Jax that it was Phoebe.

'Phoebe?' he called out.

The person turned and smiled at him. It *was* her.

'You did come,' she said, beaming at him.

'Sorry?' He couldn't recall having made any arrangement to meet her.

Phoebe hurried towards him. 'I asked Piper where I might find you and she suggested I come here.'

'She usually knows where to find me,' he said, delighted to see her. Then it occurred to him that if Phoebe was here then Fliss must be somewhere nearby. He looked around to see if he could spot her lurking somewhere, ready to mock them again.

'What's the matter?' Phoebe asked. 'You're not cross that I came here uninvited, are you?'

He shook his head. 'No, of course not, I'm delighted you're here. You're welcome here any time.'

'Then what's the matter?'

'Sorry, I was looking for Fliss. Isn't she here with you?' He looked over Phoebe's shoulder trying to see where Alex's troublesome sister might be.

'She's not,' Phoebe said quietly, stepping closer to him. 'I asked Piper to invite Fliss out to lunch with her and Alex.'

Jax felt his mood lifting once again. 'And she agreed?' That didn't sound like the Fliss he knew.

Phoebe laughed. 'Only because when she suggested that she might not, I told her we should spend time cleaning my parents' house.' She grimaced. 'She's so messy. You can tell she's never picked up a single thing for herself.'

Jax wasn't surprised. It explained a lot about her attitude to everything. 'Well then.'

Without saying another word, he stepped forward, took her

hands in his and pulled them around his waist. Then, looking into her eyes and smiling at her amusement, he put his arms around her and holding her tightly, kissed her.

'What were you thinking we might do?' he asked eventually.

'You did promise to take photos of me.' She looked around where they were standing. 'No Seamus?'

'I left him with Dad. Why?'

'Because we had intended taking some selfies and I had expected them to include Seamus, don't you remember?'

He did. 'We can always go back and fetch him, if you like?'

'No, don't worry. It's so cold and I'm sure he's nice and cosy at home.' She considered something. 'I thought you could take a few photos of me in front of this place.'

'I'm not sure about that. I don't want all your fans tracking my beach hut down to take their photos in front of it. I've heard that's the sort of thing people do, isn't it?'

'Sometimes. I tell you what, why not take a couple of selfies of us here. Just for me. I promise I won't share them with anyone.'

He didn't mind that so much. 'Only if you send me a couple to keep too.' He liked the thought of having a photo of them together.

'Great. Come on then,' Phoebe said, looking first up at the sky, he presumed to find the best light, then at the beach hut. She took him by the shoulders and manoeuvred him to stand where she wanted him. 'That's perfect. I'll set the camera timer and hand you the phone as you have longer arms than me, OK?'

'Whatever you say,' he said, enjoying himself properly for the first time in days.

Jax smiled at Phoebe's phone screen as they took several photos then kissed her again. He was enjoying himself more than he had imagined. 'Where would you like to go now?'

'I don't mind,' she said. 'Somewhere neither of us have visited for ages.'

Jax tried to think where that might be. 'Do you like history?' he asked, after a thought occurred to him where they might visit.

'Love it,' Phoebe said. 'Why?'

'Have you been to Hamptonne lately?'

'What, the working farm somewhere in St Lawrence?' He nodded. 'Not for a couple of years.'

'Yes. I mean we've missed the lead up to Christmas with the carol singing and that sort of thing but we can still visit the shop and take some photos around the grounds. I think they'd be interesting for people to see, don't you?'

She gave his suggestion some thought. 'Yes, I like that idea. Show my followers what it was like to live at various times in the island's history with photos in rooms in the different houses.'

'My favourite one is the farmhouse where the entire house is set up as it would have been during the Jersey Occupation in World War Two,' Jax said, thinking that maybe Helier might wish to visit there sometime in the New Year.

'That sounds amazing,' Phoebe agreed. 'I recall the last time I went watching a lady in medieval dress cooking something over a large inglenook fireplace in one of the other houses.' She beamed at him. 'Yes, let's do that.'

'Shall I drive?' Jax asked.

Phoebe shook her head. 'I'd rather drive, if you don't mind. It's as cold inside your jeep as it is on the outside most of the time.'

'It is a very old vehicle,' he laughed, aware that she was right. 'Good, we'll go in yours. Much more comfortable too.'

They left the beach hut and followed Phoebe to her car.

'This is yours?' he asked, looking at the pale blue Lexus parked down the lane. 'I wondered who it belonged to when I arrived. I expected you to be driving the Range Rover.'

She shook her head. 'No, that's my dad's and I wanted to bring my car out now that the snow has melted and pretty much gone.'

After a couple of wrong turns down the unfamiliar country lanes, they finally reached the car park down the road from the museum, parked and walked the short way to the entrance. Jax took his wallet from his jacket pocket and withdrew his Jersey Heritage membership card that his mother had suggested he subscribe to years before.

'I'll pay for you,' he said.

'Don't worry,' Phoebe argued. 'Is that a card for this place?'

'It is.' He held it up. 'I think the last time I came here was for the cider-making festival a couple of years ago. You should come next time, it's fascinating and always fun.'

She narrowed her eyes and smiled.

He could see she was amused by something he had said. 'What?'

'I think you could teach me a lot,' Phoebe said. 'About this island and its heritage.'

'I'd be happy to,' he said, liking the idea.

They listened to the volunteer explain what was available at the museum with its two courtyards and various houses, some thatched and all depicting different periods of time in the island's history and then made their way out of the small shop and into the first courtyard.

'Where should we go first?' Phoebe asked.

'Where ever takes your fancy.' Jax noticed her give him an amused smile and shook his head. 'How about the medieval house, there's a fire in there and it's bound to be warmer than standing outside.'

'Fine, let's hurry up and go in there then.'

He stood next to her watching the woman dressed as a farmer's wife from the period explain the herbs she had laid out on the large distressed table. It was incredible to think how simply people had lived back then and Jax couldn't help thinking that he would probably have been much better suited to that era in history than he was to the present day.

After asking if the woman minded them taking a few photos and promising Jax that she wouldn't post them publicly, he agreed. Phoebe instructed Jax where to stand, and once satisfied that she had achieved the desired effect for her pictures, they moved on to the farm workers' house.

'Shall we take some in the orchards and herb garden now?' she asked.

'We can do,' Jax agreed, 'but there's nothing much happening out there as it's the middle of winter.'

'I was thinking the scenery might look rather pretty with the snow.'

Jax laughed. 'Ahh, good point.' They walked through a gate to the meadow and Jax couldn't help thinking how natural it felt to be walking hand in hand with Phoebe.

'It's even more beautiful out here than I imagined,' Phoebe said, glancing up at him and looking as if she was waiting for him to kiss her.

He did. 'I'm enjoying this very much,' Jax admitted.

'So am I.'

After what seemed like hundreds of photos later, Jax noticed Phoebe was shivering and led her to the Occupation house so that they could get out of the cold. He watched as Phoebe, awed by the sound of the local patois being spoken on the old Bakelite radio as they stood in the kitchen, turned to him.

'This place is like stepping back in time,' he said, gazing at the table laid ready for a meal, various worn hats hanging on the back of the kitchen door. It appeared as if the residents had only stepped out of the room for a moment.

'This place is amazing, isn't it?' Phoebe asked, taking photo after photo. 'Shall we go upstairs now?'

* * *

'I really enjoyed that,' Phoebe said as they walked back to her car.' She took his hand in hers and Jax stopped to see what she wanted. 'Will you take me to other places here on the island? I'd rather not visit alone and you seem to know so much about each place and make it so much more fascinating.'

'I'd be happy to.'

She rested her free hand on her chest over her heart. 'I think your students are very lucky having such a knowledgeable teacher as you,' she said. 'You bring the past to life so well, just like Hamptonne did for me. And I imagine you make foraging and your beach walks incredibly interesting too for the groups that you take out.'

'I hope so. I love it and it makes me happy when others appreciate visiting these places on the island. There's such a wealth of history here.' He heard the car doors unlock and Phoebe let go of his hand so that he could get in the car.

Once inside with the doors closed, she turned to him, a serious expression on her face. 'I think the reason you're such a brilliant teacher is due to your passion for this place and the people who live here.'

'Maybe.' He was surprised to hear her speaking so seriously about his work. Mostly people weren't interested, which was why he liked teaching the schoolchildren because even those that weren't initially happy to be out in the cold or on a wet beach soon forgot their reservations and started to have some fun.

'It is. Your passion shines through when you speak or explain something. It's... well, it's inspirational.' She sighed. 'I wish I loved what I did that much.'

Jax was taken aback by the sorrow in her voice. 'Don't you feel the same way about your work then?'

She laughed, confusing him. 'What I do is basically advertise products. I love some of them but I wouldn't choose to use other brands that I'm paid to promote. Whereas you teach people and inspire them to learn more, or if not learn then enjoy and appreciate what they have around them. You point out things that they probably pass every day without noticing and that is so worthwhile.'

'Now who's sounding passionate?' He was taken aback by her strong feelings for what he did.

She stared ahead out of the window. 'Don't get me wrong, I loved what I do at first. I was excited as my followers increased and more people commented, or liked my posts. I think it was the first time I'd really been seen, if you know what I mean.'

He wasn't sure that he did. Jax watched her speaking, surprised that someone with everything most people could hope for had felt invisible 'How could someone like you not feel seen?'

She shrugged. 'I mean the real me.'

'Do you ever share the real you with anyone though?'

Phoebe turned to look at him. She stared into his eyes thoughtfully for a while and Jax was wondering what she might be thinking and hoped he hadn't offended her. 'Look, I didn't mean...'

She raised her hand and smiled. 'It's fine. It's a valid question.'

'I didn't mean to offend you by saying that.'

She shook her head. 'You didn't. I was just trying to answer you but couldn't find the right words to convey what I was feeling.'

'Then you don't have to,' he said, not wanting her to feel obliged to open up to him.

'No. I want you to know me properly.' She took his hand in hers. 'Do you know, Jax, you're the first person who I've truly been myself with.'

Surely that couldn't be right. 'I don't understand.'

'It's true. Well, since my grandmother died years ago.'

'But that's heart-breaking.'

She gave a sad laugh. 'It is really, isn't it? Do you know you're the most open and honest person I think I've ever met. Spending time with you has woken me up to how guarded I've always been with friends. I did have one close friend when I was about six or seven but her parents emigrated to New Zealand and we lost touch after a few years. Then I met Fliss and she became my closest friend at boarding school and, well, I suppose I felt more comfortable keeping my thoughts to myself, which is probably why I feel I can be open with you like I'm trying to be now.'

'Phoebe,' Jax said gently. 'You don't need to explain yourself to anyone, and certainly not to me. Let's just get to know each other naturally. I think it's clear we like each other.' He grinned at her. 'I know that I like you, very much.'

Phoebe's smile lit up her eyes. 'Good, I'm glad. I like you very much, too.'

He gazed at her.

'So, what should we do now then?'

'I don't mind. We could go somewhere else. Find somewhere to eat, or fetch that scoundrel, Seamus, and take him out for a walk. It's up to you.'

'If it wasn't so cold I'd ask you to take me foraging.'

Jax liked the idea but knew she was already cold from their outing. 'There's not too much to go out for right now but I'll take you out when it's warmer later in the year and then I'll cook whatever I've found for us. How about that?'

'It's a date.'

He leant forward and kissed her, happy to think that she was looking forward to spending time with him as the year rolled on. 'Good.'

Jax heard a buzzing sound and Phoebe sat back in her seat and pushed her hand into her jeans pocket. Retrieving her phone, she looked at the screen and groaned.

'Fliss?' Jax asked, aware that she was the one person who seemed to cause that reaction among most people who knew her. 'I suppose we were lucky to have as much time as we have done today.'

'Yes. She's back at my house and wanting to know where I am.' She pulled an apologetic face. 'I'd better hurry up and get back there, it's very cold and she's locked outside.'

He waited while she typed something and sent a message.

'I'll drop you back at your jeep,' Phoebe said, sounding disappointed. 'But I've had a wonderful few hours with you, Jax. Thanks so much.'

'I've enjoyed it too. We'll have to do it again sometime soon.' He wondered how long Fliss was staying with her for and asked as politely as he could manage.

'At least until next week, she said,' Phoebe answered, starting the car and pulling out of her parking space.

Jax didn't want to wait another week to be able to see Phoebe again. There must be a way for them to see each other. 'What are you doing tomorrow night?'

'For New Year's Eve?' she asked, shaking her head. 'I've no idea. I haven't thought about it. Why? What will you be doing?'

'I've no idea yet, but if I come up with something I'll let you know. Leave it with me.'

37

PHOEBE

Phoebe struggled not to get irritated with Fliss for cutting short her time with Jax. She had dropped him off and it helped to know that he was as miserable as she was when she left him at his beach hut.

'You were with Jax?'

'Yes.' Phoebe saw Fliss's mouth tighten and knew she was about to be on the receiving end of her friend's spite.

'I'm surprised you don't have more pride, Phoebe.'

Phoebe unlocked the front door and waited for Fliss to enter the house. Closing the door slowly behind them, she took a moment to try and calm her rising temper before speaking. 'And why would you say something like that?' she asked, aware that Fliss was about to continue with her spite.

Fliss turned to face her, a disappointed look on her face. 'I wouldn't have taken you for someone who was happy with my cast-offs.'

'We both know there was nothing between you and Jax,' Phoebe said, taking off her coat and hanging it up. 'Not really.'

Unable to argue with that point, Fliss changed tactics, and as

Phoebe listened to her whining about having to wait outside for twenty minutes in the cold, she decided that she needed to take control of her life more and certainly of Fliss's automatic assumption that her feelings were the only ones that mattered.

'Where is Alex staying?' Phoebe interrupted.

'The Blue Haven guest house. Why?'

'Because my parents will be home in the next couple of days and I think that maybe you should think about taking a room there.'

'Me, stay at a guest house?'

'What's wrong with that? It's good enough for Alex and I stayed there too and love it,' she said pointedly. 'The room was beautifully decorated and the bed very comfortable. I would have loved to stay longer.' She decided she needed another option. 'Or maybe you should think about going back home to your parents.'

Fliss screwed up her face. 'I'm not sure I really know you any more,' she said, the spite in her voice clear.

'I'm not sure you ever really did know me,' Phoebe said, realising it herself for the first time. 'In fact, Fliss, why are we friends?'

Fliss gasped. 'What's got into you?' She scowled at Phoebe. 'You never used to be mean.'

Hating to be unkind, Phoebe regretted what she had said instantly. 'Sorry, I didn't mean for that to come out like it did.' Then seeing satisfaction flash across Fliss's face, she realised that she was being played by her friend, yet again. No more of Fliss controlling her, Phoebe decided. She had had enough. 'I do have a point though, don't you think? We're not very alike.'

Fliss sneered at her. 'I'm beginning to think that's a good thing.'

So am I, thought Phoebe.

'I know what it is,' Fliss said. 'You've been spending time over Christmas with Jax, haven't you?'

Phoebe didn't like being treated as if she had been underhand. She decided that she was allowed to see whoever she wanted, including Jax. 'Yes, I was with him. What's wrong with that?'

'He's obviously been poisoning you against me.'

Phoebe frowned, stunned by what her friend had said. 'What are we? Fifteen? Of course he hasn't. I'm perfectly capable of making up my own mind about people, including you.'

Fliss shook her head and gave Phoebe a mocking smile. 'He's rather dull, don't you think?'

'No. He's good fun and very knowledgeable.' Phoebe hated to feel like she needed to defend Jax and doubted he would be pleased if he thought she had done.

'Maybe, for a beach bum.'

'Now who's being nasty. You really are something else, Fliss. Do you even hear what comes out of your mouth?' she asked, her temper rising. 'Or are you so intent on causing trouble that all you can focus on are your barbed comments?'

Fliss opened her mouth but didn't speak and Phoebe suspected she was shocked at her uncharacteristic outburst. Good, she thought. So many people had been upset by Fliss since early last year and Phoebe was tired of Fliss's troublemaking. She was also sick of people assuming that the two of them were similar.

'Do you know what?' Fliss snapped. 'I'm going to pack my things and get the first flight home. She grabbed her phone from the marble island next to where they were standing. 'I'm not staying here to be insulted like this, and by a so-called friend.'

Phoebe struggled to hide her relief. 'You must do what you think best.'

Fliss seemed disappointed that Phoebe hadn't tried to persuade her to stay. She was used to threatening people with consequences only for them to back down and do her bidding. But not this time, Phoebe decided.

'Fine, then,' Fliss said glaring at her. 'I'll go.' She marched out of the kitchen, her shoulder smacking hard against Phoebe's as she passed.

'Ouch,' Phoebe groaned, rubbing it gently. Let her go, she thought, not wanting to say anything that might make Fliss change her mind because she suspected that was exactly what Fliss wanted. She was so used to manipulating everyone around her to do her bidding by either demanding it, or because they were too weary from past attempts to stand up to her. But Phoebe now knew better than to fall for Fliss's narcissistic ways. She had spent far too long putting up with Fliss and had no intention of continuing to spend time with someone who only cared about themselves while trampling over everyone else's feelings.

'Let me know if you get a flight and I'll give you a lift to the airport,' Phoebe shouted from the bottom of the stairs just to make sure Fliss knew she wasn't having second thoughts about her leaving.

Phoebe was relieved when Fliss returned shortly after and confirmed she had managed to book the last seat on the next flight out of the island. She barely spoke for the entire drive to the airport and Phoebe didn't mind one jot. She only wished that she had seen through Fliss earlier in the summer. There was no point in regrets, she decided, they were a waste of energy and time. She pulled up outside the departure hall at Jersey Airport and waited for Fliss to get out.

Fliss sat and stared at Phoebe for a few seconds. 'I hope you know how disappointed I am in you, Phoebe. I had thought you were a better friend than you've turned out to be.'

Phoebe knew that words like these would have upset her a few months before, but now she could barely be bothered to react. Realising Fliss wasn't going to get out of the vehicle until she'd received some reaction, Phoebe said, 'I'm sorry you feel that way, Fliss, although the way you've behaved recently and over the summer takes some beating. You've been nasty to me, used Jax, pretending you were interested in him, never mind nearly causing a wedding to be cancelled in the summer by telling the groom he was being tricked into getting married and that everyone was laughing behind his back. You almost broke the heart of a sweet girl who didn't deserve your nastiness. If anyone has the right to be disappointed in someone it's me with you. I think it's about time you had a good look at yourself before you go criticising others.' Happy to have told Fliss what she thought of her, Phoebe sighed. 'Now you'd better hurry if you're to get through security in time to board for your flight.'

Fliss glared at her momentarily before huffily getting out of the car and waiting. Phoebe closed her eyes in frustration. Did Fliss really expect her to get out of her car and take the case from the boot?

Not caring that she was giving in to Fliss if it meant she caught her flight, Phoebe stepped out of her car, walked round to the back, opened the boot and lifted out Fliss's heavy suitcase. 'There you go,' she said, pushing it towards her. 'Safe journey.'

Without waiting for Fliss to reply, Phoebe got back into her car and drove away without a backward glance.

* * *

Twenty-five minutes later she had found a parking space on the pier and walked up to Jax's front door. She hoped she wasn't calling at an inconvenient time for him or his family but wanted to make up for lost time. She knocked on the front door and waited for someone to answer.

She heard Jax's voice. 'I'll get that, Dad.'

Phoebe watched the door pull back and Jax's expression change from a pleasant welcome to a delighted smile. 'It's you.'

'Hello there.'

Jax's smile vanished and he leaned out of the house and looked to his right. 'Fliss not with you?'

She laughed and shook her head. 'I imagine she's probably boarding the plane right about now.'

'Plane?' She could see the confusion on his face. 'You're looking rather pleased with yourself. Obviously something has happened but I can't imagine what because you only dropped me off by my car a couple of hours ago.'

Phoebe nodded, enjoying his surprise. 'I've just come from the airport. I hope you don't mind me popping in uninvited.'

He shook his head. 'You have an open invitation to this cottage.' He took her hand in his and she felt him pull her gently into the hallway and shut the door behind her. 'You come here any time you like.' He kissed the tip of her nose. 'I thought she hadn't intending returning to Poole until next week?'

'She changed her mind,' Phoebe said, enjoying surprising him.

'Something happened between you two, didn't it?'

She tapped the side of her nose. 'Shall we take that walk with Seamus now? Then I can tell you all about it. Or is it getting too dark do you think?'

'It's never too late for a walk on the beach,' Jax said, smiling at her and making her stomach flip over several times. 'But it's high tide right now, so we couldn't really go anyway. Would you like to pop to The Bucket for a quick drink? Or a slow one, if you'd prefer?' He grinned.

'Yes, that would be lovely,' Phoebe said, looking forward to sitting in the warm pub, hopefully on a table near the large fireplace. 'Maybe we could grab something to eat too, if you're also hungry.'

'I can always eat their food.' Jax patted his stomach. 'Come along then. We can plan how we're celebrating New Year's Eve while we're there.'

'I'd like that very much,' Phoebe said, excited to think that Jax wanted to include her in his plans.

38

JAX

The following morning Jax woke feeling happier than he had done in years. He showered, dressed and, after feeding Seamus, took the bacon sandwich his mother had made for him and left the cottage. It was another cold but thankfully, sunny day, and as Jax called out his 'Good mornings' to the neighbours, his breath forming frosty clouds in front of his face, he decided that he wanted to do something extra special for New Year's Eve with Phoebe.

He wasn't sure she would like his idea but he decided that if she didn't then he could take her to the guest house and join the rest of the partygoers who would be there celebrating the end of another year and the beginning of what would hopefully be an exciting new one.

'Jax,' he heard his mother yell.

He turned, wondering what she might want. 'Yes, Mum?'

She was waving a piece of paper in her hand. 'You forgot this.'

He shook his head, unsure what it was, and retraced his steps.

'My shopping list? For tonight?' She groaned. 'I should have known you were away with the fairies when I told you about popping to the shops for me.'

He would have liked to deny that his mind had been elsewhere but it was clear that he hadn't been listening to his mother when she was speaking. All he had thought about was Phoebe, his plans for the evening and then the bacon sandwich tempting him.

'Sorry, Mum. I'll go straight after Seamus has had his walk.'

He saw his mother give him a strange look before handing him her list and going back inside. He understood why. He was never this switched off and certainly had never been like this about any other woman. Phoebe really was getting to him, he realised. And, he smiled, he actually quite liked this feeling of... What? Was he in love? Surely not already. Was he?

Someone patted him on the back and he turned to see Paul from the pub. 'Morning,' Jax said, having swallowed a mouthful of his bacon butty.

'It was good seeing you both again in the pub last night,' Paul said. 'Will you be bringing Phoebe to the guest house for the party later?'

Jax shrugged. 'Maybe. We might have other plans. I'm not sure yet.'

'Sounds mysterious.'

Jax shrugged. 'Not really, but I don't want to say anything until I'm sure.' He suspected by the look on Paul's face that he was sounding a little odd and wasn't surprised his friend reacted that way. This wasn't like him at all. 'Did you want me for something?' Jax asked, hoping to change the subject.

'Yes. Your aunt asked us to put aside some booze for her party. I thought you might collect it for her and drop it off at her place.'

'We'll do that right now,' Jax said, whistling for Seamus to follow him. 'Will you be at the party?'

'Yes, but not until after the pub closes. I'll be needing a few drinks by then.'

Jax wasn't surprised. It was a popular little pub and loved by the locals. He ate the rest of his breakfast on the short walk to the pub. Then, after washing his hands, he picked up the boxes of wines and beers and carried them to the guest house. He kicked the front door lightly with the toe of his boot. 'Aunt Helen?'

The door opened and Piper stepped back and waved him in. 'That's good of you to fetch this lot.'

'I met Paul outside and he mentioned the booze.'

'Let me take this one from you.' She lifted the top box from his arms and led the way through to the kitchen and out of the back door. 'Put them here,' she said. 'They'll stay nice and cool out in the yard.'

'Is that Jax?' his aunt called.

'Yes,' Piper yelled, returning to the house. 'He's brought your order from the pub.'

'That's good of you, sweetheart. I'll cross that job off my list then.'

'It's no problem,' he said. Standing in the yard, Jax thought back to how his aunt sometimes strung up coloured lights to brighten the place in the summer. 'Aunty Helen, are you going to use your outside lights tonight?' he asked, having an idea.

She arrived at the back door. 'Not this time,' she said. 'I've got some new ones that your dad offered to string up for me.' She pointed to the back wall. 'He's drilling a row of hooks and I'll add a row of lights. You know the ones that hang down like a waterfall.'

He didn't, but nodded.

'Why, lovey?'

'I was wondering if you might lend me your old sets.'

'What? The strings of individual ones with the slightly larger bulbs than the ones we have on the Christmas tree?'

'Those are the ones.'

'You'll find them in a box under the stairs. Help yourself.' She touched his shoulder as he went to walk back into the house. 'Am I allowed to ask what you're planning, or is it something for a certain special lady in your life right now?'

'Maybe,' he said, reminded how difficult it was to have much privacy when you lived so close to your family.

'Do you hear that, Piper?' his aunt asked, making space to let Jax back inside.

'I did, Mum,' Piper answered wearily. 'Now leave him alone and stop teasing your nephew or you might have to fetch your own bits for the party in future.'

Jax laughed. 'Thanks, Piper.'

'Fine, I get the message,' his aunt laughed. 'Don't forget your lights on the way out.'

'I won't and thanks.'

He took the lights and locked them in his jeep, then, taking Seamus to the beach, went for a long walk, working through the idea he'd had and planning what he needed for it.

After dropping off his mother's shopping, he went to find various items for his planned evening.

'Dad, do you still have that metal fire pit thing we used a few times out in the back yard last year?'

'Fire pit?' His father gave his question some thought. 'Do you mean that metal globe-shaped thing on a stand with bits cut out?'

'Yes, that's it. Do you know where it might be?'

His father looked puzzled. 'Not the time of year for sitting outside, Jax.'

'I know, Dad.' Maybe he was planning this all wrong? He struggled to decide whether to continue with his plans for the evening. He liked the idea so maybe it wouldn't be a completely odd thing to do. 'It is freezing out there, which is why I was hoping to borrow it.'

'It's up to you,' Duncan said, amused. 'You've always been odd when it comes to spending time in all weathers. Not like me and your mum,' he laughed. 'We have more sense and know when to stay indoors.'

'Dad,' Jax said, trying not to give in to his irritation with his father. 'I don't have much time to arrange things, so can you tell me where I might find it?'

'Suit yourself. You'll probably find it in the store cupboard outside. What do you want it for though?'

'I just wanted to borrow it.'

'Leave the lad alone, Duncan,' his mother bellowed from the kitchen.

'I was only asking.' Duncan frowned. 'Fine. Go ahead. Take what you like.'

Jax thanked his dad and walked past his mother to the yard.

'What do you want that old rusty thing for?'

Jax stopped and tapped the side of his nose. 'I'm trying to plan something special for tonight.'

His mother gave him a knowing look. 'Off you go then, but good luck working through that mess your father has crammed into that store of his. I keep telling him it needs sorting but will he listen?'

'Yes, Mum.' Jax shook his head in amusement at her ranting and went to the store.

Finally, having found what he was looking for and managing to place the rest of his father's bits and pieces back, he closed and locked the door. He carried the metal object through the kitchen.

'I'm off now, Mum,' he said.

'Take this with you, lovey.' She handed him a Thermos flask

he recognised from many picnics his family had taken on various beaches around the island through the years.

'What's in it?'

'Never you mind. It's something warm that I think you might like but wait until later to open it.'

'Thanks, Mum,' he said, taking it in his free hand and leaning forward to kiss her on her cheek.

Once satisfied that he had most of the things he needed, Jax drove to his beach hut. He was glad it was sunny. It meant that he could take everything out of his beach hut and sort it, placing what he was keeping neatly back inside. The hut had always contained a bit of a mishmash of things he hadn't liked to throw away and it had been convenient to leave everything in a bit of a mess seeing as he knew where everything was if he needed it and no one ever came inside the hut anyway. Until recently, that was.

Two hours later, after sorting, sweeping, scrubbing and tidying, Jax hung up the string of lights he had borrowed from his aunt. Stepping back to survey his hard work, he smiled.

'What do you think of the beach hut now, Seamus?'

As expected, his dog ignored him and went into one of the bushes sniffing and digging at the hard, cold ground.

He dug a circle in the patchy lawn a few metres in front of the hut and placed the metal fire bowl his father had lent him in it, moving it until he was certain it was secure. Jax added some kindling and coal and then fetched his two canvas seats, opened them and faced them out to the fire bowl with the sea beyond. He draped blankets over the back of each chair and opened the small folded table he kept in the hut and set a bottle of champagne, two glasses, the flask that looked a little out of place, and some napkins for the food he intended bringing later.

Everything was ready. Now all he needed to do was to

persuade Phoebe that sitting outside, under the stars, in late December was preferable to being inside at a warm, fun party.

Jax noticed it was getting late and he still needed to shower, change, pack up something for him and Phoebe to eat at the beach hut. Then he had to fetch Helier before going to Phoebe's home to collect her.

Once ready, he decided that a trip to the nearest food shop was his best bet. He parked outside and raced in, coming out five minutes later with a bag containing a rich chocolate cake, some peanuts and crisps. It wasn't a sophisticated offering but it would hopefully suffice and keep their appetite at bay while they sat and drank champagne later.

'Hi, Helier,' he said, arriving at the bungalow shortly after. 'Ready for the party?'

'Yes, we are,' he said, leading Fred out of the house and locking the door. He went with Jax to the jeep and waited for Jax to lift Fred up into the vehicle and then got in and settled on the passenger seat. 'We're both looking forward to it, aren't we, Fred?'

The dog gave a bark and Jax smiled. 'I'm sure Seamus will be very happy to see his new pal again.' As they drove to the pier, Jax explained that he had plans to go out for the evening. 'I hope that's all right with you?'

Helier nodded. 'It's fine, lad. I know young Piper and Alex and she was going to introduce me to her grandmother, Margery. Alex also mentioned his grandfather is staying on the island and might pop in to the party so he can introduce us. I'm sure I'll have plenty of people to talk to for the evening.'

Jax parked near to the guest house. The laughter and singing greeted them. 'It sounds like the celebrations are well under way.'

'The pub looks busy too,' Helier said, pointing to the group of people cheerfully greeting friends outside.

'It's good in there. You'll have to come to lunch with us sometime and maybe we could go for drinks there later this week. I can introduce you to the landlord and his wife, Kevin and Gina. They're lovely people and very welcoming.'

'I'd like that very much,' Helier said. 'My wife wasn't a big fan of visiting public houses and I have to admit that it's something I've missed doing. I've always found them to be friendly places.'

'Me, too.' Jax helped Helier out of the jeep and lifted Fred down to join them, then led the way to the guest house. 'Here we are.'

They walked inside and were immediately met by Piper. 'I've been watching at the window so that I didn't miss your arrival. Hello, Fred.'

'That's kind of you, my dear.'

'Not at all. Gran and her friends are looking forward to meeting you, as is Mum.'

'Helier? Helier Le Cras,' Dilys called as soon as Jax and he entered the living room. 'Is that you?'

Helier, Jax and Piper turned to see Dilys and Margery walking over to them.

'It is,' he said taken aback. 'I, um…' He peered at her through his wire-framed glasses then his face broke into a delighted smile. 'Dilys? From school?'

Dilys laughed and clapped her hands. 'Yes! You remember me.'

Helier grinned at her. 'How could I forget the girl who flicked her fountain pen at me covering my new white shirt with Marine Blue ink? My mother gave me a right ticking off for ruining it.'

'I am sorry. I hadn't meant to do damage and have to admit to being too frightened of your mum to go to your house and apologise.' Dilys looked at Margery then back at Helier. 'This is my good friend, Margery. It's her daughter, Helen, who runs this guest house and Piper there is her granddaughter.'

Piper turned to Jax. 'I think Helier will be fine with us now. You go and have a good evening with Phoebe. We'll make sure he and Fred get home safely.'

'Thanks, Piper.'

'Will you be back here tonight?' she asked.

'I don't know. It's up to Phoebe what she'd rather do.'

'Well, whatever you've planned for her I hope you both have a lovely evening.' She rested a hand on Jax's forearm. 'She's really nice,' Piper said. 'I wasn't sure what to make of her at first but my view of her was probably clouded by her being such a good friend of Fliss's.'

'Mine too. Right, I'd better be off. See you either later on or tomorrow. Have fun.'

'Will do.'

Alex walked into the room carrying two drinks and smiled at Jax. 'You off already?'

'He's going to meet Phoebe,' Piper said, smiling at Jax.

'Great. Have a good evening.'

'Bye, Alex.'

Jax left, happy to know that Helier had already made friends and been reacquainted with another. It comforted him to know that the older man would have people who would help him come to terms with the loss of his wife and accompany him as he made a new version of his life in the next year.

39

JAX

Jax waited for Phoebe to answer her front door, wondering how he was going to approach his plans for their evening together. He watched as the large door opened and then Phoebe was standing in the bright light of the hallway looking like some sort of supermodel. Jax felt his breath still as he stared at her, unable to speak for a moment.

'Jax? Are you all right?' Phoebe asked, obviously with no idea of the effect she was having on him.

He struggled to wrangle his thoughts into some sort of order. 'Um, yes. I'm fine. You look...' He shook his head trying to find the right words. How could this beautiful, sophisticated woman who looked as if she had stepped out of the pages of one of the glossy magazines his mother's regulars liked to read in her hair salon possibly be interested in a scruffy beach bum like him? It didn't make sense.

'Jax?'

He realised he was being rude. 'You look incredible,' he said, aware that his words didn't remotely come close to describing how she appeared.

'You like my dress?'

Jax nodded. Phoebe did a twirl and Jax cringed.

She caught his reaction and a look of horror crossed her face. Realising she had misunderstood his reaction, Jax stepped forward and reached out to take her hands in his. 'You look amazingly beautiful,' he said hurriedly. 'Perfect.'

'Then why did you pull that face when you thought I wasn't looking?'

'No, I didn't. Well, I did, but not because of how you're dressed.' He needed to explain and quickly before their evening ended before it had begun. 'Can I come in for a moment?'

She nodded and closed the door behind them. 'What's the matter?'

'Phoebe, I promise you look perfect to go to an incredible party somewhere like London, Paris, or, um, Monte Carlo.'

'What are you talking about, Jax? Is this your way of telling me you're not taking me out tonight after all?' She tried to pull her hands from his but he held on.

'No, of course not.' He groaned. 'Sorry, I'm making a complete hash of this. What I'm trying to say is that I've made plans for us.' He shook his head. 'You don't have to go along with them though.'

'We're not going to the party?' she asked, looking puzzled.

'We still can, if you wish to.'

'What did you have in mind for us instead?'

Jax wished he had thought of treating her to one of the expensive parties being held around the island. Many hotels or smart restaurants or clubs held New Year's Eve parties, putting outstanding meals on for their guests with bands playing in their immaculately decorated event spaces. He cringed inside to think that he had imagined taking this woman to his tatty beach hut might be a good idea.

'Jax. Are you going to tell me or are we going to stand here all night? These stilettos aren't made for standing around on marble flooring.'

He looked down at her feet and was amazed she could even stand up in those things, let alone walk in them and wear them for hours.

'Well?'

He took a deep breath. *Just tell her the truth.*

'I've arranged a surprise for you,' he said, embarrassed now. 'It's nothing exciting, or, I realise now, very special, and I'm mortified to think that I even thought for one moment that it was a good idea.'

'You've arranged it now, so don't you think I should be the one to decide whether it was a good idea or not?'

He supposed so. 'Maybe.'

Her eyes narrowed. 'I'm wearing completely unsuitable clothes though, aren't I?'

'You look amazing.'

'You already said that.' Jax felt her hands tighten slightly over his. 'Should I go and change?'

Jax frowned. 'Probably.'

'Better?' Phoebe asked several minutes later as she walked down the stairs to meet him.

He smiled at her. She was wearing jeans, a pullover, a woolly hat, and pulling on a thick puffy silver jacket. She had worked out they weren't going to be inside, Jax realised, loving that she was getting to know him so well. 'Perfect.'

She took a pair of padded boots from the cloakroom cupboard and slipped them on. 'Shall we get going then? I'm dying to see what you've planned for us.'

Once they reached their destination, Jax wasn't feeling quite so anxious about taking Phoebe to the beach hut, especially now that he knew she suspected they would be celebrating their New Year's Eve outside. He parked the car and took her gloved hand, leading her up the small lane.

'Wait here a minute, will you?'

He ran to the beach hut and switched on the lights, then quickly lit the fire and took the food from the bag and set it out on the small table.

Then returning to her, took her hand once again. 'Ready?'

'Yes. I'm excited.'

'Don't build your hopes up too much,' he said, not wishing to disappoint her when she saw what he had done. He thought it looked good, but as her outfit earlier had reminded him, they were two very different people.

'Shut up, Jax, and take me there.' They rounded the corner to the beach hut. 'Oh, Jax, this is beautiful! I love it!'

'Do you really?' Dare he hope that she was being honest with him? He looked at his hut now resplendent with strings of lights arched around the front gable of the roof, the flickering light from the fire making shadows on the wood and supposed it did look much better than it had in the daylight.

She looked deep into his eyes. 'Jax, this is perfect and so romantic.'

'So you don't mind coming here instead of the party then?'

'Why would I possibly mind?' She wrapped her arms around him and smiled up at him. 'I love it. Honestly.'

He stared at her, taking in her beautiful features and wondering what she could possibly see in him.

'Why would you think I'd mind you doing something this lovely?'

He shrugged. 'You're used to all the best things,' he said, believing he may as well be honest. 'This,' he said, waving his arm to encompass his tatty beach hut and the second-hand makeshift decorations for their evening. 'It's hardly what you're used to and I wasn't sure you'd like it.'

'Hopefully you'll know me a bit better now and realise that whatever you planned for me would be something I loved.' Her arms tightened around him and she rested her head on his chest.

Jax held her tightly and kissed the top of her head.

'I love this, Jax. No one has ever arranged anything quite so romantic for me and it's completely perfect.'

'I'm happy you think so.'

'I do.'

She actually liked what he had done. Jax couldn't hide his delight. He placed a finger under her chin, raised it and bent to kiss her. 'I'm so happy that you're, well, happy.'

'I am. Very.' She indicated the chairs. 'Shall we go inside and sit down?'

'Yes.' He stepped forward and, taking one of the blankets, waited for Phoebe to sit and draped it around her shoulders and over her legs. 'Don't want you freezing, do we.'

'I doubt that will happen, especially when your fire gets going more.'

Jax added more wood to his fire and then wrapped himself in a blanket and sat next to Phoebe. 'I've got a bottle of champagne for us to drink at midnight,' he said. 'I've also got a few beers and some wine for you, if you want it.'

'What's that flask got inside it?' she asked, spotting the old-fashioned flask his mother had insisted he bring.

'I've no idea. That was my mother's idea.'

Phoebe gave him a knowing grin. 'I imagine it's something warm,' she said. 'Maybe let's see what she's given you.'

'Why not?' Jax leaned over to the table and picked up the flask. He unscrewed the larger outside cup and handed it to Phoebe, then took the smaller plastic cup and placed it on the table next to them. 'Here goes,' he said, intrigued as he unscrewed the top.

The spicy scent of warm red wine, a hint of orange, cloves and cinnamon filled the air inside the beach hut.

'She is clever,' Phoebe said, holding out her cup for him to pour some of the steaming liquid into it. 'I love mulled wine.'

So did he. Jax smiled as he then poured some into his smaller cup and replaced the lid to keep it warm before cupping his cup between his hand. 'Typical Mum,' he said, his heart filling with love for the woman who always seemed to know what to do for the best.

He watched her take a sip and did the same. 'Tasty?'

'Heavenly,' Phoebe murmured, closing her eyes. 'I feel all Christmassy and happy, and, oh, I don't know.' She raised her cup and tapped it lightly against Jax's. 'Cheers, Jax. Thank you for giving me such a memorable New Year's Eve.'

'I've enjoyed every moment,' Jax murmured as he stared ahead of them over the flames in the fire bowl towards the moon shining over the dark water.

'Hopefully we'll have more evenings like this one then,' Phoebe said before taking another sip of her warm drink.

'You really don't mind being here like this, do you?' he asked, realising Phoebe surely must be the perfect woman for him.

'I meant it when I said this was perfect, Jax.'

'But isn't there a part of you that would rather be at one of those smart parties tonight. That dress you wore, and those shoes, you looked so incredible and,' he said, deciding to voice his nagging concerns about their suitability as a couple, 'I can't help feeling that we're so totally different that you should be with someone who can give you all the things you're used to enjoying.'

Phoebe didn't reply immediately, then took his hand. 'Jax, look at where we are.'

'I'm not sure what you're getting at.'

'This place. The peace and solitude. Ahead of us is one of the most beautiful beaches in the world. We're warm-ish.' She grinned. 'I'm with someone who might be different to every other man I've ever spent time with but it's your differences that make me happy.'

'Really?'

'Yes. Fancy parties, smart restaurants, beautiful clothes, they're available to anyone who can afford them. This, sitting here, with a man who knows how to simply *be*, how to live off the land, teach others how to do it with a passion that you can't fake and you're always there for your friends and family. Jax, you might be tall and muscular and completely gorgeous, as well as the kindest man, but the only person who doesn't seem aware or interested in that is you. You are the most honest man I've ever met. You're real and kind and I can't help loving you for that.'

Jax stared at her, stunned. 'I'm nothing special.'

'To me and to those around you, you are very, very special, Jax. You're one of a kind and I'm enormously happy that I get to spend time with you like this.'

He couldn't think what to say. Was she still unsure about his feelings for her? He had gone on about them being friends, after all. They sat in silence and stared ahead of them as he processed Phoebe's surprising sentiments.

'Hang on a sec,' he said turning to her. 'Did you say you loved me?'

He saw her face redden in the firelight. 'Maybe.'

Jax gazed at her.

'Does that bother you?' Phoebe asked eventually.

Jax shook his head, wondering if the feelings he had been experiencing was how someone felt when they had found their soulmate. 'Not for one moment.'

'Good.' Phoebe smiled. 'That's a relief.'

They sat holding hands, listening to the waves as they lapped the shore. Jax didn't think he had ever felt true contentment until that moment.

'It's getting near to midnight now, Jax,' Phoebe said, breaking the silence. 'Shall we take that champagne down to the beach now?'

'Yes, let's do that.'

He carried the bottle and two glasses and led the way down the granite steps onto the sand below and they walked hand in hand down to the sea edge.

'Give those to me,' Phoebe said, taking the glasses from him, giving him the chance to pop the cork from the bottle.

He poured the bubbling liquid into each glass and placed the bottle securely into the damp sand by their feet. Then, taking her hand in his, they turned to look out across the silvery light cast over the rolling waves.

'This really is such a special place,' Phoebe whispered.

'It is, and you're a very special person.'

As she turned to him, Jax leaned forward and kissed her, not caring that he was probably spilling his champagne.

'I wonder what next year will bring for us both,' she said.

'I've no idea but I do know that I'm going into it happier than I've ever been,' Jax said, aware that when he first set eyes on Phoebe he could never have imagined spending New Year's Eve standing on his beloved beach, with a glass of champagne in one hand and Phoebe's hand in the other.

'Happy New Year, Phoebe.'

'Happy New Year, Jax. Thank you for making everything completely perfect.'

ACKNOWLEDGMENTS

I'd like to thank my wonderful editor, Tara Loder, for helping me with this book from my initial idea through to publication. I know this book is much better for all her help and guidance.

Thanks also to my copy editor, Sandra Ferguson, for picking up all the continuity errors I've made and to Rose Fox for proofreading this book.

Thank you to the brilliant team at Boldwood Books, for another beautiful cover and for bringing my books to readers and also to all the Boldwood authors, I love being one of you.

As always, I'd like to thank my family for their ongoing support and love, I couldn't do any of this without you all.

Finally, I'd like to thank you, dear reader, for choosing this book, I hope you enjoyed spending time with Jax, Phoebe and the residents on Gorey Pier.

AUTHOR LETTER

Dear Reader,

I hope you've enjoyed this third book in my Sunshine Island series. I've loved writing Jax's story. Jax is a firm favourite for readers of this series and I thought you might like a winter setting this time.

Christmas on the island is always one that's celebrated by my family both at home in the warm, but also taking refreshing walks along the beaches with our dogs. My favourite days, like most people I imagine, are the crisp cold yet sunny ones and when I'm down on the beach enjoying those moments I often think of Jax working and sharing his love of the coast with those that he teaches.

I look forward to hearing what you think and would be grateful if you could spare a moment to leave a brief review sharing your thoughts.

Until next time, I wish you happy reading and warm wishes from sunny Jersey.

Georgina x

MORE FROM GEORGINA TROY

We hope you enjoyed reading *Chasing Dreams on Sunshine Island.* If you did, please leave a review.

If you'd like to gift a copy, this book is also available as an ebook, hardback, large print, digital audio download and audiobook CD.

Sign up to Georgina Troy's mailing list for news, competitions and updates on future books.

https://bit.ly/GeorginaTroyNews

Explore the rest of the Sunshine Island series from Georgina Troy:

ABOUT THE AUTHOR

Georgina Troy writes bestselling uplifting romantic escapes and sets her novels on the island of Jersey where she was born and has lived for most of her life. She has done a twelve-book deal with Boldwood, including backlist titles, and the first book in her Sunshine Island series was published in May 2022.

Visit Georgina's website: https://deborahcarr.org/my-books/georgina-troy-books/

Follow Georgina on social media here:

- facebook.com/GeorginaTroyAuthor
- twitter.com/GeorginaTroy
- instagram.com/ajerseywriter
- bookbub.com/authors/georgina-troy

Milton Keynes UK
Ingram Content Group UK Ltd.
UKHW041052110823
426643UK00005B/11